HOODOO & HAIR LOSS
THE ORACLE OF WYNTER BOOK FOUR

LISA MANIFOLD

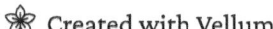

PRAISE FOR THE ORACLE OF WYNTER SERIES

Holy Cow...I can't read each book in the series fast enough! Great job of drama, snarkiness, humorous moments etc. This series is a true pleasure to read.

I like how the characters are evolving and how amid the magic her normal life can be one of our own.

This series is just getting more and more exciting and with such an amazing storyline the series could go on forever how cool would that be because I will be really sad if this one ends.

*To everyone who finds more hair than they like in their
brush and curses the fates.
We curse them together.*

Hoodoo & Hair Loss

Three weeks ago, I kicked a necromancer to the curb. Three days ago, I took a much-needed vacation with my new love. Three hours ago, someone threatened everything that matters to me.

I've just met Nina Davenport, my newest consultant, and to say she needs my help is an understatement. For starters, it turns out she's got one hell of a gnarly curse covering her. I have no idea what this curse is meant to do, but whatever it is, it's not good. To make matters worse, Nina is on the run with a nasty ex on her tail who is determined to take her daughter from her. For the icing on the cake, this isn't something that we have lots of time to figure out. According to Florry, the magical clock is ticking on this one. Whatever is coming is coming fast. If I don't break this curse, I might lose her – and her daughter.

No pressure, right?

Oh yeah? And the cherry on top of the icing on the cake? Logan seems to think that leaving me is the only way to solve all his problems. But he's got another thing coming. I am too old and now losing too much hair to deal with the angsty machinations of a man who refuses to acknowledge his own midlife crisis. No one drives the Wynter bus but Wynter. If he plans to keep me in his life, he better take a seat and buckle up.

Being the Oracle of Theama has been one curve ball after another, but this time I feel like I've been hit by a pitch.

CHAPTER ONE

I hadn't been able to get much out of the woman who had collapsed in my arms on my doorstep. I'd brought her inside, and Caro, obviously used to seeing consultants in distress, started a pot of coffee, as well as topping off the kettle.

The woman looked as though she'd been tossed overboard, rescued, dragged through a knothole, and then left on the street. She hadn't stopped shaking since I'd brought her inside. She looked to be late twenties, maybe early thirties at the most.

She also brought in what I thought of as the whiff of doom. You know like when you watch a movie, or read a book, and you just know, either by the way the music is going, or the hints the author is throwing out, that something Very Bad is about to go down?

That's how I felt when I looked at the poor woman sitting on my couch. However, she was on my couch, and it was apparent this was where she was supposed to be. I took a deep, cleansing breath, seeking support from all the former Oracles and anyone else not a necromancer or mad at me. Then I faced to the woman with a smile. "I'm Wynter. Can you tell me what brings you here?"

Caro brought over a tray—where in the name of hostesses past had she found it? She'd put coffee, tea, and all the fixings together.

I smiled gratefully at Florry's friend.

"She's a caretaker. From the word go. She's always up helping and taking care of others. If she stays here with you, it's your job to make sure she takes care of herself, too. She's no spring chicken." Florry was hovering around the edges of the room.

Caro? I thought.

"Who else? Not your shivering mess, there. Poor thing. I shouldn't call her that. She looks done in."

Okay. Got it. Let me focus here.

"Sure, sure. I'll be hanging around like a well-dressed bat in the belfry."

You can't do this to me. I keep wanting to laugh, and this isn't the time.

Florry moved out into the front room, muttering under her breath.

"Why are you looking for me?" I tried again, watching the woman as she made herself a cup of coffee, her hands shaking.

"My name is Nina Davenport. I recently got divorced from my husband, Rockledge."

"His name is Rockledge?" I had to ask.

"He's probably a grade A jerk." Florry zoomed back in. "With that name? That's jackass territory."

I ignored my ghost.

Not that I'd be able to ignore her words, however. Rockledge? Good night, Maggie.

Nina nodded, wrapping her hands around the cup and leaning back into the couch. "We have a daughter. Kira. She's six, and she's the best thing in my life." The coffee cup lowered as Nina's focus zoomed out. It was clear she was somewhere else at the moment. Then she shook her head and took a sip of coffee as her eyes met mine. "I just left her. I've never been away from her and... and it's hard."

"So she's visiting with her dad?"

"No. I had to hide her from her dad." Nina spoke in a flat tone that hid tears and grief.

I felt a chill move through me. This spoke of layers of complexity and Nina had only been here five minutes. If that. "Nina, I'm not really the person to help with custody battles. Although I do have a good attorney, if you need one." I thought about Hubie Liegal, who while not defending me for murder, would be presenting my case against the district attorney, the police department, Scott damn-his-eyes Trenton, and Hazel Babbington around their behavior toward me.

"It's not that." Nina's eyes filled with tears that

spilled down her face. She dashed at them, almost angrily.

I didn't say anything. It was apparent she needed to tell a whole story to get out what it was she needed.

"He's a warlock."

"At least it's not a necromancer this time." Florry said what I was thinking. "But a warlock isn't much better."

I'd need to ask what the difference was between a witch, a warlock, and a necromancer. Well, I knew what the difference was between witches and necromancers, but where did a warlock fall on the magical scale? *You'll need to explain this to me*, I thought in Florry's direction.

Warlocks are oath breakers. They are betrayers. Possibly traitors. Goldie chose this moment to chime in.

I wasn't sure if it was a good or a bad thing that I could keep this many conversational balls in the air.

"Why are you hiding Kira from him?" I decided to focus on the matter at hand.

Don't promise anything until you've heard everything. Goldie sounded more dire and full of warning than normal. *Dealing with warlocks is challenging. They don't keep their word.*

And the necromancers we've had to deal with were a piece of cake? Warning noted. Let me focus, please.

"He hexed me because I wouldn't help him with a really difficult spell. Well," she amended whatever she was about to say. "It wasn't just that. It was... it was the last straw between us."

"Are you a witch?"

She shook her head. "I'm an augment."

I wasn't familiar with the term. "Which means what? Forgive me, I'm still new."

Nina frowned. "Are you sure you're up for this?"

"If you found me, your quest has been judged as worthy of my help." My body stiffened. I wasn't going to take challenges from consultants. No, thank you. I had enough to worry about with my own thoughts. "What do you augment?"

"Anything. If you do a spell with me, I will increase the range, or the power of the spell. I take whatever magic is being used and amplify it."

"That's a nice skill to have."

Nina rolled her eyes. "Sure, if you want to be used by anyone who thinks they can hang onto you. It's a constant struggle to keep the shitty people at bay."

I smiled at her then, my previously raised hackles gone. "I understand that. Completely."

"I thought Rockledge was a witch. I love working with witches. They do a lot to help others, to help nature. I'm lucky in that I've been able to work with some really amazing covens. I met Rockledge through one of the covens. At first, he seemed like a good man." She stopped.

"Don't stop there!" Florry clapped her hands.

Thank the dear lord and all the saints that no one but me could hear her.

"But just before Kira was born, he left the coven

he'd been with, and started working on his own. He was hiring himself out, which can get sort of sketchy, but he was good to me, and he is—was—a wonderful father to Kira. At least, he seemed to be." Tears started to fall again.

Caro, who had gone back into the kitchen and stood behind the island, keeping herself out of the way, came back to where Nina and I sat across from one another on the sofas. She silently handed Nina a box of tissues.

Nina whispered, "Thank you." She took out a couple of tissues and blotted at her eyes. "I'm sorry. It's so hard to get through this. I just can't believe this is happening to me."

"Take your time." I tried to be soothing.

"Hurry up!" Florry shouted.

You really need to simmer down, I thought. *She's in distress.*

"We all are, waiting for her to get to the point." Florry was unapologetic.

I took a risk and shot a glare at where she hovered near the fireplace.

She glared back.

Nina patted her eyes once more and took a breath. Her shoulders squared. "I'm just going to tell you the entire thing. When I met Rockledge, he was one of the best potion makers in the coven. He did all the potion work, all the mixing. He was—is—brilliant."

"Then what happened?"

Nina shook her head. "I don't know. That's when I

met him, when the coven was doing some work with... " she stopped. "Well, it doesn't matter. I just can't discuss the work I take on for clients."

"I get it." I waved a hand.

"Anyway, we met, and he's handsome, and he's funny, and I fell in love."

"That's not a bad thing."

"No, it wasn't. Like I said, when we found out about Kira, he left the coven. That's a big deal, leaving your coven. I know witches who are with the same coven their entire lives. Most of them are, unless they move away, or something like that. It's a big deal to be invited into a coven, so it's a big deal if you choose to leave." Her shoulders sagged.

"I should have guessed something was wrong, but I was so happy, and he seemed happy. He said he wanted to work alone. It's not the usual thing, but I'm not a witch, so I wouldn't really know, right?"

"That makes sense."

"Dear lord above." Florry groaned. "We're gonna be here until tomorrow, maybe later."

"After Kira was born, he got darker. More reclusive. He was always out in the herb shed, and he seemed angrier. Neither of us were sleeping. She had a hard time staying asleep."

"I have children. I understand."

Caro came and sat down beside me.

"I wasn't working a lot, but I was helping Rock-ledge, offering him my skill without really getting into what he was doing specifically. It's not because I don't pay attention." Nina seemed like she really felt the need to explain herself for every step of her life, offering some manner of justification.

Which told me a lot more about Rockledge than she was saying, or probably would ever say.

Unaware of my thoughts, Nina continued, "It's that when you do what I do, you learn to ignore what your clients are doing. I can usually get a sense if the client is up to something negative, and I don't work with them."

"But you didn't notice it with Rockledge?"

She shook her head. "No. I was busy with Kira, and still trying to do some work, and keep our home together."

The emotional labor. I knew that role well.

"My clients were thinning out. I used to be so busy I had to turn people away, and after Kira was born, it got to the point where I'd go days without a call. I didn't know why. That all changed last year."

"What changed?" I leaned forward. I felt like maybe we were getting to the crux of it now.

"One of my old clients happened to run into me when I was out grocery shopping."

I could understand. Some of my more disastrous encounters had taken place in the grocery store lately. No one ever told you that the produce section could become hazardous to your health.

"I asked how she was, if she needed any help, and she made a face at me. Like, her nose wrinkled as though she'd smelled something bad. I was shocked. I asked her what was going on. She stared at me for what felt like a long time, and Kira, who was with me, began to cry. My client picked up Kira out of the basket and told me to follow her."

"She didn't hurt your daughter?"

"No, no, nothing like that." Nina shook her head. "She wanted to get us out of the store. We walked out to the parking lot together, and I could hear her talking to Kira, even though I couldn't hear what she was saying, exactly. I remember Kira curling her head into Madel—my client's shoulder." She corrected herself.

"Was it magic?"

Nina shrugged. "I don't know. I was so upset, by her reaction to me, and the way I felt, and Kira crying. Anyway, we got out to her car, and she whirled around and asked me how I could debase myself like I was doing. To say that I was flabbergasted was an understatement."

"What did she think you were doing?" There had to be a point to this. I'd learned that I couldn't rush the consultants. Even if I wanted to.

"Rockledge wasn't taking on work as a witch. He didn't leave the coven by choice. They asked, or rather, they insisted he leave."

"Why?"

"My client said he'd taken the path of a warlock. The old version of the word warlock means betrayer, someone who has broken their oath. I don't know what he did, but the coven felt that he broke the oaths of their coven, of their promises. And they asked him to leave. He'd been doing work for various people, but it wasn't good people, or people who were doing good things. The people he worked for were dark magic users. That's not the worst thing, however,"

"What is?"

"He told people that he was good at what he did not only because of his skill. He said his work was the best because he had an augment that worked with him exclusively, one that was skilled and sought after and who would enhance the spells they needed. He told everyone that I was with him, working with him. Aligned with his goals." Her voice broke at the last word, and she stopped.

Nina looked down at her hands, shredding the tissue she held.

I didn't think she was sad.

More that she was furious and didn't know what to do with her anger.

When Nina looked up again, her eyes were blazing. "He ruined my career! It takes time to build up trust, for people to be willing to allow you near their magic. And in just a couple of years, he ruined it. Everyone thinks I work with a warlock, an oath breaker, someone who chose to break his word, by choice. Rockledge made sure that it would be difficult for me to survive without him." Her face hardened, and her eyes turned bitter. "He wanted to be sure that I'd never leave. Not because he loved me, or Kira, but because I was good for business."

"I'm sorry. What is it that brings you here to me?" I was angry for her, and if she told me more, I would probably also be heartbroken, but I still didn't see how I was supposed to help her. How I could even be of help.

She heaved a big sigh. "I ran into that client last year. I went home and confronted Rockledge, and not only did he admit it, he laughed about it. He told me that the only person who would ever trust me was him, and that even the people he worked for needed to know that he had me under control." Nina scoffed. "As though I was nothing without him. Like I didn't support myself with my talent and skill before him. No, he had to not only take it for himself, but ruin it for me. And what about Kira? Growing up with us as parents! He ruined her, too!" She shook her head. "I told him I was done. I walked away, and he laughed at me again, telling me that he'd see me in the morning because we had work to do."

"It's hard to believe there are men like that still."

Nina continued as though I hadn't spoken, her anger carrying the story onward. "The next morning, I left. My parents are gone, and I don't have family. But I've picked up the ability to do some spell work. I did a concealment spell, and I used every bit of power I had. It worked, too." She smiled, and the pride in her ability showed through, even though she was mired in stress.

"What happened when it stopped working?"

"He found us. He tried to take Kira from me. But I'd gone to another coven, one that gave me a chance even with all they knew about Rockledge, and I bought protection spells to use if he found us. I got away, but it wasn't easy. I knew that I had to change. I hid Kira."

"Where did you hide her?"

Nina shook her head. "I can't say. I *won't* say. She's safe, and she's away from her father. He doesn't love her. He wants to use her to get me to do what he wants. If I don't come back, they'll take care of her." A sob came out of her, harsh and sharp. "I don't like to think about it, but I think he wants to see what her talents are. Whatever else he is, he's a skilled practitioner. I'm good at what I do. Kira has two strong parents. It stands to reason she'll have strong skills herself." She dabbed at her eyes again, overcome. "What have I done to her?"

"You haven't done anything. You're not responsible for what her father does."

At that point, Nina finally put her head down and cried.

I waited.

When she was able to look up again, and her tears had eased, she spoke. "Rockledge figured out, I don't know how, that I'm not with Kira. He's hexed me."

"How do you know?"

"He told me that until I worked with him, and helped him complete his commissions, I would never be free. He's lying, of course. He'll never let me go. Now that I know how he's been getting business. Now that I

know how he's been using me, and my reputation—"
She shook her head again. "He'll never let me go."

"That all makes sense, but how do you know that
he hexed you?"

"Because he keeps showing up everywhere I go.
One of Rockledge's favorite spells the last couple of
years is tracking spells."

I didn't know what to say. Her ex-husband sounded
like a creep, a stalker, an abuser—all the things. She
was divorced, but did she really want to hear this from
me? "So you're sure he put one on you?"

"I can't augment."

"What?"

"I'm not able to augment. Not since the first time he
found me and demanded to know where Kira was. After
that, he's come everywhere I've moved to, and I haven't
been able to use my augmentation. I think not only is
he tracking me, but he's blocked my magic somehow."

"This doesn't sound like something that you're sure
about."

"Magic is weird. What you think is best, or works
best for you, might not work for someone else." Florry
had moved closer. She was less belligerent than she'd
been. Her words were almost thoughtful.

"Does your ex-husband know where your daughter
is?" Caro spoke for the first time since Nina fell into my
front door and into my life.

"I don't think so. Goddess, I hope not." Nina shook
her head vigorously. "I don't think he would have been

able to keep that to himself. He'd have to brag to me. Right now, he's only threatening."

"Okay, so what is it you want me to do?" I asked. I thought I understood how she'd gotten to this point, but I wanted to be clear.

"I want you to help me get rid of this hex and cast a spell on me or for me, for me and my daughter, so that Rockledge Davenport can never find us again."

"Not much at all." Florry scoffed.

It's going to be dangerous to go up against a warlock. Goldie didn't beat around the bush.

Like the necromancers I've been dealing with lately have been a picnic. I sent my thought—again—out to both Florry and Goldie. *None of the things the consultants deal with is a cake walk.*

I feel I must warn you. If Goldie were a person, he'd be shaking his head.

Consider me warned. I couldn't turn my back on Nina. Not with her daughter at stake. Not with everything she'd shared. I wasn't sure I could turn my back once the fire ceremony had led her to me, but I didn't want to.

"Do you know what sort of hex he might use? Like, does he have a favorite?"

"No, and I wish I did. I might have known, four or five years ago, but not now. You know, people have..." Nina hesitated, obviously considering her words. "People who practice magic have a feel to their spells. It's like anything else. People get comfortable in the way they work. I've worked with Rock enough to know what his spells feel like. It's part of the reason I just know that he's done something. Even if I could still augment, I'd think he cast a spell." She looked at me. "If I'm wrong, then all I need is for you to help me cast a concealment spell."

"You know a lot more witches than I do."

Nina was already shaking her head. "Yes, and they all think I'm working with Rock, or that I was working with Rock, or I'm just pretending to take a break from working with him, and I've gone all shady. He knows all those witches, too. I can't take the chance that someone might talk. Or be forced to talk. He knows too much about me and what I've been doing to stay away from him already."

"Well, I'm not sure I can be more help than your contacts, but if this is what you were thinking about when you cast the fire ceremony, and you asked for the help of the Oracle, then your quest has been judged worthy." I wasn't sure, Oracle or no Oracle. This sounded like one of those consultants who would be a challenge.

"I'm so grateful it worked. I had to do the ceremony four times. The first three didn't work, and I nearly gave up." Nina's face looked haunted suddenly, all sharp angles and hollows, as though she'd aged years in a moment.

"She's not making it easy." It was as though Florry was reading my mind.

No, she's not. This is like looking for a needle in fifty different haystacks. Or at least, it feels that way.

Why had Nina been sent to me?

The Oracle doesn't make mistakes.

You sure about that? I directed my thought at Goldie. *Nice of you to join in, by the way.*

I am. Even when it seems like something has gone awry, there is a reason.

Even when it goes all wrong? Florry told me she has failed a few times.

"We all do." Florry must have heard me. "It sucks. Totally sucks. But it happens."

This feels... not so great. I sent the thought toward both Goldie and Florry. I couldn't tell why, but I was getting a bad feeling about all of this.

Looking at Nina, I spoke carefully. "I am going to do whatever I can to help you. I want you to be able to get your daughter and go live your life. But I'm concerned, because this feels like it's hard to get a handle on. As though there are a lot of moving parts." I felt strongly about helping Kira's mother as well as helping Nina kick her sorry assed ex to the curb. I was worried I wouldn't be able to.

"I'm sorry. Join the club. Rock's hard to pin down. And apparently he's even better than I thought at hiding shit." Nina's tears were dry now, and she seemed angry.

While I preferred trying to keep calm, I thought a

small amount of anger might be good for her. You know, keep the fire going.

Another thought hit me and I sent it out to both Florry and Goldie. *You think she's telling the truth? That's she's on the up and up?*

"She wouldn't have gotten near you if she was in cahoots with Rock-I'm-an-ass-ledge." Florry didn't hesitate.

Agreed.

"Are you second guessing the Oracle?"

Maybe. This feels... weird. Like I can't get a good grasp of what I need to do. Like it's a slippery fish in my hand and I don't have a net.

"Welcome to being the Oracle, sister. You're just getting the sense that your life is going to live in the weird zone? Where have you been for the past three months or so?" Florry started to laugh, which ended in a wheeze.

That's not it. That's not it at all. It's just... something. Something I couldn't put my finger on.

But whatever the 'it' was that was causing me to hesitate, it wasn't right. In fact, it was very off.

None of this mattered, however.

Nina Davenport was here, in my house, she was my next consultant. Once they came to me, once they'd been judged worthy of the Oracle's help—it was my job to help them.

And that is what I'd do.

I just wished I knew how.

CHAPTER TWO

"Do you have somewhere to stay?" Caro focused on the practical matters.

"No." Nina got up and stretched. "I didn't even think about it. I just wanted to get here, to ask for your help."

"You need a friend with a hotel. They can't all stay with you. Barnacles, remember?" Florry added her thoughts.

She was right. Although honestly, Logan was the only one who stayed here. The others, Farrah and Nathanial—they came over a lot while I was working with them. Nina would probably be here a lot as well.

"You don't want to have them here twenty-four seven. You need some down time, some time alone." Florry continued.

All right, all right. I'll see if I can find someone who will work with me, always keep a room open.

I have seen some of the Oracles build a house on their land, so their consultants have a place. Not too far, but not too close, either. Goldie sounded thoughtful. *Is that possible for you here?*

With my garden? I tried not to laugh. *No. I'm lucky to have the small yard that I do, the way things are here on the Vineyard.*

"May I step out back? I need to stretch and breathe a bit more." Nina looked at me hopefully.

"Sure, go ahead." I welcomed the moment to myself.

She got up and went out the back door. When it closed behind her, I leaned back. "Dear lord, how to approach this one?" I spoke to the ceiling.

"First you need to see if she's right, if there is a hex." Caro spoke from over by the sink.

"You don't believe her?"

She shrugged. "I don't know. All you've got to go on is her feeling, even though I do believe her about knowing peoples' magical signatures, for lack of any better way to describe it. She may be paranoid about her ex to an extreme degree."

"He doesn't sound like a good person."

"No, he doesn't. I think you have to trust her until we—well, you, know otherwise, but I guess all I'm saying is to be cautious." Caro nodded. "Yeah. I think that's what I'm saying."

"Okay. Caution it is. Let's find her somewhere to stay." I move into action, calling Shelly to see if she knew someone who had a rental, a room, or something available. Shelly truly had her finger on the pulse of the island, on the web of the people who lived here. We were a clannish bunch, and even though we have tourists here all the time, the residents stuck together.

And if Shelly helped me find Nina a place, it wouldn't be something that people talked about. We tended to keep to ourselves.

I mean, except for Hazel Babbington and her blaming me for her shoddy business practices. There's always one.

"I think I know of one." Shelly was thoughtful on the phone. "But that can wait a tick. How did last night go?"

"Oh, good grief." I couldn't keep the unhappiness from my tone.

"What?" She yelped, probably reacting to my disappointment. "What the hell, Wynter? This was a no brainer! A slam dunk! You better spill, immediately!"

"Shelly." I begin.

"No, don't 'Shelly' me! I braved the gossips to get you the finest selection of prophylactics on the island!"

"He left." My words fell like a stone dropped in the water.

Caro froze near the island, listening.

"What?"

"He left. His friend Mark called, said that they had finally gotten all the access to the Evander things, and he needed to go. Then he went all noble, said he didn't have a soul, that being near him would put me in danger, he couldn't do that, blah, blah."

"And?"

"And what? Then he left." I shrugged, even though I knew she couldn't see me. "What was I supposed to do? Throw myself in front of him? Weep and wail? No."

"No, you shouldn't do that. Never that." Shelly was firm. "But who is he to decide what is good for you?"

"Exactly." That's exactly it. I hadn't had a lot of time to process what happened, what with feeling sorry for myself last night and then coming down to Nina on the doorstep this morning.

"Did you tell him that?"

"I didn't really have a chance to tell him much of anything."

"He just left? Like, Oh, I gotta go? Did something he thought was generous and/or noble and rolled out? Buttoning shirt and pants as he left?" Her voice told me what she thought of such actions.

"Yes. Pretty much."

"Well." Shelly was quiet for a moment. "If that's what you want, what you're willing to accept, I guess you leave him to it. If it's not, then you need to tell him how you feel." She stopped. "Not that I'm trying to tell you what to do."

I burst into laughter. "Yes, you are."

"Okay, yes I am. But am I wrong?"

"You are rarely wrong, oh wise one."

Shelly hooted. "You don't seem to remember that enough. I'll expect a full report. And Wynter?"

"Yes?"

"Do it soon. Like this week. Don't let this sit."

"I don't know where he is."

"Does Mark know?"

"He probably would, unless he's gone with Logan to wherever they needed to go."

"Men." Shelly scoffed. "So sure they need to be all cloak and dagger. Go see Mark, and don't leave until you get the information you need. If Logan's there, you give him what for."

"Hubie's not like that." I got that in there, wanting to see what she'd say. She'd been more cloak and dagger about him than I would have ever imagined.

"Oh, he's all out in the open." Her voice softened.

"Oh, ho."

"Don't even." The softness was gone. "Don't jinx me."

"Yes, ma'am. I wouldn't dare."

"Good. Let me call Myrna. I'll call you back." She hung up.

The slider door at the back of the house opened and Nina walked back in. She looked less distressed, less all out of sorts, as my mom used to say.

"Are you feeling a little better?" I couldn't help but ask.

"I am. Thank you for letting me spill my guts. That probably wasn't necessary for what you needed."

"No kidding." Florry grumbled.

"I needed it, though. I haven't been able to talk to anyone. I didn't know who I could trust."

"Who knows where Kira is?"

Nina was shaking her head. "No one outside of me. And I've protected us both."

"How?" Caro asked.

"I'd rather not say. I trust you to help me, but... I want to keep Kira safe." Nina looked from Caro to me. "Are you two related?"

Caro answered before I could. "No. We're friends. We have mutual friends." She looked up and smiled.

Nina followed her gaze but didn't say anything.

I could feel her distrust, her worry. "One of my policies is that I don't discuss the business of those who come to me. Anyone you meet in this house follows that rule as well." I knew that if Logan ever came back, or any of the Vineyard coven showed up—they would also keep quiet. Live and let live.

Besides, Elizabeth, the leader of the Martha's Vineyard coven, had asked me to study with them. Which meant we'd all need to keep each other's secrets.

I wasn't sure if I had any kind of skill for witchcraft, whatever that entailed. I could scry, using herbs over flame. I was pretty good at it, if I do say so myself. I mean, I managed to find information when I was looking for it.

And I had my own talent, talent that had been enhanced by the Oracle. I rubbed the tattoo on my arm.

My life had completely changed since the moment I slid it onto my arm, when it was still in bracelet form. A coiled serpent with diamonds for eyes, the bracelet was beautiful. I'd found it in a room where—well, it didn't matter anymore where I'd found it.

I'd put it on, and my life took a completely different turn.

I'd thought that things would never be the same after my husband, Derek, had died. That had only been the beginning.

"Oh, hell."

"What?" Caro was eying me.

I sighed. "Natalie, that is my husband's other wife, she emailed me. I need to reply."

Nina spoke very carefully. "How many wives does your husband have?"

Looking at her, and then Caro, I started to laugh. I could hear Florry somewhere in the room, chuckling. Then Caro laughed, and I couldn't stop. When I finally managed to calm myself, I had to wipe tears from my eyes.

"He only had two. He passed away about nine months ago."

"I'm so sorry." Nina's response was automatic.

"Thank you. If he hadn't been dead when I found out he had another wife, another family..." I sighed. "I might have killed him myself. There were all sorts of things. The long and short of it is he lied to us both. He had kids with both of us. While I wanted to scream and carry on, I decided that I'd be better than that for my kids."

"Martyr is more like it." Florry still wasn't visible, but it was clear she was here, listening.

Hush. I sent my thoughts toward Florry. I didn't want to speak to her in front of Nina.

"I don't know that I could do that." Nina gazed at me with an expression I couldn't decipher.

I shrugged. "You never know what you can do until it happens. I didn't want to die in a vat of bitterness, forever angry at someone who was gone, who wouldn't even notice how angry I was. I wanted my kids to be spared from my bitterness. So I pulled myself over it." I looked at her. "At least, that's what I keep telling myself. Fake it till you make it, right? Kind of like you're doing. I'm sure you never thought this is where you'd be."

"Touché." Nina's smile was sad. "You're right. This isn't how I saw my life."

"There you go. We do what we must. Usually for our kids, but it generally is better for us."

"So what did you decide to do about his other wife? Have you met her yet?"

I grinned. "The kids and I went out to Phoenix to meet her. Her son offered us cookies while telling us they hadn't poisoned them."

All three of us laughed once more.

"Thank you for sharing that. It makes me feel

better." Nina looked more at ease than she'd been since she got here.

"I just wanted you to know that we all have to do things we don't like. Yours is more serious. My children weren't at risk."

Her expression sobered. "I don't know what he's planning but it's weird. I know it sounds paranoid, like a wife with a grudge or something, but that's not it. Every time I've gone somewhere new, he shows up. Two cities ago, he told me he wanted Kira. That I had no choice but to turn her over to him. If I didn't, he'd make me pay." She closed her eyes for a moment, took a breath, then opened her eyes and continued. "I've managed ten days now, since that day. Ten days where I haven't seen him. I left Kira two days ago. As if I'd leave her with him! I told him, no way in hell, and he just laughed his smug asshole laugh." Her eyes narrowed.

"How did you get divorced if you were on the run?" Caro was leaning on her hands, watching us.

"I did everything by email. After I requested a restraining order, they were willing to do it virtually."

"Why don't you call the police when he finds you?" I felt like I was missing something here.

"The only reason I got a restraining order was so that I could do everything virtually. He doesn't care about the law in the human world. I knew it wouldn't stop him. It was the only way I could avoid showing up for hearings, having to be in one place at a certain time.

I needed him to not know where I'd be, although he seems to know anyway."

"That was good planning." Caro still leaned on her hands.

"It's hard when your soon-to-be-ex is a skilled magic user. I'm good at what I do, but I don't originate spells. I mean, I have some I can do, when others craft the spells for me, but they are really tiny bits of magic. That's all I need, though. I can make them bigger with augmentation, but it's hard. It takes a lot out of me, and I couldn't have time to recharge, or barely even time to sleep while I was moving around with Kira. Not to mention, my augmentation has stopped pretty much all together, thanks to Rock."

"That's why you left her with someone else."

"That, and where she is, he will never find her." Nina's satisfaction came through loud and proud. "The thing that's made me worry more is that the last two times he's found me, he seems surprised that I'm there. Like he's expecting something to happen. It's the look in his eyes. If I hadn't been married to him, I would never even have noticed it." She shook her head a little. "If he's surprised that I'm there, what is he expecting to happen? If I don't go back for Kira, I know she'll be safe and loved, but... I want her to grow up with me." Her voice dropped.

"Your logic makes sense to me." More than anything else she'd said. It was also scary. What was her ex waiting for?

My phone rang. "Excuse me." I grabbed it and walked into the front room.

Caro and Nina spoke quietly. I couldn't hear what they were saying, but I knew that Caro could handle it.

"Hey." It was Shelly.

"What's the news?"

"Myrna Tostree is all in on renting the friend of your kids a room. But in addition to what feels like a marked up rental rate, I have to tell her if what Hazel Babbington is saying is true, and if not, what the scoop is."

"What are you going to tell her?"

Shelly laughed. "Not the whole truth. I wanted to square it with you so you know the dirt making the rounds."

"That's very kind of you."

"Well, as your oldest friend, of course I don't want to compromise you."

"Don't get too crazy. I'm suing that old bat, and everyone else who had talked trash about me. Maybe tell her I'm exploring my legal options. Hubie hasn't filed anything yet and I don't want to give Hazel or anyone else a heads up."

"You're really going to do it?"

"If I don't, people will always whisper. I'll be a pariah. But once I do this, people will shut their mouths about me because it won't be worth it to gossip."

"Look at you with claws and fangs."

I didn't reply. To me, this was a no brainer, a slam

dunk, to quote Shelly. I didn't want to do it, because it would cost money, and be drama-laden and draining, but I had to. I wasn't moving, and I wasn't going to walk around with a cloud of whispers following me for the rest of my days.

Particularly as Florry said we lived longer than normal.

"Hazel will have to shut her mouth." I couldn't contain my satisfaction at the thought.

There was the chance I could outlive all the gossips, but I didn't want to take it.

"I'm glad. I'll tell Myrna that Hazel Babbington is lying in addition to being a mean old biddy, and she doesn't know her head from a hole in the ground. If that's all right with you?" Shelly asked.

"They're pretty much one and the same, as far as being holes in the ground."

Shelly laughed. "You want me to come get this kiddo, get her to Myrna's? I'll make sure Myrna doesn't have too much of a go at her."

"Oh, I think Nina is more than a match for Myrna, but yes, please." I had some work to do this evening, both for Nina and myself.

And I liked the idea of not having a consultant in my home. That needed to be a standing rule. I might have to look into finding a little shed or something that I could rent. I recalled something Caro said. That Florry initially thought she'd be traveling and doing all sorts of fantastical things, but she often solved the quests before her right in her own home.

I didn't know if that was a disappointing or pleasing thought.

I also didn't know how to write off a rental for consultants as a business expense. Any tax person would laugh me out of their office.

"All right. Be over in a jiff." Shelly hung up.

Walking back into the kitchen, I could see Nina and Caro chatting easily. Caro could stay here, I thought. I liked her.

"I like her, too." Florry was less irritated than before. *Stop eavesdropping.*

"What else do I have to do?" A can of her favorite beer, Olympia, appeared in her hand, and she popped the tab and drank noisily.

I rolled my eyes. "Hey." I walked into where the other two women were still talking. "I found you a place to stay, Nina."

Her face brightened. "You didn't have to do that."

"I wanted to. This way, I know you're safe."

"I hate saying it, but I think it's only a matter of time. I think whatever hex is on me, it's a tracker." Nina looked resigned.

"Then we have to find a way to remove it. You need to be able to go away and stay hidden."

"Or he could go away." She sighed.

"He could, but if he did the things that made life

easier for you, you wouldn't be here." I kept my tone light, because I could tell that Nina was a swinging pendulum emotionally.

"I'm glad to have met you, but I would rather not have had to."

I gave up and laughed. "I agree. You're here now, however, and I'm going to help you get rid of your ex." Oh, shit. I'd made the promise.

Now I had to live up to it.

"Feeling good about your chances. I like to see it." Florry nodded as she sipped her beer.

Going up against a warlock will sharpen your skills. You must take care, however. They are as bad as necromancers without the death magic. With all the magic that harms.

Thank you, both of you. Let me focus.

A knock on the door before I heard someone coming in. That meant it was Shelly. "Taxi service. I'm here." She came in and smiled, looking around for Nina. When she saw her, she walked right over, hand out. "Hi, I'm Shelly, one of Wynter's friends. I'll take you over to your new digs."

"I can follow you." Nina looked to me. "I don't want to leave my car here in case I've been followed."

"It's your show, toots." Shelly wasn't bothered. "Wynter, you need to pencil me into your hopping schedule." She waggled her eyebrows at me.

I ignored Shelly, focusing on Nina. "Why don't we plan to meet tomorrow morning? That will give me some time to do research and see what I can do to help you." I could scry, on my own first, and read some of the books I'd gotten from the witches. I could also call Mark Tattersall, Logan's friend, and see where Logan was.

Because we needed to have a conversation.

Nina came close to me, her hands out. She took both of mine, squeezing them. "Thank you. For the first time, I don't feel like the world is coming down on me. I mean, it is. But I'm not feeling like it is."

"Whoa, big spender. Don't drop all the compliments in one place." Florry's sarcasm could cut through cement blocks.

"I'm glad. I want to help." And I did. Even with my odd feeling about this one. She was young, she'd trusted the wrong man, and she was trying to rectify her mistake with her daughter.

All good things.

Maybe the thought of her ex was what was giving me grief. I didn't know.

I would, however, find out.

"Hey, let's exchange numbers. I'll call you when I'm ready to get started tomorrow."

We added one another to our phones.

Shelly looked between us. "Right. Let's go get you tucked away. You look like you could use some sleep. Do you want to stop by the grocery store?" Shelly led Nina down the hallway, turning to blow me a kiss before they disappeared out of sight.

I blew one back.

One good friend was worth twenty acquaintances.

That was all there was to it. I waited until I heard the outer door close, and then I looked at Caro as I let myself fall back onto the couch.

"Are you all right?" Caro sat down across from me. "And should I have left?"

"No, I'm not. Something's not quite right. It just feels off." I shrugged. "I wish I could explain better. I don't think it's Nina, but I could be wrong. I hate not being sure."

"You'll find out one way or another." Florry stood right in the middle of the arm of the couch.

It was disconcerting when she did that.

"Did Florry just say something?" Caro glanced around.

"She did. Did you hear her?"

"I don't know. I heard something."

"That would be nice if she could hear me. Caro doesn't ignore me like you do."

"She says you don't ignore her like I do." I made sure Caro heard that one.

Caro laughed. "Yeah, she says that now. I ignored her plenty."

Both of them laughed then, and the friendship, the camaraderie—it made me feel as though I'd come out of this one okay, even with all my bad feelings that seemed to be dire warnings.

It would be nice not to live in the land of dire warnings all the time.

"All right. What's on the agenda?" Caro got up.

"Lunch, since it's late enough, and then I need to do some reading and make some calls."

"Wynter, you never answered me. Should I have left after Nina came in?"

"No." I didn't hesitate. "I don't know how you and Florry did things, but Florry trusted you, trusted you with her life. She's not the most trusting. That means something. I'm fine if you stay. If a consultant kicks up a fuss, of course, then it's better you step out, but otherwise, you're welcome."

"Okay. I wanted to be sure. I don't want to overstep."

"You're not." I walked closer to her and gave her a hug. "Give me about ten minutes and I'll be down to make lunch."

"Of course, you can trust her." Florry sniffed.

Caro shook her head. "No, ma'am. I'll take care of it. How about some tuna salad? Stuffed into tomatoes?"

"Sounds delicious."

"Then you go do what you need to do. I'll let you know when it's ready."

"I told you, let her cook. It makes her feel better." Florry was at my elbow, face serious.

"I know. I keep forgetting."

Caro looked at me, and then up around the ceiling, looking, I guess, for Florry. She smiled, almost to herself, and then turned back toward the fridge.

"Well, don't."

"Aye, aye, captain." I gave a mock salute.

"Oh, go away. Ask the grimoire about hexes."

I didn't say anything but ran up the stairs. I did want to ask the grimoire. I'd started to think about a routine with the consultants. First, the grimoire, and then scrying. I did well when I scryed with them, but I also had done all right on my own. Particularly for Logan. I didn't think that Logan was all that special at first. He was just like the other two—now three—who had come seeking help. I'd been thinking that maybe I needed to always try on my own, to see if anything different came to me before I touched the consultant and fell into their head.

So grimoire and then lunch, and then scrying.

After that, I was going to take some time to see if Mark Tattersall was still here on the island in the small rental house he and Logan were staying in. I was going to talk to Logan even if I had to make an appointment.

Shelly had hit the proverbial nail on the head.

Logan decided what would happen between us on his own. He hadn't asked for my opinion, hadn't asked what I thought, if I was worried, or anything. He'd just told me what was what.

And I'd been shocked. My response when I was shocked wasn't always on the ball. I needed time to think about what I'd heard, and what I wanted to say or do.

If this, if us being apart was truly what he wanted, then I would respect that. But I was done letting anyone else, even someone as appealing as Logan, make decisions for me.

I'd lived in the shadow of my family for too long.

I didn't regret it. I adored my children, even now, when they were kind of teetering on the pain in the butt side of things, and I'd loved my husband before I knew who and what he was. I'd built a good life.

I'd also taken a back seat.

Those days were gone. Sayonara, sister.

Which meant I had to face Logan. I had to tell him my truth. And he had to make the decision for him, not for me. Because the only person who got to decide my life was me.

I nodded to myself.

Then I pulled out the grimoire and went to the small window seat in the side of the room. Curling up on the cushion, I let my hands rest on it, feeling the slight hum I always felt when I held the book.

It made sense. It was the record of the women who'd come before me, the lineage of the Oracles. Our story. Through this, the Oracles all lived on.

I liked the hum. It made me feel like I was less alone.

Although how I could feel alone with Florry and Goldie in my ear and up in my grill, I wasn't sure.

We're here for you, Wynter. You should appreciate that fact. Goldie didn't sound apologetic at all.

I do. I just hope you both know when to retreat or close your eyes, or whatever. The idea of someone always being with me, always seeing—it still made me feel a little itchy. I was getting used to it, but still... someone was always there.

Although that could be a good thing if things went spectacularly bad.

I'm no more interested in certain aspects of your life than you are of having me see them. He was a bit frosty.

Good. I just like to make sure that certain boundaries in place.

They are with me. I cannot speak for the former Oracle.

I burst out laughing. "I'm not sure you could get any more disapproval into that one sentence, Goldie."

There are standards. Some of us respect them, some of us dance on them.

"You love her, just like I do."

Humph.

I laughed again and opened the leather-bound cover of the grimoire. How to cast out hexes? I thought about it. Or should it be, How to see a hex? I wasn't sure, but I considered both questions, my hands gliding across the pages of the grimoire. The pages, as per usual, remained blank as I turned them, one after the other. About twenty pages in I slowed, as I saw characters beginning to form on the page.

To Discern and Cast Out Hexes

This was more like it. A direct answer to my question. That didn't happen often. I was so surprised I leaned back a little, blinking. I also didn't want to look a gift horse in the mouth. I bent over the book, eager to see what it would share. Let's get this show on the road.

CHAPTER THREE

As I leaned over the page, watching the words appear, the writing was still going. Holy crow. This was a long entry.

IT MAY BE that you or those close to you become the victim of a hex. This is a curse that is targeted, and often designed to maximize pain, suffering, and perhaps even public embarrassment. Often, hexes are cast while in high levels of anger, so the spell work can be volatile. More dangerous are those cast by skilled practitioners. They are careful, specific, and focused. They manage and contain their anger, directing it into the hex. Above all, expect anger and the unexpected when dealing with hexes. Anger is unstable, as is any magic that uses it.

Should you find yourself or one close to you hexed, the first thing to do is determine if it is indeed a hex, or the imaginings of a fevered brain. Our world is given to high drama and after a time, it is possible to see ghouls where there are only shadows.

Obtain a solid basin. Silver is best, but any reflective metal will do. Fill the basin with water from a pure spring. Add salt that comes from the sea and use a wooden spoon to stir the salt. Place the basin at the feet of the hexed, and the feet within. With the spoon, or ladle, or some other scoop, drench the hexed from the crown of the head as you call out to the gods.

"In the name of all the gods, of my ancestors, and the creatures of the sea, the keepers of the Water, open my eyes to any ancient and evil magicks. Let me see that which has been hidden. Show me those that would harm. With our will combined so mote it be." Repeat if it feels necessary.

If a hex has been identified, first ensure the hexed will not suffer if the work continues. Sometimes those who have cast the evil make it challenging to remove it. Once you can discern your ability to keep the hexed safe, fill another basin fashioned of clay or wood with water from a pure spring. Once again add salt that comes from the sea, stirring it in with a wooden spoon. This time, also add a handful of earth from a sacred place. Then call for the hexed to place the feet within the basin. Drench the hexed with the water and call out to the gods.

"In the name of the gods, my ancestors, and the creatures of the Earth, the keepers of all that lives below and sustains us above. Cleanse this child of Earth of all magicks that do not belong, of all evil intention of harm."

This will free the hexed from that which has attached to them. If it does not, stronger methods must be used.

IT WASN'T SIGNED. So many of these weren't signed. I wished they were, or that I could see the name of those who were Oracles before me. Even if they were dated—I could see when this was used.

A thought came to me. Maybe the anonymity was the point. It didn't matter who we were in the end.

We were all the Oracle. Me, Florry, her mentor—all of us, we were just the vessels. The Oracle continued no matter who was driving the bus.

That was heavy.

However, I had no time for an existential crisis of any sort right now. I read the words again, making sure I had the process ordered correctly in my head. There were two parts to this thing. First was finding out if there was a hex, and then the getting rid of the hex part. It sounded so simple.

I knew it couldn't be so simple. Nothing ever was, and magic was no exception. I knew this universal truth long before I became the Oracle.

This was, however, one of the longest entries I'd read so far. To me, this indicated serious business.

First things first. I needed to find the two basins. A silver metal basin for the first spell, and clay or wood for the second, and big enough for someone to put their feet into.

I'd also need a kiddie pool. If I was going to be dumping water over me or Nina or anyone else, this would make a big mess. A kiddie pool went on the shopping list. It was summer. That shouldn't be tough.

I'd need to find a place to store these kinds of things. Maybe it was also time to clean out part of my shed out back.

"Thank you." I said the words aloud, my hand on the grimoire. "You're getting better. More helpful." Aside from the recipe for an old-fashioned pessary, a form of birth control right before I went on a date with Logan, the grimoire *was* getting more helpful. I wanted to acknowledge the fact that I didn't feel like I was getting just crumbs, with no clear path.

Although it seemed that could be a double-edged sword. This hex business was nothing to sneeze at. The necromancer nonsense hadn't been either. I had to admit, I was glad it wasn't necromancers, but I was surprised at the sheer volume of less than positive or pleasant magical users.

They're like any other humans. In some ways, they're worse because they have things at their disposal most humans don't. More power, a sense of superiority. It's not a good recipe. Goldie's words were harsh, but his tone was thoughtful.

You don't really like humans, do you? I mean, non-magical humans.

He still sounded thoughtful as he replied. *It's not a matter of like or dislike. It's knowing, through centuries of being in this world, what humans are capable of. And magical users, for the most part, are also human. Demons, angels, some of the magical creatures that do not shift, of course, are not human. But humans and part humans are the majority. Humans can be amazing, or they can also be unimaginably horrible.*

I don't disagree. He was right. *It's just nice, I guess, to be dealing with something other than a necromancer. That has been my go-to bad guy lately.*

Warlocks are not any less bad, Wynter. They're merely a different sort of bad.

Noted. I went back to my list. I'd need basins. In thinking over what I had out in the shed, I didn't have anything that would work. A garden center would be the best place to start. I did some searching of the local centers and found what I needed between two on the island. I was relieved I didn't need to go off island.

Since I was going out, I might as well stop by the apothecary and see when Elizabeth wanted to begin my lessons. Given the fact that the consultants were coming to me with less of a break between them, the more I was able to learn, the better it would be for me.

And for the consultants.

And for my sanity.

After I got my shopping plans in order, I hopped in the shower. I found that I stood under the spray longer than normal, turning the water up as hot as I could stand, letting it beat down on my neck and shoulders.

The steady stream of hot water allowed me to relax, and I could feel my shoulders dropping.

When I got out of the shower, I felt a little better. I wasn't happy with Logan, or where he'd left things, or... a lot of things. I had a plan to address the situation with him, and that was all I could do at the moment.

I was, however, excited at the idea of beginning to work with the witches. I hated the feeling of knowing there was so much I didn't know. This, this work with the coven, this would help. This would give me a better footing in the magical world.

Since I was in it for life, I wanted that better footing.

Caro was downstairs, finishing the stuffed tomatoes. "You hungry?"

"I am." I'd forgotten that I'd asked her to make lunch.

"How did it go? Get anywhere with dusty and musty?"

"What's dusty and musty?"

Caro pealed with laughter and after a moment, I heard Florry join in.

"That was my name for the book of not enough knowledge. The book of—" Caro began.

"Smug mysteries." Florry finished the sentence.

"Smug mysteries?" I looked at Caro, and then at Florry.

"Oh, is she here? Hey, Flo. Smug mysteries is the same no matter who the poor schlub of an Oracle is." Caro laughed again.

Florry joined in, a full-throated laugh. "That's what we called the grimoire. The book of smug mysteries. It always gave you information grudgingly."

"What happened to 'you have to learn it on your own'? You know that phrase you're always spouting at me?" I glared at my mentor.

"You do have to learn it on your own. Be thankful, you're not hearing it from a prim, upper crust English dame."

"That was your mentor?"

Florry nodded. "Patsy Cunningham. I loved her, but goddess, could she make me crazy."

"I understand the sentiment."

"Shut it, you. It can always be worse."

Florry is right. She would know. Goldie's words came out in a whisper, as though he was afraid Florry would hear him.

You don't love her like you said you did? I teased.

I cherish all my Oracles. Some of them had more challenging beginnings than others.

Your secret is safe with me, Snaky. I won't tell her.

That. Is. Not. My. Name.

I just laughed.

"I didn't say anything." Florry looked at me.

"I wasn't talking to you. It's not all about you."

Her expression made me laugh even more.

And I realized this was one of the gifts of the Oracle. Yes, I was sad that things were on the rocks with Logan. Yes, I was sad that my kids and I weren't where I wanted us to be, that I was fighting off the aftermath of a crazed criminal charge, and that my kids were struggling with decidedly weird changes in their mom. Yes, I was stressed that my husband's other wife was coming to stay sometime soon.

I looked around at my friends—new, but they felt otherwise—and felt lucky. When I'd lost Derek, people hadn't known what to do after the funeral. It had come down to me and Shelly. And I thanked the gods, goddesses, or whomever was floating about upstairs that I had Shelly.

But it wasn't just me and her anymore.

Yes, the people I called friends consisted of a talking tattoo who leaned towards snide, a chain-smoking ghost in house dresses that had to be seen to be believed, an ancient goddess of the sea, and the BFF of the former Oracle. But these were people who cared for me, who were there for me, and who stood at my side all while I learned a new way of life and battled a case of menopause that felt like a social disease.

Speaking of which, I needed to add the largest fan I could find to my shopping list. I was comfortable at the moment, but one thing I'd learned along the way in this menopause journey was that nothing was ever regular. I was comfortable now, but I knew it wouldn't last.

Caro set a plate in front of me while I was thinking, and I sat down to eat. She stood across from me on the other side of the island.

It was like she'd always been there.

"You want to come with me today?"

"What are you doing?" She took a drink of her water.

"I have some stuff to pick up in order to see if Nina is, in fact, hexed, and I need to find a fan so I don't drown in a pool of my own sweat. I also want to stop into the apothecary and see when I can start my lessons with the coven."

One eyebrow went up. "Busy day."

I laughed. "Haven't you figured that out? It's always busy here, now. You know, when the kids left, I thought I'd have a slower paced life. And I did, until I found Goldie." My hand brushed against my tattoo.

In response, I felt him move along my arm.

Which didn't bother me at all, given my earlier musings on privacy. In fact, I found it a comfort.

"Then everything changed." I ended my thought.

"For the better or worse?"

"For the better. That's not to say I don't get frustrated, but I really love this." It was the first time I'd said anything like this out loud.

I meant it. I hadn't thought it before, but I did love it. My life now, the way things were—it had scared me when it first happened, and honestly, some of the things I faced scared me now. But I loved this.

"Sure. We can talk on the way."

Something in the way Caro spoke made alarm bells go off.

"What's up?"

She shrugged. "You *are* really busy, as you said. I wanted to know when I should book my flight home."

"Don't let her go back there, Wynter. It's better with her here, or somewhere that isn't Lost Springs, Kansas. Tell her to sell both the places and get the hell out." Florry was practically at my elbow, almost shouting in my ear in her hurry to make sure I heard her.

"Why do you think you need to leave? You just got here. And I like having you here. So does Florry. I think you should leave your ticket alone, and if you feel like you need to take a break from the never-ending crises that seem to pop up here, you can just book a flight and leave for a little while."

Caro peered at me, apparently gauging my sincerity. "Are you sure?"

"One-hundred percent. I like having you here."

She turned her face away, and her eyes closed. "Thank you, Wynter."

I reached across the island and took her hand. "No, thank you. I know this isn't your home. You lived in Lost Springs for a long time."

"It's not the same without Florry."

"I can only imagine." I rolled my eyes and went back to my sandwich.

"I was, and am, fantastic company." Florry sniffed.

"Okay, then we can talk about whatever you want." Caro smiled. "Because my topic of conversation is done."

"Can we talk about how I need to fix my not really there love life?"

"You're asking me?" Caro laughed, a big, belly laugh. "When you know who my roommate was for the past thirty plus years?"

"You're both on the crap list." Florry zoomed away.

"We've just mortally offended our mutual friend." I stage whispered to Caro.

"At least she's not the type to break things when she's mad!" Caro called out.

"Don't try me!" Florry's shout came from the front room.

"She says not to try her."

"I wish I could talk to her." Caro looked around; her face wistful. "But this isn't bad. I can feel her at times."

"And you heard her once."

"I think so, but that might be wishful thinking."

We finished eating, and then headed out.

"Love ya!" Caro called out as we left.

She looked out the window as I drove to first one garden center, and then the next for the basins, and then as I stopped at a tourist shop, with tee shirts, beach towels, flip flops and the like.

I was pretty sure I'd find a fan, and I did. It was what Florry would call a whopper, probably eighteen inches across, with rolling ocean waves on one side. I also found the kiddie pool, to my surprise. That was good. One less stop.

Caro sighed. "This is so beautiful here."

"It is. It's why I could never leave."

"I don't know if I could, either. Not if I'd lived here my entire life."

"You don't miss Germany?" I hadn't heard that she'd ever gone back.

Caro shook her head. "I loved America from the first day I got here. I came over on a ship, because it was cheaper than a flight, and I was younger, and far more broke."

"Really?" I was dying to ask her why. She hadn't told me much about herself, and I didn't want to pry if she didn't want to share.

I was still dying to know.

"I'd left my husband, my family, everything. They cut me off, essentially." Her eyes were focused somewhere in the distance. "They couldn't believe I would give up my life."

"You didn't talk to your family again?"

"No. I was dead to them. I have been for decades. I got a job at a cooking school, helping with prep work, and gradually worked my way up to being a student. When I met Florry, I was on vacation, taking a road trip. The rest is history. Once I broke down in Lost Springs, I never left."

"What about your life?"

Caro shrugged. "I was cooking for a family in New York, in their Fifth Avenue apartment. I made an obscene amount of money." She grinned. "I worked all the time, so I stuffed it all into a retirement fund. The vacation where I met Florry was the first one I'd taken since working for them. While they took it well, they were sad, and then upset, that I left. Every so often, I'd go back and cook for them because I truly enjoyed working for them, but I don't regret a thing."

"That's why Florry says to let you cook."

"Yes. It's my comfort zone, it's my fallback. When I don't know what else to do, I cook. If you ever come home to more than one cake, please check in on me. I generally have more self-control."

We both laughed.

"As long as I get to eat them."

"Oh, goodness, yes. If I ate everything I cooked, I wouldn't be good for much. I love food, but I love cooking it more than eating it."

"You don't have to invite me more than once to eat." I smiled. "Let's go to the apothecary and see what our friendly neighborhood witches are up to."

The parking lot was only half full at the apothecary. I walked in and went straight toward the counter at the back. To my surprise, it was Elizabeth who stood there.

"I didn't know you worked here." I smiled at her.

"I do. We all take turns working here. It's good for the soul. It also allows us to catch up on the more mundane tasks. What brings you in?" Her smile was warm, and her eyes went to Caro.

"Oh, I'm sorry. This is my friend Caro Hackett."

"It's nice to meet you." The two women shook hands.

"I wanted to see when you were interested in starting lessons."

Elizabeth was silent for a moment.

I wondered if I'd surprised her by getting straight to the point. I mentally shrugged. I didn't have a choice.

"Are you in a hurry?" Elizabeth asked.

"Kind of. I think the sooner I start educating myself, the better." I couldn't help the note of despair that even I heard in my voice. I was very worried I'd find myself over my head with Nina.

I also wanted to stop asking for help every time I turned around. The more I learned, the more I'd be capable of helping those who sought me out.

Elizabeth's gaze moved between me and Caro.

It took me a minute to figure out that she was concerned about saying too much in front of someone she didn't know.

"Oh. Oh. No, she's—" I stopped. "It's okay to speak freely. My friend knows all about me."

"Really?" Elizabeth's eyebrows registered her surprise. "I don't know that even I can say that."

"That will have to change." I sighed. I'd avoided telling her or any of the witches the entire truth, but if I was going to work with them, I'd have to. More people who knew who I was. More risk for me as the Oracle. Yet another reason for me to begin learning how to better use my magic.

Elizabeth looked between me and Caro again, and I

felt like her eyes saw more than what was in front of her. Then she nodded, almost to herself, and said, "That would be for the best. Now, as for your schedule. How about next Tuesday? We have some things to take care of this weekend, and generally the ladies like a day to recover."

It was Saturday. "Tuesday will be great. I'm eager to learn."

"You might think about reading the books Callie gave you."

"Oh? I'm in the middle of one, but I haven't gotten any further."

"Make time." Elizabeth's words and demeanor were firm. I heard the command of the teacher within them. "Is there anything else you need?"

"No, I'm all good. Should I come here? On Tuesday, I mean?"

"Yes." Elizabeth nodded. "Around four. Then we'll get started."

"Great." I grinned at her, feeling... good. Again.

Caro and I drove home, both lost in our own thoughts.

Caro broke the silence. "Are you nervous about working with Elizabeth?"

"No, why should I be?"

"She's a formidable woman."

"That is an understatement. She's scared the daylights out of me a few times."

"I can see that." Caro looked out the window. "I

can't thank you enough for having me here. This really is beautiful."

I decided it might be a good time to pass on Florry's advice. "Florry thinks you should sell both of the Lost Springs houses and live somewhere else. She thinks that it won't be good for you there."

"It's not. Not without her." Caro's response was quick and very blunt. "The people there are very small town, and even after all these years, I'm an outsider. Now I don't even have my friend there, which was my reason for being there."

"Isn't it less than fifty people, or something? You'd think they would want people to move and stay there."

"You'd think, but the clannish behavior is strong." Caro laughed a little.

"I get that clannish thing. I mean, look where I live. People get snotty if your ancestors don't go back to at least the good ol' whaling days."

That made her laugh even more, as I hoped it would.

"Is that how long your family has been here?"

I shook my head. "No. We were on the mainland, and when the Methodists built all the houses and used this as a summer place, my great, great-grandparents bought a house so the family would have somewhere to go during the summers. While we're not original settlers, we're close enough that we can be tolerated." There was history beyond that, too, but that wasn't my history.

Although maybe it should be, I thought. There were people here before, and my family? Part of the folks who moved them along, moved them away.

Caro, not knowing my thoughts, laughed at my words, and I laughed with her.

I continued, "The house, it's the one I live in now. When Derek and I got married, my mom told me she planned to give me the house, because she was worried."

"Why?"

"I dropped out of college to marry him. He was a year ahead of me, and he wanted to get married and start the business and get on with life."

"As long as you set things aside for his plans." Caro's disapproval came through, even as she was trying not to show it.

I pointed at her to show that she'd hit the nail on the head as I nodded in agreement. "My mom felt the same way. And to a degree, she was right. It was always about his way." Then I waved my hand. "He was a cheater, and a liar, but he was a good father to the kids, and I was happy with our life. I won't rewrite that. I just won't carry on in widow's weeds now that I know the truth."

"You're very calm about the whole thing."

"Not really. I was so angry. But he's gone. I had to decide if I wanted to be angry forever. I didn't. All the things he did, they left a stain on the life I thought I had. If he were here now, I would be tempted to do bad things to his person." I shrugged. "He ruined part of what I thought was my life. I wasn't going to let him ruin my future." I grinned at her. "In the middle of me being all pissed off, I found Goldie, and that has kind of taken over my life."

For the better. I could feel the scales moving on my arm.

Absolutely, most of the time, I teased Goldie.

He didn't respond.

Caro laughed, and then said, "That's smart. And that snake does tend to change your perspective, doesn't it?"

We both laughed.

She continued, "I look at my family, who still maintains I am not a good person. I haven't seen my parents since I left, over fifty years ago. They're both gone now. They let me go without a second glance. Now it's just my siblings, who maintain the fiction that I do not exist."

"I'm sorry." What else could you say? Your family is awful? I mean, they were, but I didn't think it was my place to say so. I could have said it to Shelly. Caro and I weren't that close yet.

"Since you're not consumed with nerves, are you excited about the lessons with the ladies?" She jerked her thumb over her shoulder, back toward the apothecary. For the moment at least, the past was left in the past.

"I am. I feel like there's so much I don't know. Florry said that most of the Oracles had a sense of magic—"

"Nonsense."

"What?"

"Florry's family always hinted they were witches, but they didn't know squat." She chuckled. "Ignore that piece of so-called history. Florry had challenges."

I grinned. "I'm not going to tell her you told me this little tidbit. It's a good thing she can't hear us."

"No need to. Just something to keep in mind. Tell me what you're planning with everything we picked up today?"

"Let's get this stuff inside. I'll tell you while I get it set up."

CHAPTER FOUR

While I set up both the basins, I talked through the process I'd found in the grimoire with Caro. It was really nice to have someone to talk to as I worked.

"This sounds pretty straightforward."

I stopped to look at her with mock indignation. "How long have you been friends with an Oracle, Caro Hackett? When is anything ever straightforward?"

Caro laughed. "Fair point. But it could be. Let's be optimistic."

"She's losing her memory." Florry appeared. "I'll say this to you, Wynter. It does my heart good to see her here, happy. I've been worried about her, and I had no way to contact her after I died."

I won't tell her this. Wouldn't want her to think you'd been too worried. I knew my Oracle guide well enough to know that she wouldn't want sentimentality.

"Good, because if you do, I'll haunt your ass more than I do now, singing I'm Henry the Eighth, I am, or something equally maddening."

Please don't. No singing.

"Snitches get songs."

You've made your point. I won't breathe a word. I decided I was done with the head whispers, as I thought of them. Caro knew about Oracles. There was nothing to hide from her. "Florry, have you done the spell I'm about to do? Searching for and getting rid of a hex?"

"Maybe?" Florry tapped her finger against her thigh.

Today the housecoat was yellow with purple parrots. "Florry, are you getting brighter on purpose? Did you actually own such a housecoat? And what do you mean, 'maybe'?"

"This?" Florry looked down. "No, this one was something I always wanted. And look!" She stuck out a foot. "Matching purple slippers. I thought about this when I was here earlier. I have a never-ending closet on this side."

"Which one?" Caro asked. "Which horror is it now?"

"This is apparently the Oracle version of wishes coming true." I explained what Florry was wearing. "But she didn't actually own it?"

"She always wanted a coat with purple parrots. We never did find one."

"Well, she has it now." *About this spell and the maybe business, Florry. What do you mean?*

"I can't remember. It's a long time ago. Tell Caro it's everything I ever wanted it to be." Florry preened.

I repeated Florry's words.

To my surprise, Caro froze, and her face looked like she was about to cry. "Wynter, will you excuse me?" Her accent was more noticeable than normal.

"Oh, of course."

She hurried from the room. A moment later, I heard her going up the stairs.

"I'll be right back." Florry zoomed after her friend.

Caro and Florry had been friends, roommates for a long time.

A thought hit me. I wondered if they were more than friends. Neither had ever said anything, but it was obvious they cared for one another a great deal.

Then I shook my head. It didn't matter. Nor was it my business if neither of them chose to share with me. I'd help Florry's friend, and Florry, if she needed it. These ladies were my friends, too.

I set up the silvery basin in the kiddie pool. Then I went to the pantry and pulled out my bottles of spring water. I always kept water on hand, because sometimes the power went out, which meant the water did, too.

One of those things about island life. We had a vibrant tourist population—to say the least—who would be livid if they lost power and water, but it happened. Better to be prepared.

Putting it in the basin could wait. I got out the box of sea salt, setting it on the counter. I also grabbed a wooden spoon, which the grimoire said I needed to stir the salt. It had been pretty specific. I wanted to make sure that I followed the directions exactly.

I also needed to copy down the words from the grimoire, and call Nina. Rubbing my hands that somehow had become hot and sweaty on my capris, I decided I'd call Nina first.

That would give Caro some privacy upstairs. While she was in her own room, my house wasn't that big. If she was crying, or unhappy—I'd hear it. So I delayed having to go upstairs to where the grimoire was hidden in my dresser.

Nina answered on the first ring. "Wynter?"

"It's me."

"Are you ready for me?" The hope in her voice was almost heartbreaking.

"I am. Can you find your way here?"

"I think so. We're on an island, right? Only so many places I can go." Nina sounded amused.

"Fine, fine. I'll take off my mom hat."

She laughed. "I understand that. It's like you can't even help it."

"No, it happens without me thinking about it. I've been doing the mom add-ins to conversations for so long it's second nature."

"You want me to come now?"

"If you're ready."

"I am." Nina's words were sure. "You haven't had any creepy angry weirdos showing up and hovering around your house?"

"Not that I've seen today." I walked through the living room to the front room to peer out my window. "No cars that don't normally belong here."

She sighed. "Well, maybe he hasn't found me yet. I'm on my way."

I stared at the phone after we ended the call. Nina seemed so sure there was a tracking spell on her. I hoped she was wrong. Her tone when she spoke of her ex gave me a feeling of impending doom.

No time for that now, however. Racing upstairs and determined to ignore anything out of the ordinary I might hear from the guest room, I ran to copy the words from the grimoire. I didn't want to show Nina the grimoire itself.

I'd just come back down with the spells written on a piece of paper when the doorbell rang.

I could see Nina's silhouette outside the second door. "That was fast," I said as I opened the door to let her in.

"I'm anxious to get this moving and bring my daughter back home to me."

As I nodded, I couldn't help but to squeeze her hand. The idea of how I would have felt if I'd had to keep one of my kids away from me when they were little—it was unimaginable. "You're doing great, Nina. We're going to get her back to you."

I was about to close the door when I saw someone else pull up. Stepping back into the doorway, I stopped and waited. "Nina, if you'll go into the living room?"

"Are you all right?" She reversed course and came to stand behind me, the air around her alert and cautious.

"Yes. I just need to deal with my attorney."

"May I ask what for?" Her face was neutral, along with her tone.

"Oh, he was going to defend me for murder. That charge was dropped, so now we're suing various people for harassment, false imprisonment, anything that would make sense legally."

"Really?" Nina's expression didn't change.

Was this judgement, or did this sort of thing happen often in her world?

My world, too, now. I couldn't forget that.

The magical world was different from the world I'd lived in for forty-five years. In this case, in the non-magical world, since I was innocent, and my charges were dismissed, I needed to let go of being so upset.

Easier said than done.

I sighed as I replied to her. "Yes. Not only did one of my neighbors go bananas, but the police did also. I have to live here. I'm not going to walk around with a cloud over me."

"You could just move."

"No. This is my home. I'm not moving because of the prejudices of someone else."

"Fair enough. I'll go wait for you out back. But give a yell if you need help." Nina was very still for a moment, which made me pause.

Wow.

I'd never seen augment magic, but Nina had a lot of it. I felt it as sure as I felt the sunlight on my skin. She might be blocked, or whatever it was that Rockledge had done to her, but she was still strong.

Then she moved away, taking the whiff of danger that had momentarily shown itself with her.

I blinked and turned to wait for Hubie.

Hubie bounded up the stairs. "Wynter! I hope it's not a bad time?"

"No, not at all. Come in, Hubie."

He followed me in the house. Caro hadn't come back down, which was probably for the best, and Nina was out in the backyard as she said she would be. That was polite.

Hubie looked around, seeing the baby pool with the jugs of water. "Am I interrupting something? Wait, wait." He held up his hands, his eyes closing briefly. When he opened them, his gaze was on me. "Do I need to know?"

I recalled his lack of interest in knowing more about my new life. He'd very decidedly closed the door on knowing.

Which was probably for the better.

Smiling, I said, "No, there's nothing you need to know, it's all good. What's up?"

He grinned, his own smile like that of a shark, looking very pleased with himself. "Okay. I have a bunch of documents for you to sign. You can read them now if you like, as they aren't long, unlike many legal filings." He took out a stack of paper from his attaché case, pushing them across the kitchen island to me. "I'll walk you through them."

I pulled them closer to me.

"The first one is against Dukes County, for false imprisonment and malicious prosecution." He waited while I read it.

"Then, I filed individual suits against Bruce Malik, Andrew Dentwhistle, Scott Trenton, and Judge Beetz."

I looked up. "I thought Beetz was your friend!"

"He is. That doesn't change the fact that he should have booted this case into the bin the moment he saw it. Plus, it will piss him off something fierce to be dragged into Bruce Malik's mess." Hubie rubbed his hands together.

There was no mistaking his pure, unadulterated glee.

"I think you're happier about this than I am." I couldn't help but smile at his obvious pleasure.

"Darn tootin'. I live for this. And there's not a lot of this level of legal shenanigans on the island. Not anymore." He sighed. "I miss the good old days."

"All right, old timer. What else am I signing?"

"Then we're suing Hazel Babbington and her niece Nellie Collette for slander, libel, and defamation. She has implied you have committed a crime, when you have not, and when all charges were dropped, as well as impugning your character verbally and in written form." He grinned. "She really is her own worst enemy. I have the screen shots of her comments on local social media. And your video. But as it stands, you're asking for a public apology, both written and spoken, as well as monetary compensation. We're also going to ask the district attorney to charge Hazel and Nellie criminally. That won't get anywhere, but it will shock Hazel Babbington into behaving." He snickered. "Lastly, you're asking for all your legal fees to be paid, and a healthy sum for pain and suffering."

I read each page. When I was done, I smiled up at him. "Hubie, this is a thing of beauty."

"It really is." Hubie nodded. "Don't expect a lot. An apology from all involved, all the legal fees, no criminal charges, and you're going to get a good sum from the county. I'll make sure of it. I'm also going to push for Hazel to have to cough up some money. You want her B&B?"

I goggled at him. "You think I could get it?"

"She doesn't have a lot of ready cash that I've been able to find, so yes, I think you could. If you wanted it." He nodded. His face was carefully neutral, a strong contrast to his glee in being able to sue half the island.

Or at least, what felt like half the island.

I was as mad as could be at Hazel. I knew that Shelly hadn't even told me half of what the old bat was saying. She'd damaged me.

But take her inn? No. That I couldn't do. Her having to publicly apologize was going to give her an apoplexy as it was. "I'll settle for an amount, and she can pay me monthly. I don't want her business. But she will need to apologize, profusely, in a very public manner. To my face in front of other people, in the newspaper, on our neighborhood online page. And if she's nasty—it's all off. We can go to court." I nodded, more to myself than anything else. "That one I will not back down on."

"Got it." He pulled out a pen from his shirt pocket, offering it to me. "Let's get these signed, and I'll have them at the courthouse within the hour."

As I signed, Hubie continued. "I don't have to tell you that while we're doing this, and for a time afterward, I need you to keep yourself squeaky clean. Don't jaywalk, don't let a scrap of litter fall from your hand on a public street, don't park crooked. Trenton is obsessed with you, and until I can get him leashed and muzzled, I don't want to give him any excuse to arrest you or even come near you."

"Contrary to what this case may suggest, I'm not a hardened criminal. I'm not even a budding criminal."

"I know. I just need you to know that you have to be careful."

"Got it." I went through each set of filing paperwork

carefully once more, making sure I understood what was being said. Hubie was right. It was pretty simple.

"You do indignant so well." I finished the last signature and handed the pen back to him.

He took the papers. "I love being indignant. And I know that not everyone is innocent, but you are. We're going to make sure even the tourists here know you are."

"Thank you. From the bottom of my heart. I don't know how I would have made it this far without you. Now I'm righteously angry, rather than curled in a weeping ball somewhere."

"It's my pleasure. Shelly would flay me alive if I left her bestie at the mercy of the justice system."

"If that's what motivated you, I'll take it." I laughed. For the first time since Scott Trenton clicked the cold metal handcuffs on me, I felt an easing of my stress. I was going to get through this.

It hadn't felt that way when I'd been sitting in the Dukes County jail, but Hubie had gotten me out, and I would right the wrong they'd done to me. "Thanks for believing me."

"I didn't buy it from the start. You had nothing to do with that man's death."

I tried hard not to move, not to blink. I had no idea.

"Okay, that's it." Hubie closed his case. "I'm off to spread the good news at the courthouse. I have to repeat, stay out of trouble, because they are gonna be pissed. If they start hovering around your house, if cop cars start slowly patrolling a lot, or what look like unmarked cars, let me know. It'll be one more thing to beat them with." With a final grin, Hubie waved, and marched out to battle.

I leaned against the counter. The person I really needed to worry about was Scott Trenton. The detective had been on me in a way that was over the top since Ash had disappeared and he and his partner Andy came to question me.

A thought hit me. It wasn't something that would have been a consideration before, but now... I wondered if there was any way to cast a hex finder on Scott. I just couldn't fathom that he disliked me that much. He'd put his job on the line to push the case against me in court. I didn't know it for sure, but I was pretty sure he'd pulled out all the stops he had.

Which was weird. Before Ash disappeared, I'd never even met Scott Trenton. In court, I remembered seeing him talk with the district attorney, Bruce Malik. Bruce didn't seem as gung-ho as Scott.

I hoped that Scott would get the same warning that I did. To keep out of my way, to not antagonize me. I didn't want to see him. Not ever again. But if I could find out if he had some sort of magic push... it went onto my to-do list.

All right. Taking a deep breath, I let my mind move back to the matters at hand. My legal wrangling was managed for a time. I could check that off the list. I went to the sliding glass door and opened it. "Nina? You can come back in. My attorney just left."

She came in without speaking.

"Thank you for giving me some time with him."

"Everything all right?"

I nodded. "As they can be. Now it's time to focus on you."

Nina looked at all the things I'd assembled curiously. "What are we doing here?"

CHAPTER FIVE

Footsteps sounded on the stairs, and a moment later, Caro appeared. Her eyes were red-rimmed, but she wasn't crying now, and she put on a smile. "Did I miss anything?"

"Just my attorney, Hubie, prancing in to show me the papers for my various lawsuits."

"That was fast!" Caro nodded.

"He was as pleased as if he'd just had a bouncing baby boy."

"Good. They all deserve it. What's going on now?" Caro gave a nod that indicated all the things I'd brought in.

"I have everything set up to discover what the hex is on Nina, hopefully." I looked at Nina, directing my words at her. "I also found a way to get rid of it, if we need that. If there is a hex."

"Oh, there is." Nina's tone was grim. "I'm sure of it."

"Let's find out." I still wasn't sure, but we had to know.

Plus, it would give me something to hold onto, some point of focus in this mess. I hated feeling this way, but if I'd learned one thing, I needed to just keep moving forward, no matter how tiny the steps. There was some sort of energy, some kind of guardian something or other, that sent me in the right direction. At least, it had so far.

I hoped it would continue.

"All right. Here's what we need to do." I dragged the pool out from where I'd tucked it next to the kitchen island, Caro stepping in to give me a hand. I smiled at her gratefully as I pushed my hair out of my face.

Damn. I needed a cut, and a little beefing up of the color. Some of the grays were starting to make their appearance known. If I waited much longer, I'd have a bright grayish white landing strip right down the middle of my head.

Not that Logan seemed to—No! I shook my head a little. Logan could stay in the background right now, thank you very much. He was also on the to-do list, on several levels, but not right now.

I shoved the hair behind my ear a little harder than usual, and was rewarded with a few strands of long, blondish hair twining around my fingers.

"What the hell?" I whispered. My hair was falling out?

No. It couldn't be. I let the hair fall from my fingers, not wanting to think about it.

I needed to focus. *Focus, Wynter.*

"Caro, can you get the gallon jugs of water?" I pointed to where I'd left them. "Nina, we need to put a chair in the pool—"

"Wynter, can I ask what we're doing?" Nina hadn't moved, but stood with her hands on her hips, looking at me.

"This is a..." I struggled with what to call it. "A scrying spell, for lack of a better description. An informational gathering spell, if you will. It's one used by the Oracles." That made it sound far more imposing.

One eyebrow went up. "Okay. I had to ask. I haven't seen this before." Nina shrugged then. "Witches aren't the only ones who do magic." Then her smile faded. "I forget that at times."

I didn't need magic to figure out she was thinking about her ex, or her daughter, or both. "Well, that's why you're here. To learn about whatever... whatever..."

"Shit." Caro supplied as she opened up one of the gallon jugs.

"Shit." I nodded in agreement. "Whatever shit your ex did, we're going to discover it, and put an end to it."

Nina's face brightened a little. "I'm all in on that one."

"I know. Grab one of my white plastic chairs from out back and bring that in, will you?"

She headed out the back door.

"Did Florry ever do this?" I asked Caro in a low tone.

"No. But you're going to be great." She didn't even look at me as she spoke. "How many do you think we'll need?"

I eyed the silver basin. Well, silver-ish. It was a pond accessory, and while it wasn't solid silver, it was the best I could do. "Maybe two? She needs to put her feet in."

"Got it." Caro opened up the second jug and set it down. There was a look of pure enjoyment on her face, a mixture of what seemed like anticipation and satisfaction all rolled into one.

"She was always good at this sort of thing." Florry appeared by my side.

Are you all right? I didn't want to talk out loud, not with Caro pretending all was well. Not to mention, this wasn't anyone else's business. It wasn't even really mine, but... I had to ask. *Is she all right?*

"I'll be fine. So will Caro." Florry brushed off her zooming away after Caro as though it was nothing.

I got the hint. *All right. I was just checking. Right now, try and be helpful. This is from the grimoire, but I'm really nervous. This feels like more than just scrying.*

Scrying is scrying. Goldie chose this moment to wake up.

Not helpful. I had to resist the urge to roll my eyes.

"Golden boy is not always helpful." Florry must have caught my thought to my armband. "Unlike me."

I inhaled so as not to snort in disbelief.

Florry continued, "He gets there eventually. The grimoire generally doesn't steer you wrong. By the way, if you do something, and it all goes to hell, you need to record it, so that any future Oracle knows what to look out for."

What, like in the book? Like a note, or something? I hadn't thought of writing in it myself.

"Yes, in the book." Florry did roll her eyes.

Nina came back in with a plastic stacking chair, one of a number that I kept for guests.

Not that I'd had all that many guests who hung out in the garden recently, but I used to.

Back when I wasn't the town pariah.

You're feeling rather sorry for yourself. Pull yourself together and do the work you need to. Goldie was clearly snippy this afternoon.

I ignored him, and Florry. "Put it in the pool," I directed Nina. "Then you need to take off your shoes and put your feet in the basin."

"Any chance the water is warm?" Nina smiled, looking a lot less nervous than me.

"I don't know." I could feel my forehead knit together as I frowned.

"I'm kidding, Wynter!" Nina laughed. "Seriously, it's all right. This is nothing."

"You're a lot more cheerful than I'd thought you'd be." My words came out as a grumble.

Oh, god. I was starting to sound like Florry. Or Goldie. Or any other old lady off the street.

"Well, it's either try and smile and put one foot in front of the other, or curl in a ball and cry. And if I do the curling in a ball, my ex wins." Nina's face hardened. "I'm not going to let that jerk get another thing from me."

A sentiment which was totally understandable. "Then let's get this going. Nina, in the chair."

She slid off her sandals and sat down in the chair.

Caro poured the water into the basin, first one jug and then the other.

Everyone was quiet and there was an air of anticipation, even from Goldie and Florry.

I sprinkled the sea salt in the water, stirring it with the wooden spoon and watching to see when the salt dissolved in the water. I dipped the spoon in the water. "Close your eyes, Nina." My words were a whisper.

"Oh, hell." But she closed her eyes.

Holding the paper with the spell, as I spooned water onto her head, watching it run down her hair in small, silver rivulets, I carefully and slowly spoke the words the grimoire had given me.

"In the name of all the gods, of my ancestors, and the creatures of the sea, the keepers of the Water, open my eyes to any ancient and evil magicks. Let me see that which has been hidden. Show me those that would harm. With our will combined so mote it be."

I emptied the spoon over her head once, then twice, more and waited.

The water in the basin swirled around Nina's feet, slowly at first.

Nina muffled a gasp.

"Are you all right?" I whispered.

"It tickles." Her voice showed the strain of holding still. She was trying not to laugh.

The water moved faster, still swirling, looking like a miniature whirlpool in the basin. Then a light bluish green light rose from the whirlpool, like the smoke from a newly-lit fire.

It twined around her legs, getting darker, first more blue, then more green.

I didn't even dare to breathe.

The smoke moved up around her knees, then onto her thighs, and then around her waist.

This didn't feel right. The grimoire hadn't said anything about smoke. Or that it was kind of creepy. Okay, it was a lot creepy.

What was happening here?

The sea-colored smoke twined along Nina's waistline, small wisps moving up and down from the main band. It was as though a lot of tiny, creepy fingers were petting her.

Nina's expression changed from struggling with laughter to... something else. "Wynter..." she began.

The smoke band shot up and covered Nina's mouth,

almost as though someone had clapped a hand over her mouth, and behind the smoke, Nina screamed, the sound coming out muffled. Her eyes went wide, tears forming at the corners. She struggled, trying to kick her feet out of the basin, but the smoke that had drifted all around her legs held her fast.

"What in the name of all the saints?" Caro breathed.

I stared at the smoke. Then I closed my eyes, picturing the smoke behind my eyelids. Greenish blue, bluish green, the beautiful color of the sea, but insidious and creeping and most definitely not friendly.

"Go away. Whatever you are, whatever you're doing, go away. You're not welcome here." I squeezed my eyes and pictured the smoke flying out the back door. Opening one eye a little, I peeked at the smoke hand over Nina's mouth.

Nina's eyes were wide, and she was struggling behind the smoke. The smoke had wrapped itself further down her body, like ropes.

"You need to go." I said out loud, staring what I hoped were daggers at the persistent smoke that haloed around Nina.

The smoke cloud moved lazily, as though it wanted to be sure I knew it wasn't listening.

You need to go. I thought the words, closing my eyes once more. *There is nothing for you here.*

What felt like a summer breeze moved across my face, lifting the hair off the back of my neck a little. I kept my eyes closed. *Go. You're not welcome.*

A moment later, Nina let out a yelp. "I knew it! I knew that bastard put a hex on me!"

When I opened my eyes, there was no trace of the eerie smoke. It was as it had never been there.

But Nina looked red-faced and stressed. Caro was watching the two of us with wide eyes.

It had been there.

"Is that the sort of thing that a hex would do?" I had to ask. "I mean, I'm not really an expert in hexes." Or any kind of magic.

Yet. Goldie's voice held great satisfaction. *You will be training with the witches soon. That will improve your magical abilities.*

It's a good thing. I didn't bother to hide my relief. *I'm tired of feeling like the last one on the block to know anything.*

He made a sound that was suspiciously like a snicker but didn't say anything more.

"Are you all right?" I walked over next to Nina and offered my hand.

In the kitchen, Caro was opening drawers. In a moment, she came out from behind the island with several dish towels in her hands.

Nina swung her feet out of the pool, taking my hand as she did so. I helped her up and over to a chair at the dining table. "What do you think that was?"

"Some crap Rock has been doing." Nina rubbed her face. Her eyes met mine, looking dull. "So now we know, right? What's next?"

I wanted to rub my face, too. It was like hearing someone sneeze. Or maybe I was just stalling for time. "Whatever that it was, it wasn't friendly. It didn't touch me, but I could feel the malevolence." That was the word. Malevolence. "I have another... part of this, if you will, that can get rid of whatever he's put on you." I wished that I knew what Rockledge's spell was.

But did it matter?

"I can't believe I'm saying this, but can I have a couple of hours? I was raring to go when I got here, but after that, I'm wiped out." Nina rubbed her face again. "Which makes sense. Rock always likes draining his enemies."

"He thinks you're his enemy?" Caro was quiet as she asked her question, handing Nina towels for her feet.

It fell into the room like a bomb.

Nina nodded. "Yes. Now that I'm not only refusing to work with him, but I've taken Kira, I am one hundred percent the enemy."

"I am really sorry." Caro shook her head.

"So am I. We don't have to do the next part right now, Nina." I wanted her to feel comfortable. For all the roller coaster feelings that this particular consultant brought out in me, I didn't want her to suffer any more than she had. "You can crash here if you like."

She was shaking her head before I finished my words. "No, I think I'm going to go home." She reached over and took my hand. "I'm really sorry. I know I came in here all on fire, and now I'm bailing early, but..."

"It's fine. Seriously. It's okay to listen to your body and recognize when you're done."

Nina nodded, squeezing my hand as she did so. "I'll go take a nap, and I'll call you later?"

"Sounds good."

Caro and I watched her leave.

"She doesn't look as healthy as she did when she first came in." Caro's brows knitted together as she frowned.

"What do you mean?"

"That spell you did—it took something out of her."

"Oh, no. Do you think I hurt her?" The thought was horrifying.

"No, no, not that. But that whatever it is that's sitting on her, whatever magic her douche husband cast, it's sucking life, or energy, or something out of her."

"Hmmm." That was interesting, and it would make sense given what Nina told us about her husband. He sounded like someone who enjoyed harming others.

"There's more." Florry appeared.

"Where were you?" I asked.

"There's something around her." Florry shook her head. "It's like... it's like a countdown clock. I feel like whatever it was, whatever was driving that smoke, it's waiting. That there's an end. That this won't go on forever."

"Like a ticking time bomb." I grasped what she was saying immediately. "So not only is it draining her, it's counting down to something? How can you tell?" I asked Florry.

She shook her head. "I don't know. I wish I had more for you, something more concrete. But I was watching it, and trying to figure out what it was, and I could see something within it."

Caro was gazing at me, and then looking around—but I had to take a moment, figure out what this meant.

I needed to make a note of this—of the fact that Nina's energy was being siphoned, and that there was an end date to whatever it was that was taking from her. If I didn't, I'd forget. It would fall right out of my head.

Florry had warned me that I needed to make notes when something went differently with anything suggested by the grimoire. Okay. So when I go back up, I'll make my notes. And make a timeline so I could help Nina sooner rather than later, so that--I ran my hand through my hair, thinking, and as my hand dropped, I felt the tickle of hair on my hand.

"Holy shit." I breathed as I looked down at my hand. There was a definite clump of hair. Everything else flew from my mind.

My hair.

Without thinking, my hands went into my hair, pulling on it slightly.

Both hands had strands of hair in them when I looked down.

Everything else went right out of my head.

"What's wrong?" Caro came over to stand next to me, looking curiously at my hands.

"It's my hair." My voice was small. "Look. It's my hair, Caro."

She leaned over, peering more closely at my hands. "How old are you?" she asked without looking up.

"I'm forty-five." My voice still sounded small, withdrawn.

"Have you moved into the change?"

"The what?"

She stood up then. "The change. Menopause."

I nodded. "Recently."

"This happens." She reached out and rubbed my shoulder. "It's not going to be fun, but this is one of the things that can happen."

Tears filled my eyes. I was already reeling, even if I was keeping it at bay, at Logan's getting up and walking away from me. Now my hair was falling out?

Could I just get a break?

You will come into even more power as you age and your hair grays.

Goldie, that's really not helping right now. A tear slid down my cheek. *I have to keep hair for it to go gray.*

"Honey, it's gonna be okay." Florry appeared, her face kind, and her voice softer than normal.

"You aren't losing you hair." My voice was small, tears on the edge of my words.

"Oh, it's going to be okay," Caro said quickly.

"Go see your doc toot sweet." Florry's words came just as quickly.

I waved a hand at both of them and headed for the stairs.

Right now, for the next ten minutes, I needed a minute.

CHAPTER SIX

In the end, my ten minutes was closer to fifteen.

I went to my bathroom, stood in front of the mirror, and gently and very carefully brushed my hair. More came out in the brush than I was happy with.

Florry was right. I needed to call my doctor.

Turning away from the mirror of bad news, I dialed the number for Dr. Amberson's office. Since she'd been the one to tell me that I was, in fact, in menopause, I figured she could help me with this latest looming disaster.

Why couldn't I be like Florry, with her field of wonderful hair? I'd even be all right with it going gray —well, maybe not. Florry had snow white hair, and it was truly beautiful, but I wasn't ready for that yet.

Even if it meant I was still stuck beefing up my blond with regular touch up.

A check up with Dr Amberson scheduled at the end of next week, I turned back to the mirror. I hadn't planned on having the afternoon free. I'd planned on doing both spells with Nina—and now, here I was, at loose ends. Hopefully I'd be able to cast the hex out in the next day or so. The idea that there was a time limit made me nervous. But with Nina safely in a place nearby, there was nothing that I could do at this moment.

Which meant I needed to use this time to tackle another of my challenges.

Splashing water on my face, I considered what to do next. What I wanted to do made my heart speed up and race, and my throat feel like it was closing.

I was nervous as hell.

But it had to be done.

Taking my time, I put on some makeup, and combed my hair once more, grabbed a few things to put in my purse, then went back down.

"Are you all right?" Caro and Florry said together.

I looked at the two of them, their faces earnest, and their concern evident, and wished I could find a way for them to be able to talk to each other.

Something to put on the to do list for questions for the witches.

But back to the matter at hand.

"I am. I'm going out."

"Where are you going?" Caro asked.

Florry was silent for a moment, and then she chortled. "Oh, ho! You're finally going to beard the scaredy cat in his den! Well, it's about time, missy! You look great. He's gonna eat his heart out."

I smiled at Florry, my heart lifting slightly at her words. "I hope you're right."

"What?" Caro asked.

"Florry told me he was going to eat his heart out."

Caro smiled then. "You're going to see Logan? Good. He can't just walk away. Not like that." She folded her arms. "It is the easy way out, even though he thinks he's doing the right thing by you." She made a scoffing noise. "Men."

"Better off in the distance." Florry sniffed.

"Well, aren't you two a cheerful pair. I like men."

"Because they're batting a thousand with you?" Florry asked.

"Everyone makes mistakes. It's what you do after you realize you make one," I said.

"That go for Derek, too?" Florry was sly.

"I don't know." I refused to let her bait me, even as I felt my cheeks warm and my anger at him—that hadn't completely gone away, but that by God, I was working on—rise in my chest. "He wasn't around when I found out about his crap, so I can't say. I will say had he been alive, things would have been thrown."

"It does get their attention," Caro said with a nod. Her eyes darted around, seeking, I thought, Florry.

Watching Caro, watching Florry watch Caro—the two of them decided this matter me. That was it. Depending on how the rest of today went, I was going to find out how I could help Florry and Caro talk to each other. I didn't care if that wasn't in the rules book, or whatever. They deserved to still be able to be friends.

And it would save me a lot of translating.

What part of witch lessons would that be, I wondered? Lesson Five? Or was that a second or third year thing? The thought of me being back in school made me smile.

"I'll be out for a while. I need to track him down and talk to him." I didn't say anymore. As much as I wanted this to succeed, I wasn't going to beg or plead. Logan had to want this. Had to be willing to work at it.

"Hey, one thing you need to know." Florry spoke almost as though it was an afterthought.

"What?"

"When you did the scrying with Nina, and the smoke came out?"

I nodded.

"There's something else behind it."

I frowned. "What do you mean?"

"I mean there's something else behind it. We need to discover what that is."

"I agree," I said. "Can it wait a couple of hours?"

Florry smiled. "Go get your freak on, but remember, you're still on the job!"

"Got it," I said. Wanting to make my escape while I could, I grabbed my purse, and tossed in the things I'd brought from my bathroom. There was no reason to believe... well, at least I was thinking ahead.

"Happy hunting!" Caro called out as I left.

While I wanted to be with Logan, and thought he wanted something similar, first indications weren't great, but... I wasn't going to just be put aside unless I put myself there.

I drove over to where Mark and Logan were staying. There were no cars in the small driveway, although there were cars parked alongside the road in front of the house.

Nevertheless, I parked a couple of houses down and marched up the walk of the small rental cottage. There was no doorbell, only a ship's bell next to the front door. I rang it back and forth four times, making sure the clapper hit the side of the bell hard each time it made contact.

This place was so small, there was no way they could miss the sound.

I waited. There was silence at first, and then I heard footsteps coming from the back of the house, getting louder as they got closer.

They were the steps of a tall, big man.

But both Mark and Logan were tall, big men.

The door swung open, Logan filling the doorway.

Everything I wanted to say, everything I'd been

thinking, or planned—it went out of my head. My mouth opened, but no sound came out.

Logan looked as stunned as I felt.

"Wynter..." his voice was low, hoarse. Almost raw.

"I... I wanted to talk to you."

A spark flared in his golden eyes, and then disappeared. His head lowered. "There's nothing to say, Wynter."

It was that tone of finality, that he'd made a decision, all on his own, for the both of us—*that* tone snapped me out of my stupor. "Yes, there is." I stepped closer to him, so close that I could smell his warm, spicy scent.

His head came down lower.

I wondered if he knew he was leaning into me.

Even his smell was distracting. I had to put some distance between us, at least for now. I stepped around him and into the small cottage. *Stay focused*, I told myself. I needed to get what I came here to say out, and then it was on Logan as to what came next.

Because I was done being directed, being told what had to happen. I already had enough that I couldn't control with regard to being the Oracle. I wasn't going to be a passenger in my love life.

I took a breath. This was harder than I thought it would be,

"Okay, Logan," I said. "I need you to listen to me and then we can talk. Okay?"

Logan's lips tightened and he crossed his arms

leaning back leaning away from me as he gave me a stiff nod. His body language was so expressive. I had to wonder again if he knew what he was doing.

How could a man who turned into a panther for fun and danger not know?

How had he managed to survive as Evander Thane when he telegraphed everything he thought? Maybe that was part of the problem?

Focus! Goldie's voice broke into my navel gazing. *Say what you need to say, Oracle, and insist that this man make a choice.*

You sound like you hope he stands his ground.

There was a silence and then I heard, *He's not good enough for you.*

Goldie sounded like my dad after he'd met Derek a few times. Although in the end, my dad had been right.

I was older now, and I had a better sense of what was and wasn't good for me. And Goldie, like my dad, could be right. However, I would be making the call of what was right for me from now on. Not Goldie, Logan, or anyone else.

"Committee weighing in?" His tone was amused.

"What? Oh, um..." I felt my face heat up. "How can you tell?"

"I've been around you long enough to know when you're having conversations no one else can hear." The humor was even more apparent.

"I live by committee. For some things," I added, thinking about the vow I'd just made for myself.

"That's why I'm here. You don't get to decide what's right for me, Logan. The only person who gets to do that is me. I'm the final word in my life, no matter what my committee might say."

His humor vanished, his face creasing in concern and what looked like anger. "You just got out of legal trouble. The police here are going to be watching you, no matter what happens next. I am not Logan Gentry. Not anymore. I'm Evander Thane, and if you think the cops and lots of other interested parties, both in the magical world and otherwise, aren't going to be on my ass like mud on a pig, you are very mistaken."

"So?"

"What?" Logan shot back, glaring.

"So. What?" I enunciated the two words. "I'm the Oracle of Theama. The magical law enforcement would like to, very much," I said, remembering Farrah, my second consultant, "Get me under their auspices." I held up a finger. "There seem to be a bunch of groups of necromancers who are out for me." I held up a second finger. "Plenty of people, probably more than I am aware of, think I have no right to this." I lifted my arm, held up a third finger, and then brushed my hand over Goldie, marveling as I always did at how right he felt on my arm.

The scales shifted under my fingers in response.

Still not good enough for you.

That's my choice to make. My tone was firm. I turned my attention back to Logan. "So it seems, on the danger side of things, I'm just as much of a danger to you as you are to me." I narrowed my eyes. "You know this. You've seen the men who have come after me."

Logan shifted from one foot to another, but he didn't say anything.

"So what is it? I'm in no more danger than I was before."

"I've lost everything once before. I don't know what I had—well, I kind of have an idea now," Logan said, laughing a little. "But I didn't lose anyone. Not someone like—" he stopped.

"Like what?"

His nostrils flared as he took a deep breath and looked away.

Clearly he hadn't planned on having this conversation with me. Too bad.

"Like what?" I persisted.

"Like you. Like someone I cared for. And now that I don't have the power of will, now that the Egyptian witches took it—I'm more vulnerable than before! I can't protect you! I'm not even sure I can protect me!" There was a tinge of bitterness in his words.

He'd given up the power of will, the thing he'd sold his soul as Evander Thane to a demon for. He'd given it up because it was the right thing to do to return it to the Sisters of the Asp, and Logan Gentry knew that, even if Evander Thane hadn't cared.

Now we were getting to the heart of it. He had a lot of issues.

So did I.

But we were going to figure out our relationship issues first, then we could each inspect our personal baggage with a magnifying glass, if that was what he wanted.

First things first. I knew this was what I needed to be doing.

"You can't ever really protect someone else, Logan."

"You've been in the magical world for what, two minutes? How do you know?"

"I've been part of a relationship, lots of relationships, for years."

Logan rolled his eyes. "That's not the same."

"Yes it is! It damn well is the same! Derek couldn't protect me from his weakness! Neither could my parents, even though they saw it, and did what they could. I couldn't protect my kids from their father's failings, much as I wanted to. I couldn't protect Farrah from learning the truth about her mom. I don't think I'll be able to protect Nina from whatever shit is about to come our way. I don't even know what kind of... of... shit it is, " I said, feeling frustrated as all the thought about Nina came rushing back. The scrying. Florry's words of warning.

No. This is my time for me.

"But I know it's there. Heading right for us, for her." I threw out my hands. "No one can protect anyone all the time. It doesn't matter if there's magic involved or not. Even the Oracle magic can't protect me all the times—that crazed man broke in before, and was sitting in my back yard like he owned it."

"You protected yourself."

"I hope I did. I shouldn't have to, though. Why is anyone after me in the first place? But it's a risk you take when you decide that you're going to be a part of the world." I stopped and looked at him. "All of this is well and good, but you're stalling. I want to be with you. I thought you wanted to be with me. Now you're going to let fear get in the way?"

He stared at me for a long time, so long that I started to get uncomfortable.

"I can't bear the idea of something happening to you." His words were a whisper. "I bore losing my life. I bore starting over, as a man with no past, no history. But I don't know if I could bear it if I lost you, Wynter."

"Well, you're trying awfully hard to lose me right now." I snapped at him, unwilling to put up with this damn pity party. It did hurt to lose someone you cared for. I knew this.

It wasn't the end of the world.

It wasn't a reason to be afraid.

I wasn't afraid, I realized. I mean, sure, I knew necromancers were after me, in a general sense. They seemed to have a grudge against me. I suppose if I were in their shoes, and someone had put a halt to my plans the way I'd done to them, I might be holding a grudge of some size.

There was a demon who had tried to break through

the spell the witches put around my house. I nearly shuddered, remembering the loud crash that startled me out of bed.

My list of enemies was growing.

But I wasn't afraid. At least, not like I'd been when Goldie landed in my lap. I was the Oracle, it was for life. I'd chosen it. So now, I had to look forward, and without fear. Fear would keep me locked in the house, never venturing out, taking a chance, taking a risk.

I didn't want to live like that.

"Are you willing to let fear of the unknown stop you from living?" I softened my voice a little.

His brows lowered. "You know that's not true. I've lived the last eight years with the unknown."

It was difficult not to throw up my hands. "Then everything is a threat—how do you get out of bed?"

"This isn't a joke, Wynter. You—"

I cut him off. "You think I don't know that? People are trying to kill me for reasons I don't even completely understand." I also didn't understand why this was so hard.

Then it hit me.

This was like a birth.

When I'd lost Derek, it hadn't only been his death. The Wynter Chastain that I'd known, that everyone thought they knew—she died with him. It took me a while, but now as Wynter, the Oracle of Theama, I was in the middle of a rebirth. Just call me one of those brothers on that show that kept dying and coming back.

I was coming back.

Whether it was birth or rebirth, it was a painful, messy process.

Logan was going through the same thing. He'd died when whomever it was dumped Evander Thane out in the desert. He'd been reborn as Logan Gentry, and his process hadn't been easy. Now he'd died again—because who he thought he was as Logan had to find a way with who he used to be as Evander. A birth, and not one that was welcome, or happy.

The thought made my head swim and it wasn't even my identity.

So perhaps I could give him some... leeway on running from me.

But not for long.

I took a deep breath again, letting it fill me to my toes. "Look. There's risk inherent for both of us—just being who we are. There's more risk if we're together. I get that. But," I stopped, feeling the weight of what I was about to say, "I would rather be with you than without you. If you don't want to be with me because of things between us, that's—well, that's not okay." I felt the tears well up in my eyes as my throat began to ache like it did before I cried.

"But you don't get to decide what is best for me, Logan. Only I do." I stepped closer to him, resting my hands on his chest.

Oh, it felt good to touch him.

"I want you." My voice came out in a whisper. "Don't you want me anymore?"

There was so much more I wanted to say, but I closed my mouth and waited.

The next move was his.

CHAPTER SEVEN

Logan's eyes were so intense I felt like I wanted to look away, but I couldn't.

"Don't I? When I'm with you, I don't want anything else. I don't care that I'm a wanted man. I don't care that I have no soul, no future. *All* I want is you, Wynter." Logan growled and before I could even think about an answer, his arms were around me as he crushed me to his chest.

Then his lips came down on mine, and there was nothing else.

I couldn't breathe. I couldn't think. I couldn't do anything other than twine my arms up and around the neck of the man who held me.

Logan.

He smelled wonderful.

His skin was hot. I could feel it through his shirt. "I

want you." I managed to get the words out against his lips.

"In here." He barely took his lips from mine as he lifted me up.

I wrapped my legs around his waist.

One of his hands moved up to tangle his fingers in my hair as the other moved down to cup my ass, and hopefully make sure I didn't fall.

Then he walked down the tiny hallway, his elbows bumping against the pictures and knickknacks.

Something crashed, but Logan didn't stop.

I felt him kick open a door, and then he carefully set me on the bed, stepping back to unbutton his shirt with quick, jerky movements.

When he pulled off his shirt, I was struck almost breathless again at how truly beautiful Logan Gentry was. His skin was gorgeous, only slightly less dark in the areas that weren't getting sun. His muscles were defined, yet smooth, and every move, as I'd often noticed, spoke of bodily harmony. The small white scars that covered much of his torso only added to the beauty of his physical person.

He might have other baggage, but Logan moved like a man on top.

"You're kind of behind here." He smiled as he unbuckled his belt.

"Sorry." I stood up. "I was gawking at you."

"Much as I want to be gawked at by you, there's something I want more." His eyes gleamed.

My breath caught. "O—okay." I pulled my shirt over my head, and then taking a breath, undid my bra.

I was used to one man. While my mind said that was over, it was a bit tougher getting my body to remember that. I felt shy and exposed as I let my bra and top drop to the floor.

Logan stopped in the middle of sliding down his pants—something I needed to watch, and pay attention to once I got the heck out of my own head—his mouth open.

"What?"

"You are beautiful." His words were whispered, reverent. "Are you sure you want to, I mean, with me?"

"Yes." The fact that he was harboring his own nerves made me less nervous. "I want you, Logan."

We stared at one another in silence for what must have been only a moment, but felt like a lifetime, an eternity. In his gaze I saw acceptance, and maybe love. Not now, but one day. Gratitude, happiness, lust—it was all there, written all over his face.

Logan wasn't even trying to hide it from me. His eyes bored into mine as he finished undressing. And speaking of lust, it was very clear he was lusting.

Oh, boy.

Was it clear.

Very, very clear.

I slid down my capris, taking my panties with them. I didn't want to deal with the fumbling of getting undressed. Parts of this were nerve wracking enough without worrying about falling on your face as you tried to undress.

How would you know?

Really? Why are you here right now? Go do something else! I pictured slamming a door onto Goldie, Florry, and all things Oracle related. This was my time.

Goldie mumbled something but I didn't hear it. I didn't care. It could wait.

Logan stepped closer to me, bending down to kiss me as one hand cupped my cheek. The other slid down my side, skimming over my butt, and then cupping me closer to him.

He was hot and hard and right next to me. Even as I was so excited I almost didn't know my own name, I was nervous.

"Wynter, it's okay."

I wondered if he could sense all my emotions.

"Kiss me. It will be okay."

Yep. He was sensing.

But that was all right. I let go and fell into his kiss, letting his lips take me to a place where I was floating, where it was only the two of us, and the rest of the world could go hang.

How long we stood there kissing, I couldn't tell.

Logan took a step forward, bringing me closer to the bed.

"Oh!"

"What?" He whispered against the corner of my lips.

I slipped under his elbow and went toward the door of the room where I thought I'd dropped my purse. I dug around, and when I turned back to Logan, condoms in my hand, he laughed out loud.

"You came over here just to objectify me? Again?" He laughed once more, harking back to the time when Shelly had discussed all of his physical attributes in great detail right in front of him.

"No. I was just... hopeful."

"Good thing. I apparently wasn't hopeful enough. Come here." He held out a hand to me.

As I reached the bed, my hand in his, he took the condoms from me and set them on the bedside table. Then he turned me slightly, keeping my hand in his as I sat back on the bed.

I scooted toward the headboard, feeling... I didn't know. I wanted Logan. Badly. But..

Logan joined me and kissed me, driving all other thoughts out of my mind. His kisses were like a drug, taking me to places I didn't even know existed.

As we kissed, he cuddled next to me, his hand moving along my body, learning me. Learning my curves. When he moved down, his lips touching my collar bone, I thought about that.

My curves. My hair that was falling out. That needed a dye job badly.

Oh.

One hand went to my hair as the other brushed

lightly against my hip. This is when I needed to come back to reality? Right now?

"Stop." His larger hand slid over the one on my hip, stilling my fluttering fingers.

I couldn't get over the warmth of his skin. Not only how nice, how good, how delicious it felt—but how much I liked his skin next to mine.

"You are beautiful." His words brooked no discussion, and the timber of his voice, low and gravelly, with his eyes glowing golden as he looked at me, sent a thrill through my body that landed smack dab in the middle of my core, and caught fire.

I burned for him.

"I have never met another woman like you." He leaned down to kiss below my rib cage, then slid his body up mine.

Oh, my dear and happy sweet baby Jee. He was hot, and his muscles were hard and his skin was rougher than mine—I might just expire on the spot.

"I want to show you. Show you until you believe it, until you never try to hide any part of yourself, ever again. Not from me."

How did his voice get even lower?

It was some kind of trap for women like me. His voice. That's what it was. Not that I wasn't thrilled to be caught.

"Will you let me?" His face was close to mine, now, and the whisper of his breath warmed my lips.

He was that close.

"Yes."

Logan's eyes went rounder and more gold. I could swear I heard a growl deep in his throat. "Oh, Wynter." Then he bent down a little further and kissed me again. His lips were even warmer than the rest of his skin, and they were not gentle. He nipped at my lips, his teeth sending waves of pleasure with each bite. His tongue demanded entrance to my mouth—and I welcomed him.

My arms went around his neck, and then down onto his broad shoulders, my nails curling against his skin.

A soft hiss of breath told me that Logan felt it.

"Gods, Wynter."

I almost didn't hear him. But since this sounded like a good exclamation, I didn't think it needed any comment from me.

Logan's lips moved to my jawline, and then slowly, deliberately down my neck. He punctuated each small kiss with a nip, a small sensation of pain along the trail he was blazing down my body.

I loved it. I arched into him, unable to help myself.

I could feel him against me, feel his hardness. He had the same kind of intense need that I did.

For him.

For each other.

He continued down to my chest, lavishing his own brand of kisses along my sensitive peaks until I was gasping.

While I was thinking about how to move things along, his hand eased between my legs. With no hesitation, he slid two fingers inside me, and my release nearly happened right then and there.

"I'm taking it this means I have your consent." There was no mistaking the humor in his voice.

It was touching that he asked, even as my answer must have been apparent. "Enthusiastically." I gave his hair a little tug.

Logan's response was immediate. He looked up at me and grinned. Then he continued to kiss down my abdomen until he was between my legs.

The touch of his mouth on my core made me cry out.

These cottages were small, and very close to the neighbors. I had a feeling the neighbors were going to get more than they bargained for today, and I didn't care.

Who was this woman, this person who threw her head back with abandon, who let herself go into the embrace and bed of a man who carried around more than a touch of danger?

I was Wynter. I was the Oracle.

And I was taking what I wanted from life.

With this man. The man I chose.

Sweet baby Jee.

Logan continued with what he was doing, the result of which was me lying on his bed, gasping and exhilarated.

"You're not going to sleep on me, are you?" His eyes twinkled as he slid up next to me, a wide grin on his face.

"Not even a little bit." I kissed him as his arms brought me closer to him.

I pushed his shoulder, moving him onto his back. Then I eased myself over him, letting him rest between my legs.

"You keep that up, this won't take as long as I'd like." While his tone was growly, Logan beamed.

I reached over toward the bedside table, tearing one of the foil packets away.

"In a hurry?" Logan smiled up at me.

"Right now, yes."

His grin widened. "Don't let me stop you."

Carefully, keeping my eyes on his, I leaned back, easing away from where we were nearly joined, and tore open the packet. I rolled the condom on, letting my hands trail down him.

He hissed, his eyes narrowing and his face taking on an even more predatory expression.

It thrilled me to my core. It thrilled me everywhere.

I didn't look away from Logan's face as I lowered myself onto him. My god, he felt amazing. *This* was amazing.

His hands grasped my hips, and I could feel the grip of each of his fingertips.

I moved on him, slowly at first, letting my body learn his, and then faster.

Neither of us looked away. We were joined physically, and watching him watch me as we made love—I could see into his soul. Even as he was sure he didn't have one—I knew what I saw within his eyes was his soul.

And I let him see mine.

His eyes grew hot as I continued to move up and down, as he thrust up to meet me. Never had I felt like this before, never.

Faster and faster we moved together, heading for the same place.

Together. That was the important thing. We were together.

When my release came I pushed myself down against him, and he held me, not moving for a moment as I went to pieces. My hands went down to his chest to keep me from falling over.

Then Logan moved faster against me, his skin slick next to mine, his hands holding me tightly as I clung to him.

He let out a moan as he came. Then, after what seemed an eternity, we were still, locked together, neither wanting to move—perhaps not capable.

Or maybe that was just me.

He pushed himself up and wrapped his arms around me. Logan kissed my neck and rested his head on my chest.

Neither of us had words.

Words weren't necessary.

Gradually, I eased off of him, and curled into his side. He got up once, coming back before I had too much time to miss him. This time, however, he pulled back the blankets so I could get between the sheets.

When he joined me, pulling the blankets up to my chin and wrapping me in his arms so that I felt safe and surrounded, I let my eyes close.

This was right.

This was good.

I needed to stand up for myself more often.

CHAPTER EIGHT

When my eyes opened, it was dark. Not middle of the night dark, but the kind of dark where something was blocking the sun coming into the room through the window.

I let my eyes open fully, and smiled when I realized exactly what was blocking out the sun.

Next to me, Logan snored softly, his breathing even, his chest rising and falling in a rhythm.

I didn't move, didn't say anything, just allowed myself to be in this moment with this man. Although I was almost alone, as he was sleeping. I was here because I'd chosen it, because I'd insisted that I be treated as an equal, that my wants be seen as nothing less than equal.

There was nowhere else I'd rather be.

That didn't mean there was nowhere I had to be. In

fact, I had a suspicion I was supposed to be somewhere right now, but it could wait.

Logan was right in that we both carried danger with us. We both had no choice as to face danger. He was probably not pressing the issues on how serious it was. It wasn't as though I didn't know, wasn't aware.

But there was nowhere else I'd rather be.

And this was where I was supposed to be, come what may. I knew that like I knew my own name.

"You just wake up?" His voice was warm, sleepy sounding.

I loved it. I felt safe and secure for the first time in... ages. Or at least, what felt like ages.

"I did. I don't want to get up, but..." I looked around. "What time is it?"

"We've been lying here for about an hour."

"That's what happens when you finally show me a good time." I didn't know where this flirty me was coming from, but I liked it.

He sighed as he ran his fingers through my hair. "I've wanted to show you a good time since I met you."

"You mean when I pepper sprayed you?"

He laughed.

I laughed with him. It felt good to laugh with a man.

"I like strong women."

"That's good." I might not always be strong, but I was going to be as strong as I could from now on. The new Wynter was here.

And I was not going back to the woman I used to be.

Which meant I had to be realistic. I didn't know where this would go.

But I didn't care. I liked Logan. He was a good man. So I was going to be with him, and let the future come as it would.

Logan turned toward me. "This doesn't change—"

I held up a hand. "I know. I know. We both have danger baggage. It's okay, Logan. I'm an adult. So are you. We'll do the best we can, and..." I stopped, then pushed on. "We'll take care of each other where we can, okay?"

He stared into my eyes, and unlike earlier, I couldn't tell what I was seeing. His eyes were no longer the gold of the panther within, but more his normal green, and he hid their depths easier now. "That makes me very nervous."

"It's scary, I know."

"You don't understand. It's not just that I don't have a soul. But I haven't had to care about anyone other than myself. And Mark, sometimes. You, though —" his hand feathered along my cheek, then down my neck and along my arm. "I worry that some piece of shit will hurt you, take you from me. From everyone who loves and cares for you. And I won't be able to do anything about it." His voice broke a little on the last sentence. He closed his eyes.

I rested a hand on his cheek. "That might happen. But before it does, I'm going to fight." I meant it. I would fight. Goldie and Florry would help me. I was going to learn from the witches to better help myself.

I wasn't going down without a hell of a fight. Necromancers, the magical police, my local police, the Hazel Babbingtons of the world—they weren't going to just walk all over me.

I couldn't be sure that they had before, but it wasn't going to happen from now on. And that idea included Logan.

"I love your fight," Logan murmured as he leaned in to kiss me. His lips were warm, soft—not as demanding as they'd been earlier.

"Good. That means you're sticking around, then." It needed to be clear whatever this was between us.

"Yes. I'd rather be with you." He sighed deeply.

"You sound so happy about it." I glared.

"I worry. And now that it's not just me, there's a lot more to lose."

"That's what makes life worthwhile." I kissed him again. "Having something worth living for."

"I don't even remember what that's like. You're going to have to help me." He kissed me back.

Anything I might have wanted to say was cut off by his lips starting another conversation, one that needed no words.

At this rate, I'd be lucky if I made it home for dinner.

Which was just fine with me.

I DROVE HOME with a smile on my face. Logan had agreed to come over later tonight so that we could talk about his plans, about what he was going to do with his life as Evander. I knew that he was still nervous, in spite of me telling him over and over he wasn't responsible for me.

I had my own stuff to deal with, and my own bad guys, for lack of a better word. I'd have that whether Logan was around or not.

In the end, I think that was the argument that persuaded him.

We didn't really touch on the part about his soul, and I had a sneaking suspicion that conversation would not only be more difficult, it would probably really suck, to quote my kids.

When I came into the house, I couldn't suppress my smile.

"Oh, ho." Florry appeared as I walked into the kitchen. She floated down, a can of Olympia beer in hand. "Oh, ho, ho, ho."

"Shut up."

"No way, sister. You need to spill. But you should call Caro down, too. She'll want to hear, and then you can tell it all in one fabulous tale." She floated up toward the ceiling as she laughed some more

I knew this was coming, but I was in such a good mood, I didn't even care that the interrogation would begin shortly.

Caro walked in, peering at me. Then she smiled. "It went well, I take it?"

"Very well." My face was about to split because my grin was so wide.

"My dear girl." She came over, reaching out to take my hands and squeeze them. "All that effort. You must be hungry. Sit down." Caro walked toward the kitchen, gesturing at the island. "And spill your entire guts."

Behind me Florry laughed so hard she wheezed. Then I heard, "She'll feed you and get the entire story out of you. It's a superpower."

"Caro, you seem to have taken over my kitchen."

Caro whirled around, a wooden spoon in hand. "I'm so sorry. I tend to do that, but it's not because—"

I held up a hand. I was doing a lot of that lately. "It's fine. It's nice, actually. I've been the one in charge of making sure all the people were fed for years, and now, you're doing it. It's nice," I repeated. "I appreciate it. I'm glad, is what I'm trying to say and making a mess out of."

Caro let out a breath, visibly relieved. "I'm glad to hear that, Wynter. It was just me and Florry for so long, and she's such a weirdo—" she stopped and glanced up at the ceiling, rolling her eyes dramatically. "That I have wondered, since she left, if I was able to live around anyone else again."

"You were a weirdo long before I met you, toots." Florry didn't sound offended.

"She's saying that you are weird in your own right." I shared with Caro.

Caro hooted with laughter. "I feel like you cleaned

that up, but I get it. Anyway, not the point!" She tapped the spoon on the island. "Spill."

Carefully, because I wasn't ready to get into the details, I shared as much as I felt comfortable with them. Florry was hovering at the end of the island, and Caro kept turning around to look at me.

"She's right at the end of the island." I interrupted myself to tell Caro. "So you know where she is."

Caro's lips turned up in a brief smile, and she glanced down at the end. Her face softened, and she didn't speak for a moment. "Thank you."

I nodded.

"So where did you leave things?" Caro asked.

"Can you even remember? Because I'm not sure with that goofy look on your face," Florry added. "You're sex addled, that's for sure."

But your magic is stronger. Goldie, who hadn't spoken to me since I'd told him to go away earlier, chimed in.

I held up a finger. What had Logan called it? Thinking by committee? That was an understatement. *What do you mean?* I directed my thought at Goldie.

I can feel your magic. It is like a river, it flows. It's flowing more smoothly than it has since I came to you.

That was interesting. All it took was a—well, I wasn't going to get into specifics, but... wow.

Maybe Logan's not so bad now? I teased my armband.

He made a sniffing sound. The scales of the armband writhed on my arm. *He's still not good enough*

121

for you. But if the panther makes you happy, then I can live with it.

Well, thank you.

"What is Goldie sayin'? And can you tell him to get on with it?" Florry asked, impatience dripping from her words.

"I really need to find a way to allow my committee to talk to each other." I tossed up my hands.

"Your what?" Caro asked.

"My committee. That's what Logan called it when I was talking with him and I stopped for a second because Goldie was talking. He asked if the committee was weighing in, and I had to laugh because I am living via committee. Which isn't the worst thing, but it would be great if you could all talk to each other rather than relying on me to share."

"That would be nice." There wasn't a trace of teasing or sarcasm in Florry's words. "I miss Goldie and Caro."

"I think you all miss each other."

You don't have to do anything for me, Goldie said. *But the two of them were always very close.*

Noted, I thought.

I am here for you, no one else. You are my priority. There is no need to find ways for me to communicate with any other. I am part of the gift of the Oracle.

It was almost as if he knew what I'd been thinking about earlier. Well, he probably did. Since he lived on my arm.

You don't miss Florry at all? I was curious.

I have known many Oracles, and I cared for all of them. To continue contact would be taking away from the current Oracle.

It was my turn to roll my eyes. *It might actually help the current Oracle if you were able to share more with the past Oracles.*

That is what Florry is for. She is your access to past knowledge.

When she or you chooses to share. I rolled my eyes.

Caro and Florry both watched me, both of them kind of smiling.

You have to find—

I interrupted him. *Yes, yes, I know. My own path. I think those have become my least favorite words.*

Goldie sniffed.

It was weird, hearing your magical armband get sniffy in your head.

Whatever. This was my life now.

Okay, I'm going to continue, if you don't mind?

Carry on. He was still sniffy.

"I do, but I think you need to remain Goldie's priority. Enough about Snaky," Florry said, using Shelly's nickname for Goldie. "Where did you leave things with cat boy?"

"He's not going to run away from me anymore," I said. "He's not happy with it, I think because he's worried and scared—but he's agreed that we shouldn't deny ourselves being together."

"You look happy," Caro turned from the stove to put a plate of linguine and clams in front of me.

"When the hell did you have time to make this? It's like magic!" I inhaled the smell of the white sauce. Oh, my god.

"This is my thing." Caro's face was wreathed in a smile. "Shall we eat? And would you like wine?"

I shook my head. "No. I might fall into this face first if I have wine. Just some water, and you need to sit down and eat with me."

The rest of the meal passed in happy conversation, with the two of them teasing me.

After dinner, while I washed the dishes and cleaned up the kitchen—it was so, so nice to be relegated to the task—Florry moved closer, her face serious. There wasn't a beer or cigarette in sight.

"You need to get your magic together. I think you need to spend as much time as you can with the witches. This ex-husband dude of Nina's makes me nervous, Wynter."

"Why?" She didn't normally have these sorts of conversations with me.

Florry shrugged. "I don't know. I have a feeling, and I've learned to listen to the feelings over the years, even when I don't want to. I feel like you need more than what you have, even though you have a lot of magic already, for such a new Oracle. And you have me, Goldie, and cat boy, and that's nothing to sneeze at. The way Nina talks about him, though, gives me the creeps."

"He does sound pretty horrible."

Florry nodded. "Promise me you'll call that Elizabeth tomorrow, and tell her you want the accelerated course."

"I think I have it," I said, thinking of the books Callie had given me. None of which I'd looked at since she'd given them to me.

"Then if you aren't working with Nina, you need to be studying." Florry's words brooked no argument.

"Yes, ma'am." Good thing I wasn't in the mood to argue.

"All right then. Finish up and get to it."

"Logan is coming over tonight."

"Great!" Florry threw up her hands. "I don't want to lose you because you're in the middle of being sex addled! Tell him, and get him to help you. There's plenty of time for all the other bits," she added.

"Fine, fine, fine. I'll tell him." It would be better if Logan and I were open with each other, which meant not keeping things from him. Especially as he had more experience in the world I was now part of. He might have ideas I hadn't thought of.

"And call Elizabeth."

"Is everything all right?" Caro came back into the kitchen after being up in her room. "What's going on?"

"Florry is telling me her gut wants me to learn more and faster."

"Her gut is often right." Caro's expression was serious.

She looked a lot like Florry at that moment.

"Okay. As I told her, Logan is coming over. I'll tell him. And what do I tell Elizabeth?" I directed the conversation to Florry. "I mean, is there a spell I need to ask for? Something specific you're thinking of?"

"Tell her you want to have a better understanding of magic. I didn't have the same sort of skill you do. You can actually practice magic. You move people. I could see through them, but I didn't use my magic on them as you do. To me, that suggests you may have more."

"Does this have anything to do with Tethys?" Caro was rubbing her lip with her forefinger.

"What?" I asked.

"Tethys. The goddess. Did she give you some kind of magic by helping you?"

"I don't know," I said slowly, thinking. "Maybe? Not that I recall, but I can't say anything for sure."

"You're a different kind of Oracle. You have magic on your own," Florry said. "Patsy and I didn't. But what that means for you, missy, is you need to work more with users of magic."

I nodded.

"What did she say?" Caro asked.

I relayed Florry's words.

"That makes sense." Caro was nodding now. "It's really interesting to me how the Oracles are all different. But since you're all different people, I shouldn't be surprised."

"I've never had any inkling that I had anything magical about me ever," I said.

"You wouldn't, unless something pushed your magic to spark. But you've never noticed anything? Not things working out that had no business working out? Or things going your way?" Caro asked.

"No, nothing. In fact, everything went sideways once I got magic."

"Learning curve." Florry said.

"Okay, well, I'm going to take some time for myself before Logan gets here, and—"

"Call Elizabeth!" Florry glared at me.

"And call Elizabeth, and then I'm going to shower. Yell if something needs my attention." I walked away from the kitchen, hurrying up the stairs.

Once in my room, I shut the door behind me. Yeah, I needed to find a way for them to speak to one another because this was going to drive me crazy. So that I didn't forget, I took out my phone and dialed Elizabeth's number.

"Wynter," she said without preamble.

"Hi, Elizabeth."

"Is everything all right?"

"Yes, for the most part. I know that we're scheduled to meet Tuesday, but I wanted to ask you if we could get together sooner. I have a question about a spell, or..." I stopped, not sure what to ask for.

"What are you trying to accomplish?"

"I want a ghost to be able to speak to someone else."

"You have a spirit familiar?" Her voice rose in surprise.

"That's one way to put it," I said.

"And you want the spirit to speak to another? Is that wise?"

"It's necessary. I am going to lose my mind if they can't talk to each other."

There was a silence, then Elizabeth said, "I am willing to hear you out. This is interesting, although I'll tell you upfront, I have concerns. When would you like to meet?"

"Tonight?" I asked. That hadn't been my plan initially, but...

I wondered if I was being pushy. She said that the witches had things to do this weekend.

Another pause, then she said, "I can meet with you, although it may be later than normal social hours."

There was something very formal, nearly dignified about the way Elizabeth spoke at times. Almost as if she were from another time, when people weren't so casual. I wondered how one might ask about that and decided not to push my luck. "That would be all right. Normal social hours have gone out the window around here. When were you thinking?"

"Around ten p.m."

"Perfect. Shall I come to you at the shop?"

"No." Her answer was sharp and quick. "I'll come to you."

"Okay. You know where I live."

"Until tonight, then." She ended the call without a good-bye.

Lord-a-mercy, I hoped there was a way to make this happen. Not only would it save me, I felt that it would be so good for both Caro and Florry. Whatever the particulars of their relationship, it had been close, and I could see the effects of the loss of it in both of them.

With the happy thought of doing good for someone humming in my brain, I went to the shower. When we'd remodeled the bathroom, I'd asked for a shower with a bench in it, and it was to the bench I went as I turned the shower to as hot as I could stand it. The steam swirled up around me quickly, enveloping me in a world of good smells and soothing warmth.

After Derek died, I had no plans of being with anyone else. I figured I'd had love, even if it ended less than happily, and that was it. Logan burst into my world in a way I hadn't expected, and now, I didn't want a world without him.

That could change. Oddly, the lack of knowledge about how any of this would end didn't bother me at all, which wasn't like me.

I smiled and stretched, then leisurely showered. A moment of panic washed over me as I rinsed my hair, and my hands came away with a lot more than I wanted to see. Thank goodness I'd made the appointment with my doctor.

Try not to freak out. It's only hair. It's going to grow back. Hair always grows back.

While I managed to push the hair concerns a little off to the side, I was careful when I toweled my hair. Rather than using my brush, I combed my fingers through it, and left it to air dry.

It will come back. Hair always comes back.

Focus, Wynter. Focus on what you can control

Clothes. I can choose my clothes and—

The phone rang, interrupting my growing panic. Saved by the bell. I answered without looking at the caller ID, grateful for the save, even if I'd have to listen to someone trying to sell me a car and home insurance bundle. "Hello?"

"Wynter?" It was Natalie Chastain.

"Natalie, hi. How are you?" Oh, hell. Damn and damnation. I'd forgotten to call her.

"I'm in New York, with Derek's parents. And..." her voice faltered. "I have to thank you. Again. Whatever you said to them, however you told them about me and the kids, it's made this such a nice visit. They've been wonderful." Amazing how you could hear some people smiling over the phone. Natalie was one of those people.

"They are wonderful," I said. "I'm glad that they've been wonderful to you, as well. How are the kids doing?"

"Loving it. They haven't had grandparents before, and they're going to be impossible for a while once vacation is over."

I laughed. "They'll tell you that's what grandparents are for."

She joined me in the laughter. "I've already heard that."

Once the laughter died away, Natalie continued. "I wanted to know if it would be possible for us to come and visit you, and maybe stay the night?" Her voice went up, almost as though she were afraid to hear my answer.

This was probably the worst possible time—but what could I say? 'Sorry, but I have magic lessons, and a woman in need of some serious magical curse breaking to help, and I'm in the middle of a new relationship, and there's a ghost in my house?' No, I couldn't say any of that. "Sure," I said. "When were you thinking?"

"How about next Wednesday? We can take the ferry over that morning, and spend the day and the night with you. If that's all right. I'm happy to get a hotel—"

I cut her off. "You can get a hotel, or a vacation rental if it will make you more comfortable, but you're welcome here. I have a friend staying with me, a woman named Caro, and the kids will probably come out, so we'll be a full house. But it's totally doable."

"You're sure?" In those two words, I heard all the fear and worry.

"I'm sure." I meant it. Derek was my past. Nothing

could change the past, and this woman and her children would be part of my future, whether I wanted them in it or not. I didn't want to be weird or awkward any longer than it had to be. And my kids liked their siblings. "I'm being honest with you, Natalie. I wouldn't have invited you if I didn't mean it. But it is going to be crowded." I laughed at a little at how crowded.

"I think that will be great," Natalie said, her words sincere.

"So next Wednesday." At least my magic lesson with the coven would be behind me. That was good. "Text me when the ferry's close, and I'll come down and get you. You can leave your car at the terminal, if you want. It's up to you."

"I'll let you know. And Wynter?"

"Yes?"

"Thank you." She took a deep breath. "This has been... well, it could have been so much more awful than it was. You've made things better. I really appreciate it."

A feeling of warmth moved through me. She was as nervous as I'd been. I was glad I'd taken the high road and not tried to snatch her hair off, or some other scorned woman thing when I met her. That would be the normal reaction of most women, right? And I'd had a bit of it. But Derek was gone. There was nothing that would change what had happened. I'd learned a long time ago to let things go. Probably too well, if I was being honest, but in this case, it was working for me.

"It's my pleasure, and I mean that. There's too many other things to worry about to be angry with you." I stopped, not wanting to sound condescending. "We're going to be okay, Natalie."

"I wasn't sure before, but I think I agree with you. I'm looking forward to seeing you again," she added.

"Same here, and I mean that, too," I said.

We ended the call, and I hoped she was smiling, too.

But holy hell. My house was about to explode. I dialed another number. There was no way I was doing this on my own.

CHAPTER NINE

"You never call, you never write. Get a little magic, a hot guy, and I'm just chopped liver." Shelly answered on the second ring.

"Whatever. You're all up in Liegal land, happy as a clam and forgetting all the little people."

Shelly laughed. "What's up? I can feel the emergency from here."

"Natalie's coming next week. Wednesday, in fact. I need your help to plan it all out."

"What? Holy shit! How did that happen?"

"Come have breakfast with me tomorrow and I'll tell you everything."

"You'd better. See you then."

"Thanks, Shell. Love you."

"Love you, too."

I caught myself in the mirror as I set my phone down. I had a glow around me, of happiness and contentment. I was managing my life, bananas as it was.

"You're the baddest bitch around," I told my reflection. This was a good mantra, and I needed to tell myself things like this more often. I winked at my reflection. I could swear she winked back at me. I stared for a moment. I liked this new me.

A lot.

Then I went to my closet to get ready for the evening.

If tonight was anything like today had been—it was still Saturday, right? That blew me away. But if tonight went like today, it was going to be wild.

I could feel it.

CHAPTER TEN

B y the time the doorbell rang, I was back downstairs, reading on the app on my phone, having a cup of tea. Caro had gone into a fit of baking, humming and occasionally singing in German. As a result, the house smelled of peach cobbler.

Given that I was heavy on guests tonight I was appreciative and told her so.

"Oh, I got used to it when I lived with Florry. People showing up at all kinds of hours. Food makes things less awkward. Less chance of being killed, sometimes." She'd said that last part with a grin, like it was no big deal.

I stared at her, then just took my tea and went into the front room.

Florry cackled behind me, clearly pleased.

I'd been hanging out here ever since. While I felt I was getting into a rhythm of sorts with being the

Oracle, I didn't really want to think about a pastry stopping death. I mean, a girl needs to have one night after fabulous sex and a burst of self-confidence without the haters bringing her down, right?

The doorbell was a welcome thing.

Until I opened the door.

Nina stood in the doorway, her eyes red with tears and wild with fear. She took one look at me and burst into tears.

"Holy cats. Nina, come in, get off the porch," I said, peering around to see if any of the neighbors were out. I'd already given them enough of a show the last couple of months. When she'd left, she said she would come back to do the second part of the scrying.

Given the state she was in, I didn't think that was going to happen tonight.

Nina let me lead her inside, and I brought her into the living room, settling her into the couch. She put her head in her hands and sobbed louder.

I got a box of tissues and a glass of water. Caro nodded at me silently, and moved toward the front room, giving us some privacy.

It made me feel better, though, to know that she was within earshot, and that she'd be listening along with me. Putting the glass and tissues on the coffee table, I sat in the chair across from Nina and waited.

She sobbed for what seemed like a long time.

The doorbell rang again, but I didn't move.

Caro zipped out of the front room, heading for the door.

"Is this a bad time?" Nina asked, her last word ending in a hiccup as she looked around.

"No. You are my consultant. It's never a bad time."

She reached for the tissues, mopping at her eyes.

Logan came in behind Caro and I felt a light turn on inside of me. I smiled at him, and the way he smiled back... I was lost in his eyes.

Then I caught myself. "Logan, if you'll wait with Caro?"

He nodded, and the two of them went back into the front room.

"This is a bad time." Nina blew her nose, looking like she was about to cry again.

"No, Nina, it's not. Grand Central Station is the new norm around here. But you, you're my priority, no matter what else is going on. What happened?"

Without speaking, she handed me her phone.

It was a message, although it wasn't an email or text app that I recognized.

NINA,

I know that she's not with you, and I know where she is. You can't hide from me, and you will never keep me from my daughter. I'll play your little game. You're not going to be a problem for me or my daughter for much longer. I'd go and spend the little time you have left with her, if I were you.

Rockledge

"WHERE IS THIS FROM?" I asked, handing the phone back.

"It's one of the message boards we used. I stopped using it, although I didn't delete my account. I got this earlier. It was waiting for me when I woke up from my nap. How can he know where she is? I hid her so well! He can't!" She dissolved into tears again.

"Could he be bluffing? Trying to see what you'll do?"

Nina looked up at me, a tissue in front of her nose. I could see her considering my words. "Maybe. He knows that Kira is the way to get to me."

"Then let's assume he's poking at you, trying to get you to react. Don't call whomever she's with. Don't do anything. Just stay here."

"Are you sure?" Nina looked over her shoulder toward the front room. "You seem to—"

"I am sure. You can have one of the kids' rooms. You're not going anywhere. Hey, Caro?"

Caro appeared in the doorway of the front room. "Yes?"

"Is the cobbler cooled?"

"Probably. You want some tea?"

"Please." I got up and reached out to take Nina's hand. "You're going to have some tea, some cobbler, and a boat load of sympathy while we all call your ex a douche canoe. Then you're going to go up and sleep. If you want a shower, I have some clothes you can have. Whatever you need."

"Is this what the Oracle does?" Nina asked as she stood up. "You make me feel better."

I smiled, pleased at the thought. "I think the Oracle does whatever she feels is best," I said. "And I know you need to be here, with people who care about you, rather than on your own, worrying your face off."

"That's exactly what I would do." A tremulous smile appeared on Nina's face.

"Of course, you would. It hits hard when it's your children. She's okay, though, Nina. You must believe that. Or he wins before you even have a chance to fight back."

She sighed. "He's so much better at this than I am."

"They always are," I said, patting her hand. "It's their weakness as well as their strength. Let's go have some cobbler."

I guided her toward the island, and then went to the front room.

Logan stood in front of the window, his hands in his pockets. "Full house tonight?" he asked as he turned toward me.

I walked into his open arms. "Yes," I said against his chest. "I'm glad you're here."

"I'm here for you. Although I have to go to New York tomorrow. Mark is already there, making sure everything is ready for me," he said. Then he sighed. "It's time for me to be Evander again."

"Evander isn't who you are anymore," I didn't look up. "He's just a name. Look at him as a means to an end."

"He's part of me, Wynter."

"No, he's not." I tightened my arms around him. "Evander died in that desert, Logan. You don't have to resurrect him. Not unless you want to. And even then, you can pitch him over the side when he's not useful anymore."

He didn't reply. "I may not be the one who decides that."

"Oh, baloney," I said. "Let others call you Evander and do what you need to access the life Evander built. But you're Logan. And you need to work on how to end the bargain with the demon—"

"You don't end bargains with demons. They're a done deal." His voice was flat.

Yeah, this was going to be the crap conversation part of this.

"You don't know that. You don't even know the demon, or the deal. That's what you need to discover—what demon Evander made a deal with. Then you work from there." I stepped back, wanting to see his face.

He looked troubled and sad.

"You're Logan Gentry. You were once a man named Evander Thane, but that man is gone. Since Evander left you with a big damn mess, you get to keep the world Evander built, and all the things that go along with his world. That's the least you get for waking up with no memory, being a shifter, and now having to clean up his demon nonsense. You know good and well that Evander probably got dumped in the desert based on something he did."

Logan stared at me for a long moment. Then he smiled. "You're good for me, Wynter Chastain."

"Don't you forget it. Now would you please kiss me so I can get back to work and focus?"

With a chuckle that did so many bad things to my insides, Logan bent his head to mine, his lips capturing mine, claiming me, freeing me. His arms held me close, encompassing me.

But not holding me in, or holding me back.

Logan accepted me as the Oracle. Whatever his reservations, he accepted me as I was. He didn't try to diminish me, even as he thought he could make decisions for me.

Well, okay. He'd tried, for a hot minute. I doubted he'd do that again.

He believed me capable of many things, strong things, powerful things.

No one, other than maybe Shelly, had ever made me feel this way. Made me aware of who I was, who I could be.

I'd always been a wife, a mother, first and foremost before all else.

Now?

I was a magical being. With power. With powers that were growing, or at least, that I was learning about, and learning to use. There was a chance of more.

And Logan was all good with that.

I let myself fall into his kiss and the sensations it raised from my head to my toes. All I wanted in this moment was to race upstairs with him and not come out for days, taking the time to explore his body, and his soul, and letting him see me, see my soul with no barriers.

That wasn't possible right now, so I'd take what I could, and kiss him until we were both dizzy.

A few moments later, Caro's voice called from the kitchen "Wynter? Would you all like some cobbler?"

Logan eased his hold on me, and I instinctively put a hand to my hair. "Um, yes please. We'll be there in a minute."

I heard the hum of conversation from the kitchen rise and fall, and then I pressed my face into Logan's chest. "I don't want to go anywhere else."

He laughed softly. "We both have obligations. We also have plenty of time, Wynter."

"You're sure singing a different song than you were the other night." I looked up at him.

"I know." He sighed. "I meant what I said. I'm afraid now, like I never was before. I have something to lose. Given who—what I am, what I—" he stopped and shook his head. "I can't lose you, not when I finally found you. I didn't even know you existed, or that I wanted you—I didn't think someone like you was possible."

"I don't think I will ever get tired of hearing that," I said. My voice was almost a purr.

With a growl, Logan captured my lips, kissing me hard and intensely. I felt lightheaded, and I clung to him, so I didn't fall into a heap.

When he let me go, I had to hang onto his arms for a moment to steady myself. "You're like a deadly weapon."

"Only for you," he whispered. "Come on. Your audience awaits."

Hand in hand, we walked into the kitchen.

"Logan, right?" Nina looked more recovered, a cup of tea and a plate of cobbler in front of her.

"Yes. Good to see you again, although I'm sorry that it seems to be less than ideal circumstances," Logan replied. He looked to Caro. "That smells amazing."

"You'd better hope there's enough," I said. "Take more than you want before letting Logan at the cobbler."

Caro laughed, a rich, full laugh, and cut a very large piece for Logan, then a smaller one for me.

Nina finished hers before either of us, and stood up. "I'm going to do what you suggested," she said to me. "Would you mind if I had a shower?"

"Not at all." I got up, patting Logan's hand as I did, and led her up to Rachel's room.

Once I got Nina settled in, I went back downstairs.

"Is there any cobbler left, or has he eaten it all?" I asked as I pulled my plate toward me. I nearly moaned with the first bite. It was delicious.

Caro needed to stay here forever and be my friend, too, and cook.

"There's still some left, although he's persistent." Caro glanced toward the stairs, her brows furrowed. "Is she going to be all right?"

"Yes, maybe, eventually. He's a real bastard, her ex."

"Sounds like it."

"I heard a little of it. How are you going to break the spell?" Logan asked.

I'd told him about the scrying I'd done, and how it backfired.

"I'm going to ask Elizabeth what I'm missing, and try again," I said. "I think I'll scry on my own tonight. I feel more comfortable with that, since I've done it more. Then I'll be ready to try the scrying that is supposed to break the hex." A shiver, perhaps of nerves, ran through me. The scrying I did with Nina was a new method. "That smoke that had surrounded her? It scared the daylights out of me."

"It was interesting along with being scary. Even so," Caro said. "I wouldn't toss it out with the bathwater."

"No, especially as it came from one of the other Oracles. It just wasn't the right thing for Nina. Her ex has put one hell of a curse on her. And the clock is ticking, although I'd prefer not to bring that up in front of Nina, however."

"Good plan." Logan nodded and took a huge bite of cobbler. "Maybe the new scrying would work better a second time. Things don't always work on the first try."

"Now that you've eaten my cobbler, it's time for some home truths." Caro leaned on the island, spatula in hand, her expression solemn, glaring at Logan.

He stopped, his fork in his mouth, and his eyes widened in question at her words.

"You're going to be good to her. I know that you both have a lot going on, but you're going to be honest and upfront, no matter what. Got it? And before you answer, remember that I utilize carving knives at a professional level."

"Caro!" I sputtered.

Logan choked on his cobbler.

I waited a moment while he coughed, doing some glaring of my own at Caro.

"Good thing she said it," Florry appeared.

I agree, said Goldie.

Hey! I thought toward both of them. *This ganging up on me thing isn't fair!*

"The Oracle needs to have only those who are steadfast supporters in her life. She doesn't need drama. We have enough of that all on our own. If he can't get that, if he isn't willing to support you all the way, he doesn't deserve you." Florry didn't sound the least bit sorry.

You guys about face so often I'm getting whiplash, I thought.

It's our job to protect you as much as we can. Now that your heart is involved, we need to make sure he knows the stakes. Like Florry, Goldie didn't sound sorry, or repentant, or sad to be saying any of this at all.

"I have no intentions of being anything but good to Wynter," Logan said to Caro, his words sounding oddly formal.

"Then swear it." She didn't hesitate.

"What? No!" I interjected.

"You know what to do," Caro said, as though I hadn't spoken. "Swear it. I don't require a blood promise, because no one knows what's going to happen, and I don't think that's fair. You will, however, swear to me, as Wynter's elder, that you will, to the very best of your ability, do her no further harm," her eyes narrowed.

Everyone knew that Logan had walked out after our date. Hmm. I might have forgotten to mention that fact to him while I was tossing off my clothes with glee earlier.

The top of Logan's cheeks turned ruddier.

"And that you will protect her with all you have."

Logan held out his hand, and Caro took it.

"I swear that I will do no further harm to Wynter Chastain, and I will do all I can to protect her, to the best of my ability on both counts." He sounded even more formal.

"I accept your word," Caro said, inclining her head regally.

"What is going on here?" I asked. This felt almost medieval. Absently, I reached to touch Logan's arm.

The spark hit me with the strength of a lightning bolt. Okay, a baby lightning bolt, but it was strong. "Ow!"

"Are you all right?" Logan dropped Caro's hand and turned toward me, his hands catching me at the tops of my arms as I swayed in my seat.

"Give me a sec." I took some deep breaths, steadying myself. Then I sat up straight and glared at both of the people with me. "What the hell was that?"

"He promised that he'd be good to you and make your safety one of his priorities. It's not an uncommon thing in this world." Caro shrugged.

"And you thought it was your place to do this?" I was debating how annoyed to be.

"I'm your elder, and your friend. I'm the person that should."

"She's right." Logan agreed. "I'm surprised you know about it, though." Having gotten past his surprise, and not choked on his cobbler, Logan didn't seem offended at all.

"My roomie was the Oracle for years. I learned a lot." Caro shrugged again. "This was for me as much as it was for you, Wynter. We've only just met, but I want to make sure you're safe." Her eyes flashed, then she looked down at her cup.

I was about to blast her for interfering when Florry spoke.

"She's worried about you, Wynter. Losing me was harder than she lets on, and she likes you more than she thought she would."

How do you know this? I thought in Florry's direction.

"I've known Caro for decades, that's how. She's tough on the outside, but soft inside, and she's worried. I didn't even know she knew about making someone give their magical word, but she's right. She lived with an Oracle for a long time. Don't take her head off. It comes from a good place." Then Florry disappeared.

That in and of itself was weird. Normally Florry was there, pushing and pushing until I did what she wanted.

In this, she was clearly leaving me to my own devices, my own choice. I sighed. "Please warn me before you do something like this again. There's no one else I'd be comfortable with you asking for their word. I'm not sure I'm comfortable with it even from Logan."

"Understood. I don't know that I'd ask anyone else. I wasn't planning on it, but it came to me suddenly, like a flash of inspiration." Caro smiled, a small half-smile.

Hmm. It was a flash all right, but I had an idea of where it came from.

No wonder Florry up and vanished.

"Did either of you feel anything when you gave your word?" I looked between Logan and Caro.

"A slight tickle up my arm," Caro said.

"About the same," Logan added.

"That was it?" I said as I shook my head. "I got a bit

more than that when I touched your arm," I nodded at Logan. "Like someone stuck my finger in a light socket."

"I'd bet your magic is getting stronger," Logan said, frowning at me.

"Isn't that a good thing?"

"Not if you can't use it." He frowned more deeply. "When did you say you see the witches again? This is more their wheelhouse."

"Elizabeth is coming over tonight."

"Good. But if you're still having guests, we should probably talk, so you have time to work with her." Logan stood up, taking his plate to the sink. "Caro, that was amazing. I'm tempted to steal you away from Wynter's house so I can eat like this all the time, in spite of your threats."

"Flattery doesn't work with me, kiddo. As long as you're welcome here, I'll feed you. And now, I'll leave you two." Caro kissed me on the top of my head, making me feel very much like a child getting a good night kiss from her mom. She patted Logan's arm as she passed him and headed for the stairs.

Part of me, the part that missed my mom, both my parents, found it comforting, even as the adult me was annoyed. It had been a long time since I'd had a mother figure in my life.

Caro's steps echoed up the stairs, and then I heard her door close.

Finally, finally, we were alone.

Logan came over and took my hand, leading me to

the larger sofa. He sat down and pulled me into his lap. "Come here and just sit with me. It's never a quiet moment as the Oracle, is it?"

"It doesn't seem that way," I admitted.

"Then let me be your quiet space."

"That's not what I want from you right now," I grumbled as I settled into his lap.

Logan leaned back and my head moved onto his chest. His arms went around me and even though I wanted to take him upstairs with me, I could feel myself relaxing into his large, warm form.

"It's not what I want from you, either, but if you think I'm going to give myself free reign with Grandma Beats My Ass right upstairs, you are mistaken." He laughed as he spoke.

"Don't you mean Grandma Carves Your Ass?" I teased.

"That's even more frightening. She looked like she meant it."

"She did." I smiled. "She was a professional chef."

"Really? That would explain the food." He slid his hand along the nape of my neck, drawing me to him for a kiss.

His lips and tongue were gentle. It wasn't the intense demanding kiss of earlier today, but something different. Something more.

Inside my chest, as though a key in a lock was turned, I felt something within open. Logan knew me. Perhaps not with the knowledge of years, but the knowledge of who I was, who I could be—and it didn't bother him.

Did I have that before?

I didn't know. The path of my marriage was so entwined with what I'd learned after Derek died. I couldn't separate the two, outside of the love both of us had for our kids. It just wasn't possible anymore.

But this, with Logan—I was just me. Just Wynter. Yes, I was a supposedly powerful member of the supernatural world, but that wasn't why he cared for me.

His arms went around to my back, his fingers slightly clawed as he raked them down my back.

"Oh, God!" I couldn't help it. I got a sensual shiver that went from my head to my toes.

"You taste like the night, after the sun's gone down," Logan murmured against my lips.

"Oh?"

He leaned away from me, his eyes gleaming a deep golden amber. "Shifters love the night."

We stared at one another, and the intensity of his words moved over me. "*Oh*," I said, feeling the shiver again.

"Yes, oh." Logan pulled me to him once more, kissing me thoroughly.

We sat together, taking our time to get to know each other better, with hands and lips. Then I rested my head in the crook of Logan's neck, feeling the warmth of him through his shirt, and hearing the steady beat of his heart.

"When is the witch coming?" Logan asked, the timber of his voice rumbling in his chest and through my ear that was still pressed against him.

"Ten."

He held up his hand to peer at his watch. "I don't want to, but we need to talk. "

I sat up. "That sounds ominous."

"No, not really. Since you won't let me do the honorable thing and stay away from you—"

"Honorable my Aunt Fanny—" I began. I couldn't believe we were back to this.

Logan took my hand and kissed my fingers. "I don't want to be apart from you. I was wrong. Wrong to think it would be better, even if it is the more honorable thing —" He raised his eyebrows at me. "I don't often take the honorable route. You've robbed me of my one good intention for the year." He lifted my other hand and kissed my fingers. "I am so glad that you did."

I let out a breath. "Good thing you're seeing just how wrong you were."

"I was. But since we're going to be together, there are some aspects of precaution you need to know."

"Okay."

"Mark knows where I'm going to be while in New York."

"You won't be with him the entire time?"

Logan shook his head. "No. I can't be. I can't expose him or his part in this. I'll text you every night from one of my burner phones. Don't add me to your contacts. I'll say," he stopped, looking over my shoulder. "Tommy-knocker."

"What?"

"Tommyknocker. The little gnomes, or wee folk that worked in the mines alongside the miners. It's a Cornish legend, one they brought to the United States when they came here. That's not the point. It's an odd enough word that you'll know it's from me. It means I'm safe."

"I won't be able to talk to you?" I'd been hoping for some video chat, truth be told.

He shook his head. "No. I have everything I need to come back from the dead. I'm better prepared, thanks to you." He kissed me.

"And the Sisters of the Asp." They had exposed Tomas, and the fact that someone did toss Evander into the desert on purpose.

He frowned, rubbing at his eyes with one hand. "Don't remind me. Part of me misses the power of will."

"You shouldn't have had it anyway."

"I know, I know. Don't rub it in. I didn't even know I had it, but when I gave it up, I felt the loss. It was there, with me, all these years. I don't know if that's why I was so successful with Mark, or..." he stopped. "It doesn't matter. Because you discovered Tomas Severn," he said, naming the man who had spilled the beans about why Evander Thane was left in the desert, "I know more about who I need to look out for."

"It's always the ones you don't expect," I said,

thinking of the two women who had been clinging to Evander at the party where I'd met him in my first attempts at scrying, back when Logan himself was my consultant. They were far more dangerous than Tomas Severn. Especially Davina. She was in cahoots with Tomas.

"True, but I'm forewarned."

"How will you explain all the years that you've been missing?"

"I've already started to." He grinned. "I've told a few people, in the process of reclaiming my life, you understand," he smirked as he nodded at me. "That I woke up in shredded clothes on the beach in San Diego, and had no memory of how I got there, and I found work and help along the way. That's it." He shrugged then. "I don't want to out Mark for his help. I don't want people to know that I'm a shifter. They'll know, soon enough."

"How?"

"Magic senses magic. Other shifters will know. Thankfully, panthers aren't pack oriented." He sighed. "Or I would have been outed years ago."

"What about the person who bit you?"

"They'll know. I've had Mark looking for prominent panther shifters, but so far, nothing. Until Evander... we didn't know where to look, where one might be hiding. Panthers hide better than most shifters."

I could see his frustration. I kissed the end of his nose lightly. "You'll find him."

Logan smiled up at me. "I know. It's frustrating until we do, but you're right. We'll find him."

"So. Tommyknocker. That's how I'll know you're all right."

"Yes. If Mark calls you, answer the phone." He kissed me briefly.

Which told me that this interlude, at least the kissing part, was over. "And then what?"

"Do you have his contact info?"

"I don't know."

Carefully, Logan put me on my feet. "Let's go look at your phone."

Ten minutes later, I felt like some sort of spy, or someone who lived a double life. Logan had added Mark, under a different name, gone through my phone to check for malware, and infused me with a sense of foreboding. I rubbed my arms. "I want you to find whoever did this," I began.

He pressed something on my phone, then handed it back. "You're ready. And I will find them."

"I want you to make them pay." The anger I felt spilled into my words.

Logan blinked. "Who is this fierce warrior, the Oracle of Theama?"

Shaking my head, I leaned into him, wrapping my arms around him, wanting his warmth near me for a little longer. "I don't know. I'm just tired of other magical people telling me I don't deserve this—"

You do, Goldie said.

I know, I replied. *Let me finish here.*

"Or that I'm not worthy, or whatever, basically, 'Wynter, you suck!' and other blah blah blah drivel about how they don't suck, are more deserving, et cetera. You're dealing with people who tried to kill you because they felt entitled to what you wanted." My arms tightened around his waist. "I'm over it."

Logan didn't respond immediately.

I leaned back to look up at him.

Which is when he bent and kissed me hard, fiercely. When he lifted his head, his green eyes were golden again. "That's why we're going to put them all back where they belong."

"Away from us."

"Away from us." His voice was a growl.

Then rational thought fled as he kissed me again and enveloped me whole.

CHAPTER ELEVEN

"Ehem."

We jumped apart, me hastily getting to my feet. I felt Logan move to stand behind me.

As I looked to see who it was, my first thought was, *At least it's not Rachel*. The last time Logan and I had been interrupted kissing, it was by my daughter, and she had not been pleased. In fact, none of the kids were all that happy.

Shit. I had to call the kids and let them know about Natalie, see if they could be here for dinner Wednesday night.

See if they were still angry at me.

Angry wasn't exactly the word. Disappointed. Hurt. Questioning my sanity. The last one was the one I wouldn't tolerate, but none of it was fun.

"I rang the bell. When no one answered, but I could

sense people within, I became worried. Otherwise, I would not have entered." Elizabeth looked between us.

"It's fine. I'm sorry I didn't hear you." I met her gaze. I wasn't going to apologize, even though that had been my first impulse.

Old habits die hard. Very hard.

That Wynter was gone. If she wasn't, I was going to help her stay gone. I felt a thread, or a small surge, or something electric, run through me.

"It's of no worry, although we need to protect your home better than it is. I know the barrier spell is working."

"Thank goodness. I haven't heard anything that sounded like a car crash since the other night."

"The demon who set it off will not bother you here, at least." Elizabeth crossed her arms, satisfaction radiating from her. "But it's strange that she was—"

"She?" I interjected. "There are female demons?"

"Yes. Male and female."

"I never even thought about it before."

Elizabeth waved a hand. "There are not as many female demons out in the open. Their men tend to be more aggressive here on the human plane. Regardless, even though we were unable to determine why she was here, she will not return."

"Did you catch her name?" Logan asked.

Elizabeth shook her head. "It would take a far stronger witch than I to secure a demon's true name, panther."

"I'd say you're pretty strong." Logan eyed her.

"Strong enough for the responsibilities I've chosen, yes. Demon hunting? No."

Logan turned to me. "I need to go. I'll see you soon, hopefully." Then he kissed me, lightly, but with a possessiveness that hadn't been there before.

I didn't mind it.

"Elizabeth," he said formally to the leader of the coven.

"Logan." She nodded in return.

He left, and I heard both the doors at the front close behind him.

"You are sure the alliance with the panther is what you seek?"

Why was everyone asking me variations of this question? "Yes," I said. "I'm sure. I've weighed the costs, and I'm sure."

"We never know the true cost of anything until it must be paid." With that happy thought, Elizabeth sat in one of the chairs at the island.

"Oh, lord. Would you like some tea? I also have cobbler, baked today."

She smiled, and the severity of the last several minutes lifted from her face. "That sounds wonderful. It's been a busy day since I last saw you."

"You're telling me," I said.

Elizabeth's smile turned to a grin. "How so?"

You mean other than this felt like the longest day of my life?

"Well, there's the Logan... element." I busied myself in the fridge, gathering myself for a moment. Telling Caro and Florry was one thing. Other people? A little more difficult. I'd been a Mrs. to someone else for a long time.

"And?"

"I did a scrying for my consult—" I stopped, turning with the cobbler in my hand. "I need to back up. Since you have asked me to train with you, and allowed me into your world, I need to be honest."

Carefully, taking my time, I started the timer to heat the up the cobbler, gently putting it in the center of the oven. Then I turned to face her.

Elizabeth didn't say anything, only nodded.

I took a breath. "I'm the Oracle of Theama."

Her eyes widened. "Really?" Her voice was practically a whisper. "How did this occur?"

I told her everything. About my birthday, the flowers, the insurance, and then me going out and meeting Ash. About what I found after I came out of the bathroom in Ash's hotel room. If she'd had an inkling before, or suspicions, or whatever—she hid it well.

"May I see the armband?" Elizabeth got up, coming around to my side of the island.

I set the cobbler down and held out my arm.

She leaned forward and peered at my forearm. "It is truly beautiful. And so powerful. It radiates."

The scales undulated, just the tiniest bit.

Elizabeth saw it, and jumped back, her eyes even wider, and her hand over her mouth.

Showoff, I thought.

Goldie didn't reply, but I felt great satisfaction from him.

"It moves?"

I nodded. "He—"

"He? You speak with it?"

"There is a connection between myself and... the spirit of the Oracle."

Elizabeth's hand fell from her mouth, and I could see that her mouth was open in an 'O'. The light roses in her cheeks paled.

"There have been many, many Oracles, Elizabeth. The Oracle isn't one person. It's all of us, all who have carried this," I lifted my arm. "All of us who have agreed to do this."

"That is amazing. I would love to ask you more—"

I shook my head. "That's all I'm comfortable saying. There are things that are for the Oracle alone." I didn't know this for sure, but I was pretty sure.

You are right. It's good that she understands who she's dealing with.

You just like it that she called you beautiful.

I am. He didn't even sound smug.

Yeah, yeah, you are. Let me get on with this, okay?

He didn't reply.

"What is it you want from me? From my coven?" Her color had returned.

"Well, there are a lot of things, because all the Oracles have different talents. I think that if you are willing to work with me, I can get better at working with my talent, be a better Oracle."

"And claim dominion over others?"

"What? No. What do you know about the Oracle?"

"That if you are worthy, you can request help. That they are secretive, and no one knows their true power, true strength."

Fair enough. "That's true. Are there witches in your coven who have different talents, who are better at things than others?"

"Of course."

"The Oracle is the same way. Each Oracle brings who she is to being the Oracle."

"You are saying you have magic?"

"Apparently so." I shrugged. "It has never come up, not in all the years I've been alive before now, but yes, I do. I can't deny it."

Slowly, Elizabeth nodded. "Then it is fair and right you should seek our help with your ability. What else?" Her formality had returned.

I didn't like that. It made this feel transactional somehow, and that was definitely not what I was after. "I want to be your friend. I don't know if I can request to join your coven, because I serve another responsibility before anything else, and that I can't and won't change. But I'd like to be a friend," I repeated. "An ally. A person that you know you can turn to."

Her face settled into a neutral expression. She was really good at looking neutral. "That is something I've not been asked before. Not just from the Oracle of Theama, but any other magical creature."

"We both live here. I like you, I like the members of your coven that I've officially met." I knew a couple, and the coven had come to my house to help me before. "I want to be your friend."

"Why?"

"Why? This is kind of a lonely gig. I have... allies, but... I want to learn more. I want to be better at this, do a better job for the people I'm helping."

"Have you failed when someone has come to you?" Her tone sharpened.

"No. Although I'm assured it will happen at some point."

"True. We all experience failure." Her index finger came up to tap at her lip. "What have you discovered your abilities to be?"

The oven dinged, alerting me to the fact that the dessert was ready. I remembered what Caro said about food easing tensions, and I thought that applied here.

"Can we sit down? I'll cut some cobbler, we can have some tea, and talk?"

She stared at me for a moment, and then smiled. She wasn't the stern coven leader anymore. "Yes, of course. I'm sorry. I'm interrogating you." She moved back to where she'd been sitting.

"I asked for it. Now sit, and I'll start this," I said as I

filled my kettle. "What kind of tea do you like?" I'd been so engrossed in our conversation I'd forgotten the tea.

"My favorite is one called Paris."

"I have that! It's amazing. The smell always hits you first, and then it makes the tea more enjoyable." I turned back to Elizabeth. "Okay, just listen, okay? Because this is all kind of jumbled."

I took a breath, and while I served up the cobbler, I shared with her about feeling the lightning zing today when Caro made Logan give his word, and the fact that I was able to send things away.

"What sort of things? Physical? Ideas? Magic?" Elizabeth leaned on the island.

"All of the above? I know I sent away magic smoke."

She frowned.

The kettle clicked off. I got up and poured the tea, handing a cup to to Elizabeth.

"I did a spell, and the result was a magical smoke, one I didn't create. It was evil." I shuddered a little at the memory of it.

"How did you get rid of it?"

"I imagined a window opening, and a breeze carrying it away."

"That's interesting." Tap, tap, tap with her finger against her lips.

"And there's something else?"

She waited for me to go on.

"The last... client... I worked with. When..." I stopped, frustrated. I went to run my hand through my hair, and stopped, remembering what my hair had been doing lately. I didn't need to pull out any more than was falling out on its own.

"The last job I needed to complete," I began again, "I noticed that I brought people together, people around me, in order to get the things done I needed to get done."

"So you pull those you need to you when necessary, and you send things away?"

How did she do that? How did she sound so... neutral? There was no judgement in her tone.

I nodded. At least there wasn't instant judgement.

"That is gathering magic." She took another bite of the cobbler.

"Well, when I bring people to me, that makes sense."

"No, no," Elizabeth said, shaking her head. "I mean your type of magic. It's known as gathering magic. The idea being that when you don't wish something near you, you're able to move it away."

"That's it? It's that simple?"

Elizabeth laughed out loud—a rich, full sound. "No, it's not simple. But it's got a name, which I think you were looking for?"

I nodded. "Yes, I was. I am. Gathering magic. It sounds so benign."

"No magic is always benign, Wynter. But I can see where this could be upsetting."

"Sometimes. Sometimes I love it."

She cocked her head, studying me. "I can see that. I can see where you can be very powerful." She went silent. "What are your goals?"

"I want to be a better Oracle. I want to be able to help those who come to me better. With greater knowledge." I took a breath. "I want to be able to protect myself and those I love."

Her eyebrows went up as she leaned against the back of the chair. "Ah. So you have made enemies?"

"Have I?" I laughed, a short, not-very-funny laugh. "I have at least two groups of necromancers who are angry at me. There's probably another one out there who, if they discover my involvement in... some... incidents, will be equally angry. There's a warlock after my current client. The local police." I threw up my hands. "Take your pick."

"There does seem to be a concerted effort to tarnish your name on the island." Elizabeth spoke carefully. She took a couple of bites as she watched me.

I laughed again, and this one had more humor in it. "That's about to change."

"How so?"

"I have an excellent lawyer."

This time, Elizabeth laughed with me.

"Good," she said. "It's better for you to live a low-key life when you have magic like this, both your own and that of the Oracle."

"I know, but I can't exactly stop what I'm doing. Oh, and there's one other thing."

"Yes?"

"I have a connection to Tethys."

"Who?"

"Tethys. Goddess of the—"

"I know who she is." Elizabeth cut me off. "How do you have a connection to her?"

"I don't know. You realize that I'm trusting you with everything? With my life? With the lives of those I'm bound to help?"

"That trust goes both ways. By speaking with you, I am exposing myself, and potentially my coven members. We are just like you, people here on the island, who have normal lives, where no one would expect magic, much less a group of witches. And you are aware that women in power are seen as a threat?"

"Yes, no, I hadn't thought of it."

"You need to. As a woman, the Oracle has always been seen as something of a mystery, a woman apart, with different rules. There are those who covet what you have."

"Don't I know it."

"It's worse if you add the words 'witches' or 'witch-craft'. You need to know that."

"Now that you've told me, I do. And I won't talk about working with you. I mean, outside of my close circle."

"Who is in your circle?"

"Is that your business?" I was taken aback at the abrupt question.

"You will be meeting my circle, my coven." Elizabeth shrugged.

That was hard to argue. "Okay. There is Caro, who lives with me. My current client, and that changes as I help them and another needs help. My friend Shelly, her boyfriend who is also my attorney, Hubie—"

"Hubie Liegal is a good man."

"He is," I agreed.

"Do your children know? I thought you said you have children."

"I have three of them, but they do not know everything about my life. I'd like to keep it that way."

"Won't that be difficult?"

Cripes. Elizabeth was asking all the questions I didn't want to think about.

"Yes, and no. The more they are here—god, they're going to be here this week—" I needed to call them— "the more chance they have to find out. I don't want that. None of them live here, and I want to keep this from them."

"I'm not sure how that will work out, but that is your choice."

"That's one that's a goal." To me, there was no discussion. I didn't want my kids anywhere near that.

"Very well. So shall we talk about what made you call me today? We are still getting together on Tuesday, correct?"

"Yes, I want to. I can't wait, actually. But the 911 call that went out today?" I sighed. "Part of being the Oracle means that you have a mentor, a spirit, that works with you. She's visible only to me."

"Are you talking about me?" Florry chose this moment to pop into existence—for me at least.

"You've been listening, haven't you?" I glared up at her.

"Always, babe. Always." She floated backward, her arms crossed and her expression satisfied.

"Your spirit guide is here now, aren't they?" Elizabeth was looking around the room. "I can feel the shift in the energy of the room."

"Yes, my guide is here. What I want to know is if I can allow—my guide—to speak to another. Part of the deal means that my guide speaks only to me."

"Why do you want to open up the communication? A spiritual guide is a gift."

"See?" Florry cackled. "I'm a gift! It's about time someone saw it. She's one smart cookie, Wynter."

"Hush," I waved a hand at her. "I'm trying to work here." I turned to Elizabeth. "I don't want to make it possible for everyone to access my guide. Just one person. This is the request of my guide." I added that last bit because I felt that Elizabeth wasn't sure of my motives.

"Why does your guide want this?"

"Repeat what I'm about to say exactly, Wynter." Florry came to hover near my elbow.

"Okay," I said. "Hang on." I held up my finger to Elizabeth.

"Tell her that I was once a person, with a life, and that while I put my responsibility to you first, there is something I would like for myself. I don't think that's too much to ask. And don't tell her my name."

I repeated the words. But then I looked to Florry, unable to stop my next question. "Even if it's not the way things are done?"

Rules can sometimes be... bent. Goldie's words were quiet.

What? Who are you? Where is the stern snaky that lives on my arm.

Enough. I can hear the pain in Florry's words. If it is possible, I see no problem with it.

You softy.

Only when appropriate. Pay attention to the witch. She is wise, and very experienced. She will be a good teacher for you.

How can you tell? I could sense the power and dignity on Elizabeth, but not more than that.

Practice. I've been around a while.

Did you just make a joke?

Focus, Wynter. Let's get this going so you can move onto the things you need as the Oracle.

I smiled and looked up to find Elizabeth looking at me.

"I'm sorry, what did you say?"

"I didn't say anything. I was watching you."

"Lots going on inside."

She studied me. "I can tell. I can feel it. I don't need

to know everything, however. You've told me more than what I needed to know."

"I could have kept more to myself?"

"No," Elizabeth was blunt. "If you had, I would have refused to help you more. Trust must be earned, and part of that is offering to trust others with the things important to you."

I'd passed some sort of test. Well, good. I needed the help, and nothing I'd seen from the Martha's Vineyard coven made me uneasy. The general sharing of information that I'd been told to keep secret made me kind of twitchy, but there seemed to be sharing as needed with this gig, so I tried not to get stuck on that piece of things.

"I thank you for trusting me. I speak for my coven when I tell you that we will keep your secrets, and protect you as one of us."

"Thank you."

"I think that I can help your spirit. I don't believe it would work beyond one person, and there may be some help needed from that person. Would that be possible?"

"I think so," I said. Caro would jump at the chance, maybe even baking for the coven.

"Okay." Elizabeth got up, picking up her now empty plate. "Thank you for the cobbler. It was delicious, and I think I need the recipe."

"The chef will be happy to share," I said.

"Oh, it wasn't you?"

"I'm not a bad cook, but my guest is a master."

"Indeed. Well, ask her if she'd share." Elizabeth sighed. "I would like to tell you that you'll have to wait, I'll get to this when I can, but I know myself—I will go straight home and see how I can solve this riddle to help your spirit guide." She smiled. "I'm a bit of a workaholic."

"Not a bad thing to be, but you need to get some sleep."

"Overrated," Elizabeth waved a hand. "Goodnight, my dear. Thank you for your trust. My sisters and I will keep your trust, and return it to you." The words were more formal again.

"I will keep your trust as well."

"I know you will. I feel good about our partnership. I'll let you know if I have an answer for you before Tuesday. Otherwise, I will see you then. And Wynter?"

"Yes?"

"Read some more." One eyebrow rose.

Then she was gone.

The front doors closed behind her, leaving me leaning against the island, feeling like a wrung-out dishrag. I cleaned up the kitchen and slowly went up the stairs, stopping to listen at the top of the stairway.

Both my guests were quiet. I was glad. They needed the sleep.

As did I.

I hurried through my nightly routine, holding the top of my head as I brushed out my hair.

It had been the longest day I could remember, if not

of my life. Overall, a good day, I thought as I considered Logan and Elizabeth. I had to find out how to break the curse with Nina. That wasn't in the win column.

But I had a chance to help Florry and Caro.

You've done well today, Wynter. You should be proud.

Thank you, Goldie, I thought. *I feel like my to-do list is never ending.*

It's not.

Thanks, I thought.

Get some sleep.

Yes, sir. I wasn't in the mood to trade insults, quips, or even anymore more conversation. I was conversation-ed out.

I closed my eyes, feeling myself sink into the pillow, in that way you feel as you're fading to sleep.

Wynter! Goldie's voice broke into my consciousness.

Go away. It's Sunday. I'm sleeping in.

You need to get up now. His last word was punctuated with a jolt of electricity.

A feeling of panic took up residence in my chest.

CHAPTER TWELVE

"What?" I said out loud, pushing my self up onto one elbow. It was light out, which meant I'd gotten some sleep.

Your consultant. She is in need.

How can you tell?

Get up now. Go see her.

I thrashed in the covers for a moment, trying to free myself. When I finally managed it, I tossed them back, and hurried from the room.

The hallway was quiet.

Go!

I ran to the door where Nina was sleeping and opened it, not wanting to slam it and scare her.

"Holy hell!" It wouldn't have mattered if the room came down around her. Nina wouldn't have heard it.

Because she was on the bed, her limbs jerking back and forth, and her face a nasty, pale gray.

"Nina!" I ran to her, grabbing her shoulders.

She kept jerking, making me move along with her.

"What is this?"

No one, not even Goldie, answered.

I have to send it away. I can gather to me, and I can send away the things I'm done with. I remembered Elizabeth's words.

I stepped back, took a breath, and then leaned down, putting my hands on Nina's chest, which wasn't moving around as much as her arms and legs.

Whatever you are, you don't belong here. You are not welcome. You are no longer able to be here.

Something pushed back against my hands.

I was so surprised I nearly fell backwards, but I righted myself, and kept on chanting within my head. The reaction told me I was on the right track.

Whatever you are, you don't belong here. You are not welcome. You are no longer able to be here.

I kept repeating the words, focused on keeping my hands on Nina, sending my message through her, through her entire body. From her heart, up toward her head, down toward her toes.

Nina screamed, her shriek echoing in my head.

Then she sat up, and screamed again.

This time, I did fall backward. "Nina!"

"Noooo!" She screamed as she clutched at her heart, then one hand went to her head.

"Nina! You're here! You're with me!" I scrabbled to my feet and covered the hand on her chest with mine.

Her eyes wide, she panted heavily, glancing around in a way that reminded me of an animal seeking a way out of a trap.

"Nina, Nina." I used the same tone I used with my kids when they woke up from nightmares. "I'm here, Nina. You're safe."

"No, I'm not." Her voice was hoarse.

Caro came in. "Is everyone okay?"

"Can you get some water?" I asked without looking around.

In a moment, I heard her running down the stairs.

"Keep breathing, Nina. You're here. You're safe. You're safe."

She stared at me, her eyes wide, her breathing fast and slowly, slowly, as I heard Caro coming back up the steps, Nina seemed to catch her breath.

"Here." A glass of water appeared next to me.

I took it and handed it to Nina.

Nina grabbed the water and drank it in a few gulps.

"What do you want?" I asked as I took the glass. "You want to try to go back to sleep?"

Nina shook her head. "More water. Then we can talk? Wynter?" She grabbed my arm, her hand viselike. "I'm running out of time."

"Let's go downstairs." I got up, and held out my hand to Nina.

She took it, gripping my hand tightly.

Together we walked down the stairs, taking the

steps one at a time. I got Nina over to the couch in front of the fireplace. "What do you need?"

She sat down slowly. "More water. A blanket. I don't know. I don't know, Wynter! He's got me trapped, and I can't get out!" Her voice rose into a wail of panic and fear.

Caro had taken the water glass before we came downstairs, and she came back with another glass.

Nina took it again, and sipped at it.

I got up, my hand rubbing at my throat. "We need to do the casting out scrying." I didn't know who I was talking to.

No. You meant to scry last night, and you didn't. You should scry on your own, ask for guidance.

What will that do? Look at her! It was all I could do not to turn around and point to Nina. *Goldie, she's fading. She looks terrible. This thing, whatever it is, is attacking her in her sleep.*

No. Scry for yourself. Then see what is to be done. He didn't hesitate, didn't waver.

You're not going to let this go, are you?

No. I don't often tell you what you should do, but I feel I cannot be silent.

I sighed. *All right.*

"Caro, keep an eye on Nina. I need to scry, to see... to see." I sighed again.

"Got it." Caro's words were a whisper. "I think she might be able to sleep."

When I looked over, I could see Nina lying back on the pillows, her eyes closed.

Her face was still gray.

I might have time.

I hurried to the kitchen, and pulled my scrying bowl and the herbs from the pantry. "I need to set this up so this doesn't take so long," I grumbled to myself. Add another thing to do on my list—find a place to store my growing collection of Oracle items.

I had all the boxes with the spell journals, and the jars of herbs that Nathanial had given me, boxed from his father. It was his father's studies, and many of his supplies. I couldn't wait to get into it—but I hadn't had a chance to do anything other than stack them up along the wall next to the back door.

And my scrying. And now the scrying supplies from the Oracle scrying. My things I needed were piling up. I couldn't keep them in the living room, and the pantry.

My to-do list was screaming.

But I had to keep going. I took all the supplies out into the front room, to the long couch near the bay window. Shaking the herbs into my bowl, I sat back, closing my eyes.

I needed to be calm, to try and find my center before I scryed. I'd already worked out that it went better for me if I did.

Breathing in and out, thinking of the breath coming in as light, and exhaling a dark haze, the things I didn't want or need within—after a few minutes, I felt myself more at ease.

Great.

I lit the burner under the herbs, and then stretched myself out on the couch, closing my eyes and inhaling deeply. Eventually, I could smell them, pungent and intense, filling my senses and surrounding me.

Let me see, I thought. *What do I need to see? Show it to me. Help me to see what I need to help Nina.* That's what I'd done with all my other consultants when I first attempted to scry for them. Just open my mind and let whatever needed to come, come.

My mind went dark, like when someone closes the curtains on a room. I sat in the darkness, waiting for whatever it was I was supposed to see.

A form began to emerge in the darkness. It was clear that whatever this was, it was in a small room, shrouded by darkness at its edges. There was a lighter form in the middle and as I watched, the form became a man.

He was sitting, his back ramrod straight, head bent down over a small brass bowl. Smoke rose in a thin, white stream over the bowl. His eyes were closed, and his lips moved as he chanted.

How I knew he was chanting? Probably because the entire set up led me to believe that he was chanting. I mean, what else could he be doing? Making some hipster video for social media?

No. I'd go with chanting.

In some of my other scryings, I felt like I could step into the scene, be a part of it. Some, I'd known I needed to be an observer only. This one? I needed to not even be noticed.

The danger, the hate, the anger, the meanness—it rolled off this guy.

"Who is this?" I whispered. *Let me hear more.*

The view zoomed in. I could hear his voice.

"... she needs to learn. Let her learn, let her know her place, and if she will not, let her disappear, her energy returned to her daughter. Let her go in peace where she will not suffer longer." His lips twisted at the last words, and while he said 'let her go in peace' he meant the exact opposite.

"Kira, show yourself to me. To your sire, to your father."

Holy hell. This was Rockledge Davenport.

I'd have to tell Florry he looked exactly as you'd think he did.

His face was pale, his eyes dark and blazing with need and want. Greed. That's what it was. Greed. His lips pressed tightly together as he spoke, and the tension rolled off him like a tsunami.

This was an angry man.

I focused on his words. This would help with the hex.

"Her time is nearly up. If she does not return my blood to me, let her stand forever in the knowledge of her mistake. Let her be still while her mind continues on. Let her know that she brought her destiny upon herself, by defying me, by keeping my blood from me. Show her, now, what she faces." He raised his head then, his arms spread wide, the smoke rising from the bowl thicker, less opaque.

Yep. This was Rockledge.

Florry had been right. This was a ticking time bomb. But what did it mean? What would happen when the clock ran out? He sounded like he wanted to kill Nina. But also keep her alive, so that she would be stuck and suffer.

What a rotten bastard.

He looked around then, and it seemed that he looked right at me.

Oh, shit.

I pushed myself away, wanting to fade, move farther from him.

As I felt myself pull back, his eyes stayed on where I'd been. The further I got, his features faded, but I could see his eyes.

It was almost as if they gleamed red.

Moving faster, I worked to put more distance between myself and the man who radiated anger, hate, and evil.

My eyes opened, and I was back in my front room, the sun shining in through the bay window, and the low hum of Caro and Nina's voices in the background.

Closing my eyes again, I tried to calm my pounding

heart. The necromancers I'd seen when trying to help Nathanial had scared me.

This was worse.

No wonder Nina was afraid.

And as much as I hated to admit it, she was right. He had hexed her. With something big. What had he said? That he wanted her to feel what she was facing?

I was on my feet, blowing out the burner beneath my herb bowl. Then I was back out to the living room, where Nina was sitting up, Caro next to her.

"Wynter, are you all right?" Caro looked alarmed as I came toward them.

"No, I'm not. Nina, how are you feeling?" I came around the couch and sat on the coffee table in front of the other women.

"Better, a little. But I'm wiped out. It's like I'm so tired, and can't get enough sleep."

Show her, now, what she faces. Those had been Rockledge's words. *Show her, now, what she faces.*

Whatever this was, whatever he ultimately had planned for her, this was only a preview.

CHAPTER THIRTEEN

"Explain it to me again." Nina was at the island now, a hot cup of tea in front of her.

"He does in fact have some sort of hex on you, and if you don't give him Kira, he plans to pull the pin on whatever grenade he's got on you, so to speak, or whatever. If you don't hand her over, you're going to lose your life as you know it, although you're not going to die."

"That bastard."

"That was my sentiment, too."

Nina took a sip of tea, which I was glad to see.

"We have to do the other scrying. The one to cast off the hex." Her voice wobbled a bit.

"I don't think you're strong enough," I began.

"He's leeching off me. I don't know how he's doing it, but he's leeching from me. It's not going to get better." Nina's eyes were fierce.

Our argument was interrupted by the ringing of the doorbell.

The three of us looked at each other.

"Anyone expecting anyone?" I asked, glancing between Caro and Nina. I was expecting Shelly—I hadn't heard from her, and that made me worry. Just a little. I figured she was with Hubie, which made me not worry at all.

But no one else.

Both shook their heads.

"Well, let's go see what the day is bringing." I headed for the door, noting as I did that I still hadn't made it out of my pajamas.

I opened the door to find Nathanial and his husband, George. They looked like the poster children for brunch.

"Hey Wynter, I wanted—whoa, did we wake you?" Nathanial gave me a once over.

"No, I'm good. Come on in. I have something for you," I said, remembering what I'd tucked in the hallway table.

"We have something for you, too." George smiled at me.

"You didn't need to. You already gave me all your father's wonderful herbs." The thought of the boxes with all the jars gave me a sense of pleasure.

"I know. But this is something, just for you." Nathanial handed me an envelope.

"And this is for you. Your father's coven journal. You should return it to his coven. I think they would appreciate it."

Nathanial's lips tightened. He'd learned, after Logan found George and I'd cast away the nameless necromancer who had orchestrated the whole thing, that he had magic, and it had been deliberately blocked. Probably by his parents.

Nathanial had no interest in magic, none at all. It had been the death of his parents, and nearly the death of his husband. Magic had no feel goods for him.

"I said that I would, and I will. But that's it, I'm done."

"I think you need to do what's best for you," I said.

"Thank you for being so concerned. I'm so glad he had you. Now, open your present!" George smiled at me again as he threaded his arm through Nathanial's.

I tugged at the flap of the envelope, pulling out the card within.

On it, it gave me an entire day of healing and health at a well-known spa on the island. A facial, manicure, pedicure, massage, seaweed wrap, and a float session.

"Will I be able to move after this?" I asked. "This is going to leave me boneless."

"Hopefully not," Nathanial said. "You need a day off."

"Oh, Nathanial, you have no idea." I laughed then, opening my arms for a hug.

I got one from both of them, and we chatted for a few minutes more. Then, as abruptly as they'd come in, Nathanial and George left, their need for the help of the Oracle done, the door closed on what had been a really tough time.

I stood there for a moment, card in hand, tears welling in my eyes and spilling down my cheeks.

There was no reason why.

It made me happy to see that one of my consultants, one who had been angry, and upset all throughout the time we worked together, leave happy and not just smiling, but beaming.

This must be part of what made it worth it.

Glancing down at the spa card, I had to admit, the massage wasn't going to hurt.

I put the card back into the envelope and made my way back to the kitchen.

"That was nice," Caro said.

"It was. I have an excellent day ahead of me. After we get rid of your hex, and get your daughter back to you." I patted Nina's hand, and then walked toward my desk in the far corner of the living room, tucking the spa card into the top drawer.

When I came back to the island, I picked up where we'd left off. "Nina, we need to let you rest. Just for a day or so. I know, I know he's leeching off you. But if things go wrong, like they did before—I'm worried you won't be able to fight it off."

Nina opened her mouth, then closed it. She sighed. "You're right. That smoke thing wiped me out. But if I'm getting weaker, how will that help?"

"I'm going to ask my grimoire. Let me clean up my stuff, and I'll go shower and see what the grimoire can offer."

"Breakfast after?" Caro called.

"Yes," I went back to where I'd left all my scrying materials, and busied myself in the kitchen, cleaning it up.

"You need a better place for all this."

"It's uncanny how you're on the same page with me," I glanced over her.

"Your stuff is in my way." Caro didn't look up from pulling ingredients out of the fridge.

I laughed, which eased some of the tension I was feeling. "All right. It's on my to-do list anyway. I've already thought about that. My supplies are growing."

"Yeah, I was wondering what you were going to do with all the boxes." Caro didn't even look down at what she was doing, cooking from what seemed like memory.

"They're on the list! I swear!"

"Okay. Just know, I need room to cook."

"Got it." I glanced at Nina.

She was falling asleep.

"Nina, why don't you go back up and sleep some more?"

"I'll save some breakfast for you," Caro promised.

"I think... I think that's a great idea." Nina yawned.

"Come on. I'll walk you up."

She nodded, not even speaking.

I followed Nina up the stairs, worry first in my head again. Whatever this was, it was working fast, and even though I wanted her to rest, I wouldn't have much time. She could take the day to sleep. She needed that. But I'd need to do the second scrying tonight.

Because it was clear she didn't have a lot of time. I didn't want to say that out loud; I wouldn't. I could see it, though.

And as the Oracle, Nina was my responsibility, and I needed to act.

I got her into bed, closing the door softly as I left the room.

"Well, this is a mess." Florry appeared.

"Where have you been? You and Goldie have been missing in action all morning."

I woke you.

"Yes you did. But where have you been? Did you see what I saw?"

I did, Goldie said.

"Go into your room," Florry said. There wasn't a trace of humor or laughter anywhere on her.

I followed her direction. Once the door closed behind me, Florry zoomed around me. "Before you get into the grimoire, let me see if I can see it." She came close, her hand outstretched to me.

"You can see what I see?"

"I don't know, but I want to try."

I felt a cold spot near my face.

"Close your eyes. This might be easier."

I closed them. The cold on my face increased, and I felt the mind of another next to, and then within mine.

My instinct was to push it, push her away, but I inhaled, and tried to keep myself relaxed.

The vision I'd seen during the scrying flashed through my memory at a super-fast speed. Then, as quickly as it had come close to me, the memory was gone, and the cold moved away from me.

"That is one creepy guy." Florry was back near the window.

"Understatement of the year. How the hell do I get rid of him?"

"Just like you planned. See if the book of smug mysteries can help, and then do the casting out spell. And we go from there."

"What if it doesn't work?"

"If it doesn't, we'll find something else. That's what you're here for, Wynter. Not everything works out on the first try. Or even the second."

"I don't think I'll get a lot of tries. He's going to kill her."

"That's not quite what he said. Her form will be dead, but her mind will be alive."

I gave her side eye. "That's better somehow?"

"No, it's worse. He's a sick creep. But he's not going

to kill her. He doesn't want her dead. He wants her to suffer."

"Jerk. I want to see him ruined."

"Destroyed?" Florry was cheerful.

"Sure."

"That's my girl."

"I'm getting a shower first."

"Well, not being stinky is a good thing."

"Thanks," I said. "I won't be long."

"Wynter, take your time. You need to be in a good place for this to work. I think today is going to be another long day."

"You know, yesterday was made better by Logan. He's leaving for New York today," I couldn't help teasing her a little.

"Get used to it. I figure cat boy travels a lot."

"You're so cheerful. Keep that up, and we'll talk more when I'm done."

I stayed in the shower until the water went cool. Once I got out, I took my time to get ready. If Florry was right, I wanted to put my best face on.

Even if my damn hair kept falling out. I got dressed and dried my hair, brushing it carefully, and putting the lost hair into my trash can, refusing to think on it. I wouldn't cry again. Not until after Friday, when I saw Dr. Amberson. Then it might be time to really cry.

I had too much to do today.

"Thought you might drown in there."

"You'd miss me if I was gone," I said.

"Get to the smug mysteries." Florry pointed at the dresser where I kept the grimoire.

I didn't reply, only complied. I took it to the bed and settled in with it. That was my favorite place to look for knowledge and information from the grimoire. Setting it in my lap, I took a couple of deep breaths and closed my eyes.

"I need help. I need to keep a consultant going. Her enemy is trying to end her. I want to stop the draining magic he's doing." I laid my hand on the cover, on the snake on the front of the book. "Please. Help me." My voice fell to a whisper. "I don't want her to die."

There it was. I'd said the words out loud. I didn't want Nina to die, and I was very afraid she might. That the horrible little man I'd seen would take the life from her, take it before I could stop him, before I could pull her back from him.

Downstairs, I heard the doorbell ring.

I swear to god, the doorbell was my Achilles' heel this weekend. How was it still the weekend, by the way?

There were voices downstairs, and I figured if I didn't hear yelling or carrying on, Caro had things in hand. I closed my eyes again and thought to the grimoire.

Please help me. Please.

Then I paged through the book, turning the pages slowly so as not to miss any writing that might appear.

I'd gotten halfway through the book before I saw a

faded brown script move across one of the pages. I stopped, waiting to see if it was just a trick of my wishful thinking.

Words continued to form and I breathed a sigh of relief. The grimoire didn't always respond. Closing my eyes, I leaned against the headboard. When I opened them a couple of minutes later, the page was full.

An answer.

Maybe.

THERE MAY BE times when those in need of your help are suffering, and you are worried for their continued survival. I have discovered a way to offer them energy, to give of myself so that they can sustain until I find the answer they seek.

WHAT? Give of myself? What did she give? How much? Was it a limb? I didn't know if I really wanted the answers to that question, but I couldn't look away. It was like a train wreck. I had to keep going.

THIS IS A DANGEROUS MAGIC. It will deplete you, and you will need to give yourself time to recover. It is not to be used unless you are certain your consultant will die. Even then, weigh carefully. There is only so much we can give to others. We already sacrifice much.

• • •

THERE WAS a scrawl at the bottom of this that I guessed was a signature, and then below it was a list of herbs, and then the heading, *'For the Sharing of Energy'*.

I leaned back. Wow. This was intense. There wasn't a way to sustain Nina without giving her something from me.

That is the cost of magic. Nothing is free. You can't get something from nothing. If you are able to heal, or keep someone alive, that energy must come from somewhere.

Have you seen this used? I asked Goldie. *Be honest.*

Yes.

And how did things turn out?

Both the Oracle and the consultant lived.

But?

But what?

Goldie, I hear the 'but' in there. What's the catch?

He sighed. *The catch, Wynter, is that both parties were weakened. I know that you're worried for your consultant, but I would advise against this.*

"Florry?" I called out softly.

"What?" She appeared so fast that she must have been hovering.

"Have you seen this before? This spell for transferring energy to a consultant?"

She shook her head, her puff of hair waving as her head moved. "No. I've never had call to look for it. How bad is it?" She drifted closer, peering down at the grimoire in my lap.

"It's not good. Goldie is advising against it."

Florry looked at me. "What?"

"Goldie is telling me this isn't the best idea."

It's not.

"It's not very often that Goldie says don't do it." Her face showed her concern.

"You would know better than I would."

Florry studied me, then said, "But you're going to do it anyway."

"I can't let her die." If Nina died, then not only would her ex win, but it meant that a little girl would lose her mom. And potentially be raised by that awful man.

I couldn't be party to that.

"Wynter, you cannot save everyone." Florry drifted closer, ignoring that it brought her into my bed.

It was weird to see her from only the waist up and I looked at her face, which was creased in worry.

Florry continued, "I told you that. All of us, all of the Oracles, fail at some point. It happens. I'm sorry that yours may be early on. It's the worst feeling in the world. But you cannot sacrifice yourself for one consultant."

"I'm not going to sacrifice myself."

"Stuff and nonsense, my girl. I know that look, even though it's only been three months with you. You're making your own decision and deciding the hell with me and Goldie."

I didn't reply.

"Go on, try to deny it."

"I'm not denying anything." I got up and got paper and pen to write down the ingredients and the spell.

Neither Florry nor Goldie said anything.

"I wish you wouldn't do this," Florry said to my back.

Listen to her.

"I can't let her die," I told both of my mentors. "I can't."

"You are not the person who decides who lives or dies." Florry moved into my line of vision.

"But if I make a choice that leads directly to the death of a consultant? An innocent, who only came to me for help?"

"Maybe you've helped her as much as you can." Florry met my gaze, not giving an inch. "Why don't you ask—"

"No, I'm the Oracle. I make the decisions for myself. I don't need to double check every decision I make." I didn't like the inference that I couldn't manage what had to be done as the Oracle.

"Wynter, this is serious. This is not going to come without a cost. Magic never does. And when you're giving some of you to others? The desire to live is the strongest drive in the world. The person you give to will keep taking what they need for themselves. What if you can't stop it?"

"It wouldn't be in here if it wasn't possible." I put

the grimoire back into the dresser, and taking the paper with the spell on it, went back downstairs.

I could hear the quiet conversation as I walked down the stairs. Oh, hell.

I'd totally forgotten.

I was a terrible person.

CHAPTER FOURTEEN

I'd forgotten Shelly. Last night—was it just last night?
—I'd asked Shelly over for breakfast. That seemed like
years ago at this point.

How did you forget a date with your best friend in
less than twelve hours?

"There she is! And don't you look a peach!" Shelly
got up from the island and came over to hug me. "It's
been too long, lady. We have to—" she stopped and
pulled away from me. "What is it? You're as tense as
can be."

"I have to do something I don't want to."

"Then don't do it."

I shook my head. "I have to, Shel. But it can wait a
little. Have you had something to eat?"

"We were waiting on you. Did Nina get back to
sleep?" Caro asked.

"I think so. I put her back to bed."

"Great. Then sit down, and let's eat, and you tell me all about what's going on with Logan."

Despite the weight of what I had to do, I couldn't help but smile. "What's going on with him is good."

"How good?" Shelly peered at me. "Spill it all, and don't you hold back."

I pushed the spell to the side so I could sit and enjoy my friend. We talked for nearly an hour, laughing and catching up.

She was in it deep with Hubie. Given the way she was talking, I thought there could be a marriage, but I didn't dare say that to Shelly.

She's good for you. Take strength from her.

I can't take anymore from her. I already leaned on Shelly a great deal.

You can ask for help from her. She will give it, freely. With love.

I know. That's why I can't ask. Not for this.

I ignored my armband in favor of continuing talking with Shelly.

"Hubie's thrilled with you letting him sue everyone in sight," Shelly said with a laugh.

"I got that impression."

"He does love his job."

"And you? Does he love you the same way?" Caro asked, her tone sly.

Shelly's cheeks pinked. "We're not talking about me. I came here for good food and Logan gossip."

"Which you have gotten in full," I said, laughing.

"Yes, I have. And I am going to tell you, it's all right."

"What?"

"I know you, Wyn. It may not hit yet, but somewhere in there, you will find a little cart of guilt. Since your kids are coming this week to see Natalie, I'm guessing they'll be driving the cart, even if they don't know they are."

"I don't know about that," I said.

"I do. And I'm telling you right now, don't you fall into that cart of guilt. It's a trap. Derek is gone. You don't owe him the rest of your life as a sop to his memory, no matter what your kids might shout at you."

"They're not going to shout at me," I said. "I hope not, anyway. They just think I'm crazy."

"Why?" It was Caro rather than Shelly who asked.

"Because even though they know what their dad did, the idea that I might be moving on is not one they're ready for. Rachel came in the house one afternoon and Logan and I were kissing in the kitchen."

"She had no business giving you grief." Shelly shook her head.

"It's all right. Rachel has always been the strongest willed of my kids. She's the one most upset with me. She said she was better, but... I haven't seen her or talked with her much since we patched things up. The boys are less upset, although I don't think they're thrilled."

"Look, they're adults. You're an adult. Things are

what they are. I know you've been feeling off balance with them, but now is the time to get them over here, get them back on track with being a family, and if they don't like Logan, well, they're nuts." Shelly patted my hand. "Make time to call them soon."

"I have to. Natalie will be here Wednesday. She's spending the night, and we're all going to play happy family."

"Are you inviting Logan?" Caro asked.

"He's out of town, which isn't the worst thing. It's bad enough that my kids know about him before I was ready to tell them. I don't know why, but I don't want to have my new romantic interest around Natalie."

"Why, because you think that since she stole one of your guys, she might steal another?" Shelly peered at me.

"No." Yes.

"Derek was not as good looking as Logan. And Natalie has nothing Logan wants. Not only that, Logan isn't the same man as Derek."

"How can you tell?" I asked my best friend.

"I've known you, and Derek, for years. I've also gotten to spend time with Logan, one on one. He wasn't trying to impress me."

"Don't count on that. He could tell what you were to me right off the bat," I said with a smile. "A smart man woos the friends, not just his lady love."

"But he's not wooing anyone. All I'm saying is that if he happens to be on the island, you should invite him over." Shelly rolled her eyes. "It's not some kind of state affair."

"I'll take your advice under consideration," I said.

"What's next today?" Shelly asked.

"Wynter's going to try something that is very bad for her health." Florry chimed in from over by the fireplace. The fact that no one else could hear her didn't bother her in the slightest.

Shush.

"No. I'm not letting you kill yourself for a consultant. You do more good alive." She came closer.

"Is Florry here?" Caro spoke then, looking around.

"She is. She's yelling at me."

"Why?" Caro and Shelly said together.

"I am going to do a spell today to help Nina. You haven't seen her," I said to Shelly. "She looks terrible. She's fading, and I think it's the hex on her. I found a spell in the grimoire to give her some of my energy, and I'm going to. I need her stronger for the next scrying I need to do."

"You can't do that, Wynter." Caro's eyes were wide. "You need the strength for you. I was here, remember? I saw what that thing, whatever it was, did to you. To both of you. If you sap your own strength, it won't help either one of you."

"I can't have her die." No matter what anyone said, that fact remained at the forefront for me. I couldn't let her die. And her death was what her ex wanted.

He was not going to win.

"What do you need from me?" Shelly asked simply. Her face showed me she was worried, but Shelly wasn't a fusser. She was a doer, and right now, even though she was worried, she was going to do what I needed her to do.

"Nothing. Well, that's not true. Maybe do some shopping for me, get a list and a menu together with Caro, if you both wouldn't mind? I want to have a nice time when Natalie's here, even if it is really inconvenient. I just feel like I can't do it all." I stopped, feeling tears well up for no good reason.

"We're on it," Shelly said, exchanging what I'd call 'a look' with Caro. That meant my friend had an agenda, but I couldn't worry about that now. I needed to focus on keeping my consultant alive.

First things first.

With Shelly and Caro on track with their own tasks and headed out shortly, I went into the storage area that lived on the other side of my master bath. Under the eaves of the house, it was small, and in the last couple of years, didn't even have that much stored in it. There were two lights on the walls, and a desk in the corner. Derek had sometimes come in here to do work when he was here.

I thought this would do for my Oracle space, but now that I was here, looking around, I didn't like it. I didn't like the feel.

Damn it. My house wasn't that big, although it was big for Oak Bluffs. Where to—a thought hit me.

I went back to my room and straight to the closet formerly known as Derek's. It was cleaned out, thanks to the earlier efforts of myself and the kids. It had shelves, places to store things, and it was right here, right in my room. I could get a lock for the door.

This was it. This was perfect.

Feeling energized, I went downstairs and starting bringing up my things that had been collecting wherever I could find room in the kitchen and surrounding areas.

All my scrying herbs, and my bowls. I liked to do my scrying lying down; I wondered if I could rearrange my room, move the bed to the far wall, and get a chaise longue up here, putting it close to the closet. Maybe a small table, and even a fridge to keep drinks in.

I nodded. This was shaping up well. Much better than the storage space.

Then I brought up the boxes from Nathanial's dad. As much as I wanted to unpack all the boxes, I confined myself to opening the ones with the bottled herbs, setting them on the shelves. The rest of the things, I left in the boxes and neatly stacked them in another closet unit. There would be time, soon I hoped, to get this all organized.

I'd need to get a desk, or a table of some sort in here. It meant a bit of a makeover, so that this would be an efficient space for me to work.

But I could leave the door open, and open the window in my room—I had a large window up here, and when it was nice, there was a wonderful breeze off the sea—and this would be a calm and tranquil place to work.

I took a drink of water from the bottle I'd brought up with me, and sat down at the floor to read through the ingredients I needed. It took some time, but from my own stores, as well as some of Nathanial's dad's, I was able to gather all the things on the list.

The 'how-to' section was a bit more involved.

Mix all the herbs together in a metal bowl. Burn the herbs from below, adding a few drops of water as they burn. Then prick your finger and add four drops of your own blood. Continue to heat the mixture. Once the herbs have greatly broken down, increase the heat and make a strong brew. Allow the brew to cool and steep for a further two full hours, then it is ready to be used. This is what you will give to the one in need.

As they drink your offering, say the following:
I share myself with thee.
Of myself, I give freely.
Take that which is given
To be part of the living
I share myself with thee.

It sounded like a bad nursery rhyme. A really bad one. I followed the directions, wincing as I pricked my finger with a needle from an old sewing kit that was also living up here. The smells of the herbs mingled together was nice, almost soothing as the smoke from the burning herbs drifted up into the rafters. The good smell was tinged with the copper of blood. I didn't think I'd taken that much, but I could smell the coppery tang.

This would work.

It had to.

After the mixture had boiled down, I took the burner away, and looked at my phone. Two hours. I had two hours to get other things done.

What I really wanted was to collapse face first into bed, and not come out for a day or two, but I didn't have a choice.

Closing the door of the closet behind me for now, I walked back into my room, lay down on the bed, and dialed the number for my daughter. I carried the grimoire, because I needed to make a note about the scrying, and I kept forgetting.

But first, the kids.

"Mom, hey, what are you doing?"

"I heard from Natalie yesterday. She and the kids are coming to visit on Wednesday. I'd love for you to be here."

"When are they getting there?"

"Probably around lunch time."

"I can be there before dinner, but I won't be able to take too much time off."

"That's fine, honey. I just would like you to be there."

"As a buffer?"

"No." I laughed a little. "I think we're beyond that now."

"Is Logan going to be there?" Her voice was steady.

Too steady.

"No, he's in New York on business, so I don't think so."

Rachel let out a breath. "Are you still seeing him?"

"Yes."

"And?"

"And what?"

"What happens next between you two?" Rachel asked, her words impatient.

"I don't know. When I do, when something changes, I'll let you know. Right now, we're taking things slow. We both have responsibilities and obligations." There was no way I was going to tell her about the other day. Not if there was a hot poker to my toes.

Silence, then she huffed. "Fine. All right. I said I wouldn't be a brat about it anymore. Did you call the guys?"

"They are next on my list."

"Okay. I'll be there in time for dinner."

"Do you want to spend the night?"

Rachel said, "No, I can catch the last ferry back. I don't have much vacation time left."

A pang of guilt shot through me. She and the boys had taken a lot of time to be with me after Derek died. Then I stopped myself. She should have had a month, maybe two. It was criminal that none of my kids had jobs where they got time off to mourn their father.

"All right. I'll be glad to see you, sweetheart."

"Me, too, Mom. Love you."

"Love you, too."

One down, two to go.

I called Kris, and left him a message.

When I called Theo, he answered.

"Hey, Mom."

I explained about the Wednesday visit, and he offered to come over that morning and help me with whatever was needed. I doubted we'd need any more help since Caro was on the case, and told him so.

"Rachel and Kris coming?"

"I talked to Rachel. She's coming for dinner, but she's not staying the night. No word on Kris. I left him a message."

"He'll probably be there for dinner. His work is pretty insane right now."

I felt a pang. I'd been so wrapped up in my own stuff, I hadn't talked to my kids much the last two weeks. Not to mention, it felt like we all needed some space, even though things were supposedly on the mend.

At least they were there for each other.

"Oh, is it? I hate to hear that."

"It's fine," Theo said. "We'll probably all take the later ferry home."

"I'm glad you're coming."

"We're not going to leave you to face them alone."

"I thought you liked Natalie and the kids."

"I do. But she's coming to your home, your home with Dad. The one he lived in for longer than he knew her. It's a thing, Mom."

"You and Rachel have been talking a lot, haven't you?"

He laughed. "We all have. For the record, I don't mind that you might be dating a man that Rachel thinks is way too hot."

"What?" I wasn't sure to laugh, or cry, or what.

"She described him, and I think one of her concerns was that he was way, way good looking. If that's the case, good for you, Mom. If he's around, I'd love to meet him."

My eyes welled up at the words from my son. "I don't think he will be, but if he is, I'll make sure he's there."

"Okay. Whatever you want, Mom. This isn't my call. It's yours."

"I can't wait to see you, honey."

"You, too, Mom. I gotta go. I love you."

"I love you, too, Theo."

When we hung up, I sniffled. Theo was a great kid. All my kids were great kids.

The good thing was, I felt better about them being here on Wednesday. I'd be glad to have them with me.

Glancing at my phone, I saw that almost an hour had passed.

Depending how this went with Nina today, I would love to see if we could do the second scrying spell and send her ex off to Timbuktu, or wherever.

While I waited for the brew to finish steeping, I cleaned up around my room, getting the laundry together, and sat down with the grimoire to make the notes about what had happened. When I opened the book to the page about banishing hexes, the page was full.

"Where do I make the notes? I don't want to write over anyone else's notes."

The page on the right was blank, and I decided this was the best I could do. I wrote everything I remembered, and made a note that I would continue the update once I'd done the scrying to cast out the spell. As I stopped, thinking about what I'd written, the words disappeared into the page.

"Hey, I wasn't done."

Nothing reappeared.

Well, then. I'd just have to see what happened when I went to update my ongoing scrying mess.

Chores done for the moment, I decided to lay down and take a cat nap. I had a feeling today was going to be another long day, just like yesterday.

Thirty minutes later, my alarm went off. I went to check on my energy brew. The whole closet smelled like herbs with an undercurrent of something sharper, tangier. Oh, eww. Was that the blood?

Better not to think about that. It was done, had to be done.

I tucked my cheat sheet with the spell on it into a pocket, and carefully made my way down to the kitchen, balancing the bowl of liquid in my hands. As I put the bowl onto the counter, a sigh of relief slipped out.

"I thought for sure I was going to spill that."

"Hey," a soft voice came from the couch.

"Nina." I hurried over to her. "I thought you were in bed."

Her face was even more gray than this morning. Shit. This thing, whatever it was, had accelerated whatever it was doing to her.

"Hello?" I called out.

"I'm right here," Nina whispered.

"No, honey, it's all right. Hang on."

I walked through the main level, but no one else was here. Caro and Shelly must still be out shopping.

There was nothing else to be done.

Grabbing a pitcher from a cabinet, I poured the herbal brew into it. Then I got a glass, and carried them both over to where Nina was still on the couch.

Oh, god. Was I really going to do this?

I heard Florry's and Goldie's warnings in my head.

I have the same warnings. Still. They have not changed. Goldie didn't hesitate to invade my thoughts.

"I know, I know," I grumbled.

"He's not wrong, whatever he's saying." Florry chose that moment to appear.

"If you don't know what he's saying, why are you just agreeing?"

"Because if it's about this cockamamie scheme to share your energy with a consultant and he's not for it, I'm with him!" Florry sounded angry.

"I don't have a choice. I can't lose her."

"Sometimes that's not your call." Florry said. "I'm gonna keep saying it until you hear me, Wynter!"

"If it's not something to use, why is it in the grimoire?" I snapped.

"Even Oracles make mistakes."

"I'll remember that." I set down the pitcher and glass. "Now please leave me alone if you can't be supportive."

We are being supportive, Goldie said. *It's our job to protect you, even if that means we protect you from your own foolish decisions.*

"I am not losing her. I will keep saying that until you two hear me!" I pictured a door closing in my head, a door that separated me from Goldie and Florry. They'd made their feelings clear. So had I.

"Don't shut me out, Wynter. Or Goldie." Florry was still here, although she looked more opaque than I'd seen her.

"Will you both be quiet? I need to focus."

"Yes." Florry crossed her arms, looking deeply unhappy, but she didn't say anything else.

I'm always at your side, even if you are not happy with me. Goldie's tone was calm.

"Good. Then let me get to work." I sat on the coffee table, and put my hand on Nina's arm. "Nina, honey, can you wake up?"

"Hmmm?" She stirred a bit, but her eyes didn't open.

"I need you to wake up. I have something I think is going to help you."

Her eyes fluttered, and she stirred again, her face turning toward me. "What?" One hand moved up to her face, rubbing at her eyes.

"I need you to get up for a bit. I think I can help you."

"Oh, okay." She struggled to push herself up.

Where was the woman who had been coming to my house, eager and ready to do whatever it took to end the curse from her ex, and get her daughter? This might as well be a different woman.

"She's gotten worse," Florry said.

You think? I thought at her and Goldie. *He's draining her. If I don't do this, she'll die.*

Neither of my mentors answered me. There was nothing else to say—between the three of us, we'd said it all.

"What are we doing again?" Nina mumbled.

"You need to have something to drink," I said. "Here, I brought you something."

I guided the glass to her hand, and because she was

216

moving so slowly, I kept my hand on it, and steadied it as she brought it to her mouth.

At the first taste, Nina attempted to push the glass from her mouth, but I held it close, tipping it up.

She made a face, eyes closed, but drank it.

Softly, I said the spell from the grimoire.

"I share myself with thee.

Of myself, I give freely.

Take that which is given

To be part of the living

I share myself with thee."

She was drinking slowly, so I repeated it twice more.

After finishing the glass, she fell back against the couch, coughing. When she stopped, her eyes opened and she looked at me. "What was that?"

"I'm trying to stop what's happening here."

"What's... happening here?" She yawned.

"Your ex is draining you."

"Rock... gets like... that some... times. So intense." Her eyes closed again.

"You know, I wish you could discover what this spell or hex or whatever is." Florry appeared to my left. "This is working fast, and it's very effective."

"That makes two of us. I was thinking about this," I said, watching Nina breathe more deeply, clearly falling asleep once more. "I wonder if he came up with this on his own. He sounds very smart, even if he's evil as a snake."

That makes sense, Goldie said.

I nodded, my anger from earlier all but gone. I understood that they were worried, and I didn't even think they were completely wrong. But I couldn't let her die. And I knew that was the right thing, even if it took a toll on me.

"How do you feel?" Florry asked.

"Nothing seems different," I said with a shrug.

Nina's breathing slowed, but her color was looking better. There was pink in her cheeks.

That was good, right? Please, please, please, let it be good.

I got up and walked around, unable to sit still. Goldie told me, when we were first talking about it, that everyone involved lived, but they were weakened. Well, that was a chance I'd need to take. The thing was done now.

The spell information hadn't mentioned anything about a second helping. Okay. Still full of nervous energy, I took the pitcher from the table and set it back on the counter. Should I put it in the fridge? Did cooling it detract from the potency?

"Hey!"

I whirled around to see Nina sitting up on the couch, her eyes wide and wild.

"Nina, how are you feeling?"

"Like someone just gave me an adrenaline shot. Holy shit, Wynter. What's going on?"

"You've been out of it for nearly two days."

Her face darkened. "Rockledge."

I nodded. "I'm pretty sure it's—" I suddenly couldn't stand. Not, I couldn't stand Nina, or the situation, but I couldn't stand. I gripped the island, moving hand over hand to get to the table so I could sit.

At the end of the island, I launched myself toward one of the chairs, and fell into it.

"Wynter!" Nina yelped.

A moment later, I felt her hands helping me into a sitting position in the chair, versus the jumble I was after nearly pitching face forward.

"What's going on?"

"I gave you some of my energy." Good night, I couldn't keep my eyes open. "It, I was warned, powerful." Even words were hard. "Takes from me."

I closed my eyes again and then everything went dark.

Thank god. I was so, so tired.

CHAPTER FIFTEEN

A murmur of voices tickled around the edge of my awareness, but I couldn't understand what anyone was saying.

I didn't think I cared, either.

Carefully, I stretched my arms over my head, eyes still closed.

The voices went up in pitch, and they were closer.

"Wynter!" I felt a hand on my shoulder, shaking me.

"Go'm 'way." I turned my head from the hand, the voice.

"I need you to open your eyes." The woman's voice was firm, taking no nonsense.

Where had I heard this before? Somewhere, recently. Someone had said it to me? Or I said it?

While I was pondering this déjà vu, the voice spoke again.

"Wynter, you need to wake up."

"Fine, fine, fine!" I opened my eyes to find the kind, but worried face of my doctor, Dr. Amberson, peering down at me.

I was on the smaller couch in the living room. I didn't know how I'd gotten here. What day was it again? "Is it our appointment?" I asked, completely confused. It wasn't Friday yet was it?

"No, my dear, it is not. Your friend called me because you passed out and they couldn't get you to wake up."

"You make house calls?" I felt like I was missing the salient point here. In fact, I was sure that I was missing it.

"For you, yes. How are you feeling?"

"Tired."

"Makes sense. Apparently you all but fell over. What have you been doing?"

"Working," I said, trying to keep up.

"I know it's probably a hard no, but I have to ask. Could you be pregnant?"

I let out a weak laugh. "You would... know better than me, doctor."

She laughed, and in it I could hear relief, even as her expression stayed calm. "Then we'll say no. Okay, Wynter, let's try to sit up, see what happens." Her hands were on my elbow and shoulder.

Feeling as though I were moving through quicksand, I sat up.

With help.

"What happened?" I asked.

I could see Florry hovering. She was wringing her hands, and her face was wreathed in worry. Caro and Nina stood near one another, both with similar expressions to the one on Florry's face.

The spell hit. Nina was restored, and you were depleted. Goldie's voice sounded odd. Off, somehow.

Nina. Right. My consultant.

It came back to me—making the energy transfer brew. Giving it to Nina, and then cannonballing myself from the island to the table. Everything was pretty dim after that.

"Thank you for coming," I got out.

"It's a good thing you had me in your phone. I'm not normally a general practitioner, but since you're in treatment with me, and we have an appointment later this week, it's possible this is menopause related. I can't really see anything, though. Any ideas?" She stared at me, her gaze searching and intense.

"I wish I knew." There was no way I was going to tell her what happened. A quick glance around told me that no one else had intentions of speaking up, either.

"Okay, I want you to take it easy, add some water, extra sleep, and stay off your feet. In fact, when you are staying off your feet, I want them up. Over your head some of the time, if you would." Dr. Amberson gave me the stink eye. "I mean it, Wynter. Fainting is the body's way of letting you know that it's feeling stressed. We'll do some blood work, make sure nothing is low, and there's nothing that needs further attention. Which should be fine, *if* you take care of yourself this week."

"Yes, ma'am." I didn't dare to argue. Dr. Amberson was not that much older than I was, but she had the mom voice down pat.

Dr. Amberson nodded at me, and then sent her mom glare around the room. "All of you need to make sure Wynter takes it easier this week."

Caro and Nina both nodded, wisely taking the same route I did and saying nothing.

Then Dr. Amberson patted my hand. "This isn't a huge worry. More of a wake-up call." She smiled as she took her stethoscope from her neck and tucked it back into the messenger bag at her feet. "I'll see you on Friday. Rest until then."

"I will," I said. I mean, what else was I going to say? What I really wanted to do was ask her about my hair, but she was already doing me a favor, so I'd save it for the office visit.

Caro moved forward. "Thank you so much for coming, Dr. Amberson." She walked alongside the doctor toward the door.

A moment later, Caro was back. "Wynter, you scared the daylights out of us."

"I scared the daylights out of myself."

"This is why we didn't want you to do this," Florry interjected.

You are weakened, Goldie added. *This will make your plans for Nina more challenging.*

I'll get through it, I thought.

At what cost? He wasn't backing down.

Isn't that my job?

If you sacrifice yourself over and over, it will result in needing a new Oracle sooner rather than later.

I didn't have a response to that. The message was clear. I still knew what I needed to do, and at this point, I'd already chosen the path.

"Wynter, I wish you hadn't done that." Nina came to sit on the arm of the couch.

"You weren't going to make it," I said. I didn't know how I knew it, but I knew that she would have faded to a place where I wasn't sure I could help her.

"You don't know that." Florry was pissed. "You can't take that kind of chance anymore. Goldie, tell her! Tell her how important she is! This isn't a joke!" She was yelling by the time she was finished.

Both Caro and Nina looked around, as if they could hear her.

"Is that Florry?" Caro asked.

"She's not happy with me."

Understandably so. You took an unacceptable risk, Goldie chimed in, obviously still unhappy with me.

"I can feel it." Nina looked around, rubbing her hands on her arms. "It's like your house is mad."

I laughed, although it came out sounding weak. Not a ringing endorsement for what I'd done.

"The house may as well be mad," Caro said. "Florry doesn't hold back."

"No she does not." I could feel what they meant. Florry's anger filled the space.

"Not when you're being a damn idiot! This isn't a game. You are an important part of the magical world. You can't find another Oracle like getting a gum ball out of a machine, Wynter! There's a reason you were chosen. The Oracle needs you, Wynter Chastain! Even if you're dumb as a rock and twice as stubborn." Florry kicked a foot in my direction and disappeared.

I don't know the last time I saw her get that angry, Goldie remarked.

You're not helping.

I'm not trying to. You have to learn to be more cautious with your person.

I heard a chime from my phone, although I had no idea where it was. "Who has eyes on my phone?"

"Is that really important right now?" Caro asked.

"Yes." It could be Logan. At this point, I should be hearing from him.

Caro made a noise that sounded a lot like disapproval, but she brought my phone to me.

It was a text. When I opened it, it was one word.

Tommyknocker.

I let out a sigh of relief. It was so difficult not to reply, but I knew that I couldn't. This was what he needed to feel like he was keeping me safe. It wasn't ideal, in my opinion, but I could live with it.

"What is it?" Nina asked.

"Logan let me know he's all right. He's got a lot going on, so we have to," I waved a hand, not finishing the sentence. There was too much to explain. I wasn't up for it. "He's not—oh, it doesn't matter. It's just one less thing to worry about." I couldn't help the smile that spread across my face at the thought of Logan.

"Which is what you need. Less to worry about. Wynter, why don't you go up to bed? I'll bring you some tea, and something light, and then you can get some sleep." Caro spoke easily, but it was clear she wasn't asking.

"Okay. I'll think I'll skip the eating part, though. My stomach isn't up to food right now." The thought of food made it grumble. Never a good sign. "And I'm not agreeing just to avoid an argument. I am tired, and I need to be rested. We're doing the scrying tomorrow."

"We'll see about that." Caro's lips pressed together.

I just smiled again, and slowly made my way upstairs. In all honesty, I was glad to get to bed. I felt like I'd run a marathon. Or maybe this was just what it felt like. I'd never run one. I'd read about people who did—I could never be one of them. The mere thought of that much running made my knees hurt.

But I'd done it. I made the energy brew, and I successfully transferred energy to someone who needed it.

Me, Wynter Chastain.

Three months ago, I would have laughed at magic.

Now, today, I'd just done more magic. Another piece of magic.

My consultant was still alive.

No matter what, even with the cost to me, I counted that as a win.

As I curled into bed, snuggling down into my pillows and pulling the blankets up to my chin, feet up as instructed, I was smiling.

Because I'd done it.

Me, Wynter Chastain. The Oracle.

I did it.

———

I felt the sunlight on my face before I opened my eyes. Keeping my eyes closed, I listened. Old houses have a language, if you know them, and you pay attention. I knew my house, having lived here all my life.

Everyone here was still asleep.

The house woke as the people within woke up, creaking and groaning with footsteps, trips up and down stairs, and voices echoing through its wooden bones.

But right now, all was still.

Which meant I was the first one up.

I didn't have to be. I could go back to sleep, if I wanted. All I had on my agenda today was tidying up the house, and doing the scrying with Nina.

Natalie and the kids would be here on Wednesday.

My kids weren't going to be here until dinner time, so I figured we'd go to the beach, taking it easy. Then back here for dinner, coffee, bed, and they would be leaving sometime on Thursday.

It sounded so simple, but I knew that it would be a whirlwind.

So maybe going back to sleep was a good call.

With absolutely no guilt, I closed my eyes again.

The room had warmed by the time I woke again, and I could smell coffee and bacon from downstairs. I stretched, taking my time and acclimating myself to the thought of getting up.

After a long shower, again, with no guilt, I made my way downstairs. I'd dressed comfortably today, in leggings and a loose top, my hair up. I was dismayed to find after another careful session of brushing that hair still came out in my fingers and my brush. **It's going to be all right,** I thought. Dr. Amberson said. Today was a work day, and I planned to get my work done.

The spell I'd used to keep Nina going wasn't going to last forever. I might be a newbie to magic, but even I knew that.

"Good morning," I said as I came down the stairs.

"How are you feeling?" Caro asked.

"Tired, but not horrible. A lot better than yesterday."

"Shelly and I did the shopping for the visit," Caro turned back to the stove.

It looked like she was making an omelet of amazing proportions, complete with cheese and vegetables. The bacon in the oven made me think of my mom, and further back, her and my grandmother, making breakfast for us on summer mornings when the entire day stretched ahead like a promise, an invitation to a hidden treasure.

I'd spent most of my days at the beach.

"What can I help with?" I asked, leaning against the island. "And what still needs to be done for Natalie and the kids? I don't know if I told you, but my kids are coming over around dinner. They won't be staying, though. They all have to get back to work." I smiled. "It's nice that they're coming, since it's a hike to get back here, and it's the middle of the week."

"You have good kids. There's nothing you can help me with, not with breakfast, or planning for your guests. Shelly and I have it all in hand. Are you going to tell the kids the entire truth about being the Oracle?"

"No." My response was immediate. I'd told them enough before, when I was clearing my name after being arrested. "Too many people know all or most of the truth already. If the kids know it all, it puts them in danger."

"They're already in danger being part of your family."

"But they don't live here, and they aren't visible." I

wouldn't think of this. I couldn't. Besides, the kids hadn't reacted all that well to what I *had* told them.

They'd inferred, some less kindly than others, that I was losing all my marbles. Tell the whole truth? I might be carted off to the hospital within the hour.

Caro didn't reply. "What's Natalie like?" she finally asked.

"I like her. Had I met her in different circumstances, she's someone I could be friends with."

"But not now?"

"Well, maybe not as easily. I can see why Derek liked her." I shrugged. Admitting that fact didn't sting as much, and I wondered how much Logan had to do with it. He was a piece of it, certainly, but... not the main piece.

Logan was my main piece, however. I kept my snickering to myself.

"Am I allowed to fix my own tea, or will I get a smack on the hand?" I teased.

"You scared me to death, so don't get all light-hearted over there. I know that Florry had to be angry. I could feel it. Even Nina could feel it. And Goldie. Is he even talking to you?"

Barely, he grumbled.

"Barely," I repeated his terse answer. "No one's happy with me. I get it. I'm sorry I scared you, but I know that I did the right thing. Nina can't die. Not on my watch."

"You know that you're going to fail at some point,

right? It's going to hurt, but it happens." Caro looked at me over her shoulder. "You'll never forget it, either. But you'll live."

"Did Florry's failures live?"

Caro frowned, thinking. "Yes, they did."

"I know, in my heart, in my gut, that Nina would not have made it." I felt that with the same surety as I knew my name. "I had to, Caro. It's okay that you all are mad at me. I appreciate that there are people looking out for me."

"I haven't known you very long at all, but I would be most unhappy if you weren't around."

I could hear the smile in Caro's voice.

"So would I. I have a lot to live for."

"That's the spirit." She flipped the omelet expertly. "You're allowed to serve yourself tea, then sit down."

I moved over to where I kept all my tea things and filled the kettle. "Where's Nina?"

"She went back to wherever it is she's staying. You youngsters. So determined to do it your way, come hell or high water."

I laughed.

We sat and ate, talking. She told me what she and Shelly planned for Natalie's visit, and I agreed to it all. It was nice to have someone else managing the details.

After breakfast, in which I tried to clean up and Caro shooed me away, I found that I was restless. I wanted to get Nina over here, do the scrying.

Shit.

I'd probably have to ask for help moving all the things downstairs. While I felt better, I wasn't at one hundred percent. It was the way you felt after the flu. A little unsteady. Breathless at times. Needing to sit down more.

"Caro, I'm going to walk down to the beach."

"All right. Take water and walk slowly."

"How is it that you're not a mom? You do it like you've been one for years."

"Years of working in kitchens. All chefs are big babies underneath the yelling and ego," she said with a laugh. "Don't stay out too long, either. It's coming up on the hottest part of the day."

"I got it, I got it." I grabbed a bottle of water, my shoes and phone, and I escaped while I could.

Since it was Monday morning, and later in the summer, there weren't as many tourists on the beach this morning. After lunch, it would be packed. For now, it was light, with more locals.

I noted that most people nodded at me, gave me a smile—but there were a few who glared, gave me a very rude once over, and marched away, often with their noses in the air.

The work of Hazel Babbington, no doubt.

It only reinforced my surety that suing for a retraction and damages was the only way.

My eyes were caught along the shoreline by a small, shiny... something that sparkled in the sun. Bending over, it was a piece of sea glass. A bottle stopper, if I gauged correctly, with a floral top, the petals spread open in soft aquamarine.

"Wow."

The sea is capable of much beauty, daughter. The deep, resonant baritone of the goddess of the sea filled my head and swirled around me.

Tethys. How are you?

I am well. How do you fare? Something has diminished within you.

I had to do a spell to help one of my consultants. It took a lot from me.

Do not give your power away, daughter.

Even if someone might die?

All humans die, even humans with something of the gods, like yourself. She went silent. Her thoughts were a dark hum. Then, *Was it worth the loss from yourself?*

I think so. A woman and a child were—are—at risk.

That is for you to determine, daughter. I hope that you are right, and they are worth your sacrifice.

Wow. Everyone was on me about this.

Which was a clue that perhaps they weren't being worrywarts.

Although I didn't feel that I was right, and they were wrong. They could be justified in their concern and I could be right about saving Nina.

Daughter, take off your shoes and step in.

Without hesitation, I slid off my flats and walked into the ocean.

Instantly, like a shot to the heart, I felt a jolt of

energy. It wasn't what I'd felt when Logan gave his word to Caro. It was something less sparky, even as it was no less intense.

I could swear that I was growing. My head fell back and my eyes closed as I soaked up the sun and whatever it was that was coming through me via the water.

You are a child of the sea. You always have been. I heard you when you were younger.

My head snapped forward. "What?"

You used to talk to the ocean when you were younger, asking to come and stay. Even then, you always wanted to be near.

It's why I could never leave the island. That decision had charted the course of my life.

You are a powerful being. Not just this magic that the human world has put on you. Tethys' voice and words dismissed my Oracle side as though it was nothing.

I felt Goldie move along my arm. Probably in indignation.

There are humans who know from whence they came, know that in the end, they begin and end with the waters of the earth, with the sea. You've always been one of them.

I will never leave here, I thought. *I love it too much. I don't sleep as well without the sound and smell of the sea.*

You must go to the witches. I know they are here. I have felt them, when the moon moves across the water.

I'm already planning to. Is there something you'd like me to do? Can I do something for you?

Tethys laughed.

I could feel the vibrations of her laughter down to my marrow.

No, daughter, there is nothing I need from you. But you need something from them, from the witches. You must tap into the power that runs through you, the power of the sea. There is only so much that I can do, that I can give you. It is forbidden, anymore, for the gods to meddle overmuch in the lives of humans.

Why?

Once you have come more into that which ties you to the sea, to me, we will speak more. Until then, I cannot interfere. But I can allow the sea to restore you.

I feel amazing.

I know. Be wise. You have wisdom within. The wisdom of your life. The wisdom of your sex. The wisdom of the sea. You merely need to bring it forth. As you did with my gift. Another deep, rich, chuckle.

I'm so glad you liked it.

It was well chosen. Her voice sounded as though she were smiling. *Be well, my daughter.*

I felt her presence pull away from me.

When Tethys first spoke to me, it scared me. A lot. She was dark, and big, and all encompassing. When she was near, she was all around me.

But now? I didn't know if it was her use of the word 'daughter', or the fact that she'd taken care of a couple of bad guys for me—the family that kills together stays together, right?

Okay, that was macabre.

Anyway, I didn't feel the same level of fear with Tethys that I did before. She felt... comfortable. Right. As though she belonged in this part of my life. As part of my world.

But I'd bet my left arm that with this little visit, I'd just added to my homework with the coven. Speaking of which, when I got home, I'd sit down and finish the book I was reading. I didn't want to look like the worst student ever tomorrow night. I also didn't want to seem as though I weren't taking it seriously.

Feeling refreshed—amazingly so—and cheered, I walked home, humming to myself. As I turned the corner onto my street, I saw someone coming toward me from the opposite direction.

Oh, holy hell and all the saints, shit on a stick.

I did not need this today.

Detective Scott Trenton marched toward me with the air of a man going to his doom, and not caring. He was angry. I could see that from here.

As he got closer, his narrowed eyes, red face, and fists that were clenching and unclenching confirmed it.

I stopped, pulling out my phone and hitting the video button on my camera. My days of being bullied by this man were over.

The thought I'd had earlier that he might be magically assisted in this anger crossed my mind.

How could you tell?

Did I care? I was so angry at him myself, I wasn't sure I cared why he was doing it anymore, only that he stop, and face some kind of punitive measures for his actions.

That, and he was kind of an asshole.

I reached into my pocket.

"Wynter Chastain." He nearly spat the words out.

"How can I help you, Detective Trenton? I don't think we should be speaking, according to my attorney."

"That jackass."

"Hubie Liegal is pretty effective. He'll be sorry to hear you think of him this way."

"Are you being smart with me?"

"Does it matter if I am? You're not supposed to be near me. Hubie was clear about that. So please step aside and let me pass."

He glared for a moment, for so long that I thought I'd need to call the police, which was absurd. But then with elaborate care, he stepped off the sidewalk and into the grass next to the road. "Of course, Mrs. Chastain," he sneered.

I nodded. "Good day, Detective Trenton."

"One thing, Mrs. Chastain."

I hated the way he said my name. It made me want to punch him right in the mouth. I stopped and turned back to look at him. "Yes?"

"You're not going to get away with it. We will get you."

"I beg your pardon? We? Who is we?"

A strange expression crossed Scott Trenton's face.

He probably hadn't meant to say that. Then I saw a flash in his left eye, dark and then red, before it disappeared. Without another word, he spun on his heel and marched away.

I lifted my phone to my lips, stating the date and time and location, then turned off my video.

I dialed a number.

"Wynter, how are you?"

"I'm not good, Hubie. I just ran into Scott Trenton."

"And?" His entire voice changed with that one word.

"He is unhinged, Hubie. As in. I'm worried I'm going to need bear spray or something to keep him away from me."

"Where are you?"

"I'm on my street. I think he was at my house."

"Is there anyone home?"

"Caro, I think. I need to go make sure she's okay." Shit, shit, shit. I hadn't even thought of Caro. My pace picked up as I hurried down the block toward my house.

"Wynter, I'm on my way. If you get home and things aren't right, dial 911, then call me." He hung up.

I broke into a run, slipping on the grass in the front yard as I turned toward the front porch. Taking the stairs two at a time, I burst through both front doors.

"Caro? Caro, where are you?"

CHAPTER SIXTEEN

"Caro?" I raced into the kitchen and living room. "Caro, where are you?"

There was no answer.

"Caro!"

After a moment, one where I could hear my heart pounding in my ears and scenes of various harm and destruction raced through my head, footsteps sounded on the stairs.

"Wynter?" Caro stopped just above the bottom step, her hand on the railing. "My goodness, child, what's going on?"

I took four steps toward her and threw my arms around her. "Are you all right?" I asked, my voice muffled.

"Why wouldn't I be?" Caro stepped down and then back from me. "You're all red, and I can tell your heart's racing. What happened?"

"Did he come here?"

"Who?"

"That asshole detective. Trenton. Scott Trenton." Now that I knew she was safe, I could feel the sweat breaking out all over me.

Great. Let's add a hot flash to all this. Because that's what was missing, right?

"Oh, that detective? Yes, he stopped by after you left, wanting to see you. He seems like an angry young man. A bit high strung to be a police officer, if you ask me. I told him you were out, and I'd pass along that he stopped by."

"He didn't do anything? Didn't hurt you?"

Caro smiled. "I think he wanted to come in very badly, but I stood in the doorway and made it very clear that he wasn't putting one toe in this house."

"Caro, I'm sorry. You shouldn't have to deal with him."

"I don't think anyone should."

The doorbell rang, and then the front doors were opened, one after the other as Hubie burst in. "Wynter!"

I stepped toward the hallway. "I'm here. Caro's all right. He stopped by, but she didn't let him in, and he left. Although I think he was hanging around, like some creepy stalker." My arms wrapped around myself. I didn't like the idea of anyone skulking around my home.

Hubie took a step closer. "You're all right, though?"

"Other than being pissed this is still going on? I'm fine. I got him on video."

Hubie beamed, relaxing. "I love that you think to record these doofuses."

"I don't know how much there is to see. I held the phone down so he wouldn't see the camera open."

"That's my girl. Let's see what you got."

The three of us stood in a huddle as I pulled up the video.

After it finished, no one spoke.

Scott Trenton was even scarier when I saw him like this, when I wasn't in the middle of it. There was something very, very off about him.

"That man is dangerous." Caro broke the silence.

Hubie didn't say anything, just gazed out toward the back, his hand rubbing his jaw. Then, as if coming out of a trance, he snapped his head to me. "Wynter, can you email that to me?"

"Sure. I was planning on it." I sent the email.

Hubie checked his phone after it dinged a notification at him. "Yep. There it is."

"What are you going to do?"

"I am going to court right now. I'm getting an order of protection for you, and I'm asking that Detective Trenton be placed on leave and on house detention. I'm also going to ask for an anklet monitor, since he can't be trusted to leave the citizens of Oak Bluffs alone."

"Oh, sweet hell." I groaned. I couldn't help it. "This

is going to make things worse. So much for keeping my head down."

"You didn't do a thing, Wynter. He is so far out of line I think he's in another country. If you don't—if we don't stop this, he will keep going. Don't go out and about alone. I don't want you out without someone else until I can tell you that he's being monitored."

"Okay." I nodded.

"Get Shelly over here. I don't want you alone, and the more people that are here, the better."

With those ominous words, Hubie strode from the room.

Caro and I looked at each other.

"Whiskey," I said.

"Whiskey," she agreed.

I went to the cabinet where we kept the liquor, pulling out a bottle and a couple of rocks glasses. Pouring a generous helping in each, I handed one to Caro. "Here's to keeping the crazy people away from us."

"Amen, sister."

We both drank deeply.

"Wow, I needed that. Let me call Shelly so I don't get into trouble for not following orders." I dialed my best friend.

"Wynter, what's up?"

"Did Hubie call you?"

"No. Why?" Her voice changed instantly to all business.

"He asked that you come over here. Detective Trenton strikes again."

"That guy is not only an ass, he's a menace."

"Your boyfriend agrees, and is off to fight the dragon for me."

"Good. I'm on the way." Shelly ended the call.

"She'll be here shortly."

"Good. I feel like there's safety in numbers. It's nice that you have a good group of friends. It was always just Florry and me, and if we couldn't handle it, it was on us."

"That sounds lonely."

"Not lonely, no. She was—is—the best friend I've ever had. I love her dearly. But at times, being the BFF of the Oracle was stressful as hell." She smiled.

I laughed a little. "I think being the Oracle is stressful. I imagine it's worse for the BFF. Although Shelly might disagree."

"That woman would charge Hell with a bucket of water," Caro agreed. "But back to you. How was your walk, before you ran into him? You seem better. Not as rattled I might have thought." Caro tilted her head as she looked me over.

"Oh, it was good. Really good."

"The fresh air agrees with you."

"It does. So does walking on the beach." Tethys. "Caro, will you excuse me for a moment? I need to go make a note."

"Go on. Have you heard from Nina, by the way?" She walked toward the back door.

"No, but let's talk when I finish this. I just don't want to—"

"Go." Caro waved a hand and walked out to the back deck.

"What did the sea witch want?" Florry popped into existence next to me as I ran lightly up the stairs.

"She... hang on, Florry. Let me get this down." I went to the closet that was now my Oracle office, and pulled out the notebook I'd added to the pile of books Callie, the witch from the coven, had given me. I'd started it after Logan had showed up, just making notes, things I wanted to remember, about Oracle related happenings. It had turned into a journal of sorts. My own personal grimoire. Today was the kind of day I'd started this for.

I took a couple of deep breaths, willing my racing heart to calm. It was so strange that I was feeling the adrenaline rush now, after the danger was over. I wanted to calm myself so that I could remember my conversation with Tethys. Talking to her felt like a conversation within a conversation, and I wanted the ability to go back and think about what she'd said.

Also, I needed to make sure I could repeat it all for the coven.

Once I was done, I read it over four times. It was as complete as I could make it.

"That's that." I closed the notebook, and then closed the clo—the office door behind me.

It wasn't a closet anymore. It was my office.

Pulling out my phone, I went to the big box store's website here on the island, and ordered a lock. Oh, and distilled water. I'd used a lot with the last scrying spell. The lock made me feel better. Access to this closet needed to be limited. I didn't know how I knew that, but I knew I needed to protect my Oracle work.

I was pleased to see that I could pick it up later today.

Ooh. Maybe I could learn a spell to keep it locked, too. Kind of like the spell around my house, the one the witches had cast that kicked a demon to the curb.

That needed to go on the to-do list as well. Why was a demon trying to get close to me? The only demon I'd come across was the one in Logan's story, when he was Evander. There was no need for that demon, or any crossroads demon, to come looking for me.

But a demon had come poking around, close enough that it set off the alarm in the spell. Add that to the to do list.

"All right, what next?" I said out loud, trying to organize my thoughts. They rattled around like scattered marbles in my head.

First, the scrying. I could do it without worrying I'd be hurt as I was restored, thanks to Tethys.

"All right, what did the witch want?" Florry was back.

I told her, making sure to tell her about stepping into the water and how Tethys or the sea or both had given me a bigger jolt than even my most ambitious espresso consumption days. "How did you know, by the way?"

Florry frowned. "I don't like it, Wynter. I can sense her, even though I wasn't right there with you. She is a huge piece of magic. The witches probably sensed her, too."

"Why not? You weren't this bothered before. And are you sure? Tethys seems like she could keep her magic to herself, if she wanted."

"I've been stewing. Ask Caro, never a good thing. She's taken an interest in you, a very personal interest. What I ask myself is, 'Why'?"

I shrugged. "I don't know. She says there's a connection between me and the sea."

Florry sighed. "I hope that's all there is. If you read history, or mythology, the people the gods take an interest in don't usually benefit from it."

"That's true, but—"

"But you're different? Wynter, we are never different to the gods. We're one of thousands of humans they've come across. I might be going off the paranoia cliff. I'm well aware that's a possibility. But please be careful."

"I will."

She stared at me, not saying anything, her expression saying it all. She didn't believe me.

"I will, I promise."

"Like you were careful with Nina?"

"I won't let her die." I wasn't having this conversation again.

"Fine, fine, no need to rehash. So this is a busy week. What's up with cat boy?"

"I don't expect to hear much from him. He's in New York, bringing Evander back to life." It was my turn to sigh.

"You don't want that? The man came to you looking for his past, his history. It's his life, Wynter."

"I don't know about that."

"Oh, this should be great. Please, enlighten me. He can't escape who he is."

"I one hundred percent disagree." I said, shaking my head. "He isn't Evander Thane. That man is gone, killed in the desert. He is Logan Gentry, and he's not the man I met in my scrying."

Florry shook her head in response. "I think your vision is clouded by your involvement with him."

"Well, everyone is welcome to an opinion."

She didn't reply and I glanced over at her.

"We're having our first fight, aren't we? I was always so mad at Patsy, always wanting to have a throw down. It feels different on the other side of the argument." The ghost of a smile played across Florry's lips.

"It usually does. It's all right, Florry. Logan thinks I'm wrong, too."

"And you're still sticking to this theory?"

I nodded. "I am. I know I'm right. Eventually, all of you disbelievers will know, too."

Florry stared, and then burst out laughing. "You are growing in leaps and bounds. I hope it's not because of Tethys, because goddess gifts are temporary. I don't trust 'em. Never have, never will. But you're different. You're not the woman who was jumping at her own shadow a couple of months ago."

I was pleased with her assessment. I felt it, too—that I wasn't the same Wynter Chastain, that I was a better Oracle than I thought I'd be. "I'm trying."

"Well, it's working. Even if I don't agree with everything, you're doing good, Wynter."

Her praise pleased me in a way I didn't expect. I was so used to hearing how I had to do more, get more done —although that could be my own issues at work—that it felt good to hear I wasn't disgracing us all. Us meaning all the Oracles.

"All right, we need to call Nina."

"You sure you're up to this today?"

"I feel like I could take on... well, I don't know, a lot of things. And win."

"That goddess drug is some good stuff, huh?

"That's an understatement, Florry."

"Be careful."

"That is practically my middle name, along with Worry. You know this by now."

We stared at one another.

Then Florry looked away, tossing up her hands.

"You're right. I hate to admit it, because it means at some point I've been wrong, but you're right."

"Enough of this. It's not getting things done. Nina has energy, which is great, but I don't think it's a permanent thing. That hex or whatever is really strong."

"All right, all right. Get her over here." Florry crossed her arms.

"Thanks for the permission."

Florry rolled her eyes.

I called Nina.

"Wynter!" She answered on the first ring. "Oh, my god. Are you all right? I feel so—"

"It's all good," I said, stopping her before she could get going. "I mean it, I really am all right. You want to do the second part of the scrying spell? Where we kick the hex and your ex to the curb?"

"Are you sure?"

"Absolutely." I'd never been more sure.

"Okay, but if you look like things are going south with you, I'm going to stop it. I mean that." Nina sounded fierce.

"Fair enough. If I look like I'm going to pitch forward, you are welcome to stop things."

"Okay. Can we plan on about two hours from now? I have some things I need to finish up."

"Perfect." I ended the call, and went to gather all my supplies from the Oracle office. What was it that Nina had to finish up? My mind wandered with possibilities, and then I shoved them to the side.

It didn't matter. What mattered was that I took care of my piece in this. Two hours meant there would also be time to pick up the lock I'd ordered. Something was nagging at me to get all of my Oracle stuff secured. I wasn't going to fight it.

It took several trips to bring down all the things I needed.

Caro came into the living room as I dragged the kiddie pool from the backyard. "What's up?"

"What? Oh, Nina's coming over, and we're going to do the scrying spell. Get rid of that ex. I'm getting set up now, even though she's not coming over for a while, because I have to run out and pick up a lock."

"A lock for what?"

"My new Oracle office. I don't want that open, I don't want anyone to be able to just walk in."

"I think that's a good idea. I don't know why Florry and I never thought of it, because we did have people try and steal old and musty," she mused, referring to the grimoire. "So you're ahead of us."

"When I thought about it, it made me feel better, and Goldie and Florry are always telling me to follow my instinct, so I'm going with it."

Caro nodded, and then looked at the kiddie pool. "Are you up for this?"

I sighed. "I am, actually. I got a shot of energy this morning."

"How?"

She listened intently as I detailed my chat with Tethys. "Are you all right?" Caro asked finally.

"Yes, and no. I mean, yes, it is. But it's a little scary, too." I sat down on the sofa.

"What's she like?" She came around to sit next to me, still listening intently.

"When she first spoke with me, she was this big, deep voice in my head, and it reverberated through me, like standing under a church bell, you know?"

Caro nodded.

"But now, I like it. She's quiet, and calm, and you can feel her power. She doesn't go on about it, she just *is* powerful. I like chatting with her, even if I know she could crush me like a bug." Florry's warnings rang in my ear.

You can be appreciative and cautious with Tethys, Goldie said.

I wondered if you'd gone on vacation. I haven't heard from you all morning.

I don't need to comment on every aspect of your life.

I'll remember that the next time you have lots of comments.

Make smart decisions, and I won't need to be so wordy.

Oh, he was in a mood today.

She helped me to feel better.

I know. It's almost like you're humming with electricity.

It feels great.

Be ready for the crash.

If I can release Nina from her hex, I'll feel just fine sleeping all day for a day or two.

He snickered, just a little.

Holy shit. My Goldie just laughed.

I didn't say anything. I didn't want to call attention to it. It wasn't even that funny.

But he'd just laughed.

It felt as though something had shifted. I had no idea what, but something had.

If you can release the hex, you ought to consider taking yourself on a vacation. Nothing long, just something to get away.

My mind went immediately to Logan. He was in New York, maybe New York City. A couple of days with him... oh, the thought made my skin tingle.

Are you suggesting I take days off?

You are the Oracle until you die. There are many demands on you. Your life is no longer your own. So if you can take a few days here and there for yourself, it makes you more effective.

There's the Goldie I know and love. I had to smile.

I am realistic. I've seen Oracles buckle under the pressure. I don't want that for you, Wynter.

When he used my name, I knew that he was in earnest. That meant no teasing. *Okay. If I can get this hex off Nina, release her from whatever it is, I'll have her stay here with Caro, just to be sure all is well, and I'll try to get away.*

Don't get carried away. I know you're planning to head straight for the panther.

What if I am?

You are the Oracle first and foremost. Goldie was firm.

Yeah, yeah, I know. It's interesting that you all don't tell the prospective Oracle this upfront.

No, that's deliberate. The Oracle must learn to stand on her own. Even if she has support around her, she is the Oracle, and in the end, she is on her own. Even with me, even with the previous Oracle.

It would have been nice to have a hint of what being the Oracle meant. I wasn't complaining, but I did think learning the whole enchilada about this gig was pretty overwhelming.

There is a lack of information on purpose. Those who seek to become the Oracle do not do so for the right reasons. That is a lesson that has been learned the hard way. The less the Oracle knows, the better.

If she lives.

I would not let you die because of lack of knowledge, Wynter.

Could have fooled me.

"Wynter, are you in the middle of something?" Caro asked.

"What? Oh, sorry, Caro! Yeah, the committee is weighing in."

"Well, you finish up. If you don't mind, I'm going to go putter in your garden. As long as that's okay."

"Of course it is. I'm not territorial."

"Oh, good. I like being outside, puttering around in the dirt."

"You'll help me to assuage some of my guilt. The flowers need some weeding, and I've been neglectful."

"Do you have an herb garden? One for your work?"

"No, I don't." I frowned. "Should I? I wasn't aware."

Amazing how my mentors were silent.

"I don't know if you should or shouldn't, but if you're going to work with the local coven, don't they use a lot of herbs and such?"

"They do. Caro, I don't want you to feel you have to do anything—"

She cut me off before I could finish the sentence. "Darlin', no one takes advantage of me." The steel was a razor sharp thread running through her words.

"I don't doubt that for a moment."

"It's settled. I'm going to go see what you have going on out there, tidy up any neglect," she winked at me, "And see where we can fit in an herb garden. What did you call it? Grand Central Station around here? You might need your own supply."

We both laughed, and Caro went out back.

As I gathered my purse up to leave, Goldie spoke again.

Back to the matter at hand. It was as though there had been no interruption. *It's good that you didn't realize we would keep you safe no matter what. If you don't feel that you have a stake in something, you don't give it your all.*

Okay, that's it. Enough of this. I rolled my eyes. *I have things to do.*

And you are feeling up to it?

Weren't you around earlier today? When I walked into the ocean?

Yes. I find Tethys' interest in you... interesting.

You and Florry.

She's not wrong. The attention of the gods isn't always a good thing.

Noted. Again. Now, can you and Florry keep an eye on me with this hex thing? Like, yell out if you feel something weird? I sent the thought to Florry as well, hoping she was hovering somewhere near.

"If you're worried, why are you doing this now?" She was in the corner, a light yellow housedress today, and a pink nightie. There were flamingos on the housedress.

I hoped when it was my turn I could choose how I wanted to present myself to the new Oracle. I focused on Florry's question. "Because I feel like the person who cast the hex is a tricky man, with a lot of malice, and he's capable of the unexpected. You're my support, a tool in my arsenal. Just keep an eye out for wayward magic, or creepy spells, or creepy guys."

"You know we will."

"Not without a lot of stuff and nonsense." But I smiled.

"Let's get this done. If you race off to snuggle up to cat boy, I can hang out here."

"You're not with me all the time?"

Florry shook her head. "I can be with you whenever you want me to. But I like to be here."

"Because of Caro?"

"In part. Also because I don't want other magical beings to sense me. Look what that crappy necrojerk did to me," she said, referring to the necromancer who had tried to take me and use me for his own purposes.

I still didn't know what they were, the necromancers who had come for me before, and I didn't want to know. It didn't matter. They wanted to harm me or use me for their own ends, and I could not allow any such thing.

The one Florry referred to had last been seen in a vision from Tethys, clinging to a buoy in the open ocean. I hoped I never saw him again.

Florry said, "He froze me, blocked me from movement. Got Goldie, too. It's a risk when you travel with a spirit. I'd rather not take it if I don't have to. Your house is protected, and that means I am, too, when I'm inside."

"All I need to do is call you? Why didn't I know that before?"

Florry shrugged. "I'm sure I told you."

"You're pretty casual sometimes about all that I have to know."

"You are learning on your own, like you have to."

"If you say it's part of my journey again, I will throw a shoe at your head."

Florry stuck out her tongue and disappeared.

I laughed out loud. Whatever Tethys had done, whatever she'd given me to bring me back up to normal —it was great.

Checking my supplies once more, I was satisfied. I had the salt, the wooden spoon, the tub was in the kiddie pool, and I'd get some more water today. I brought the outdoor chair inside, and set it in the kiddie pool.

The doorbell rang, and then the door opened.

"Hey!" Shelly called out.

"You're right on time to come do errands with me," I said.

"Great. I'm the dogsbody today."

"No, you're getting a front row seat to all the latest in Wynter Wonderland."

"You know how to tempt me."

I grinned. "Come on."

Together, we headed out.

CHAPTER SEVENTEEN

I made it home with both the water and the lock and no interactions with any of the locals who were giving me the evil eye, none of the police department, or any of the magical community.

Totally uneventful and normal.

It was great. I'd never realized how great boring could be.

Other than the interrogation from Shelly. It started the moment she got in the car, and it didn't stop until we pulled into my driveway.

I wasn't sure if she took a breath the entire time.

She was furious with Scott Trenton. Made moony eyes over Hubie's indignation and anger on my behalf. Asked me too many questions about Tethys and what she did for me, and even more about me doing the scrying for Nina.

"You sure you're up for this?" Shelly's words and

expression were fierce. "You've had a long ass weekend, and none of it was restful, or relaxing, or anything like that. It's been one thing after another."

I nodded. "One hundred percent. One hundred fifty. Now help me get these in."

Shelly peered intently at me. Then she made a decision, and swung herself out of the car.

I didn't even have to ask. I knew that she was with me.

After hauling the water inside, Shelly came upstairs with me while I installed my brand new technological marvel of a lock. This lock could be opened with the keypad, a key, the app on my phone, or a thumbprint. I loved it.

"I don't know if that thing could be more complicated."

"It makes it harder for anyone else to open." I grinned at the thought.

"If you say so." Shelly still looked dubious.

Just as I finished, I heard a car pull up out front. I looked out my window to see Nina.

Perfect timing.

"Caro, Nina's here," I called as I went down to the door. "Come on, Shelly. You can see for yourself that I feel fantastic, and you can be around to make sure all goes well."

"I'm not sure my yelling at a malicious hex would do much," Shelly said, following me down the stairs.

"Put water in the wooden basin, would you?" I asked as I went down the hallway.

I opened the door before Nina was even on the porch.

"Wow. You do look better." Nina gave me an appraising look.

"Thank you. I feel better. The more important question is how do you feel?"

"I still feel good, thanks to you. How long does this last?"

"I'm not sure, which is why I don't want to delay. And since I'm good, too, I figure we need to get moving."

"I'm all for it. The sooner I lose this hex, the sooner Kira and I can be together again, and we can disappear. Are you able to cast a spell for me to keep him away?"

"I meet with my colleagues tomorrow. We're going to discuss the best way to handle this."

"Okay," Nina said.

Unlike when she first showed up, she didn't question my ability. A thought hit me. "Nina, give me a sec, would you? I'm going to ask the head of the coven to come over, so she can see what sort of hex it is. That could help in creating a spell for you and Kira."

Nina nodded. "It helps to understand the feel of the magic the enemy uses." She spoke as though this was normal.

For a moment, just a split second, my new reality scared the holy hello out of me. This was the world I lived in, where you had to evaluate the magic of your enemy.

I stepped into the front room and dialed Elizabeth.

"This is Elizabeth."

"Hey, it's Wynter. I have something I need to do today, and I thought you might like to observe, to get a sense of what I'm dealing with. It may come in handy for our lessons tomorrow."

There was a silence, and then Elizabeth said, "When?"

"As soon as possible."

"Let me get someone over here, and I'll be right there." She hung up.

All these women in my life were so abrupt.

It was because we all had things to do, and no time to waste. I loved that idea.

"All right. Slight delay, because I want Elizabeth to see the magic, get a sense of it. In order to do an effective protection spell for you, I want her to understand who she's dealing with."

I'd need to check with the grimoire, but in this case, I thought the coven was a better resource. My goal was to be able to do this myself eventually. Eventually as in soon.

I went through the supplies again, smoothing out the paper with the spell on it, reading it. I wasn't nervous. I'd done this before, and I'd banished the evil smoke, or spell, or whatever it was. Not enough to keep Nina safe, but I'd gotten rid of it to a degree.

I could do it again.

I would do it again.

Elizabeth was fast. Within fifteen minutes, she was walking into the living room. "I'm here to observe. Wynter feels that my seeing this will help her going forward. As long as that's all right with you?" She directed her question to Nina.

Nina nodded. "If Wynter trusts you, I trust you."

Elizabeth inclined her head.

"Okay, Nina, shoes off and into the kiddie pool again. Feet in the basin."

"No silver this time?" Nina asked, referring to the silver metal basin we'd used to discover whether there was a hex.

"No, for this part, we need a clay or wooden bowl."

"Oooh," Nina shuddered. "How is this so cold?"

I ignored her complaints, and added the sea salt, stirring. Then I took the small cup that had earth from my garden in it, and poured it into the basin. I stirred with the wooden spoon once more, taking the time to dissolve the salt and the dirt.

The water was a light brown now.

Taking a breath, I read from my cheat sheet. "In the name of the gods, my ancestors, and the creatures of the Earth, the keepers of all that lives below and sustains us above. Cleanse this child of Earth of all magicks that do not belong, of all evil intention of harm."

The water in the basin shuddered, like something big had taken a step next to it.

Nina went very still.

I repeated the spell.

Another shudder across the water.

Nina inhaled sharply.

I glanced up, and she looked like she was clenching her teeth.

"You okay?" I whispered.

She nodded, one stiff jerk of her head. "Keep going." She was definitely clenching her teeth.

I repeated the spell a third time, with emphasis on the last sentence. *Cleanse her*, I thought. *Send all that doesn't belong to the curb, to the garbage.*

Nina went rigid, her head jerking back, the muscles in her neck taut. In the water, her toes curled toward her feet. The tension radiated from her.

"Cleanse this child of Earth of all magicks that do not belong, of all evil intention of harm." I spoke forcefully, my hands on either side of the basin.

Nina opened her mouth, with great effort.

"Fight, Nina," I whispered. "Fight him."

She screamed, a long, high scream that ripped at my soul.

Then another.

And a third.

It pierced my eardrums.

As suddenly as she'd gone rigid, Nina slumped forward. I caught her before she fell out of the chair.

I could feel something coming from Nina, almost like it was leaking from her. A dark, black fog encased her, and me with her. The fog came up from out of nowhere, kind of like the blue smoke had before. Swirling, getting everywhere, even between my fingers, until I couldn't see daylight.

"No, no, no, no..." Nina muttered in my ear.

I couldn't see her, but I knew that my arms were still around her, knew that her head was kind of on my shoulder.

You will not take what is mine. The words were a statement of fact. No concern, just informing me of what was. Deep, distant, menacing.

Wynter, shield yourself! Goldie's voice came from what sounded very far away.

I didn't know how to do that. Instead, I focused on what I could do.

My arms tightened around Nina. I spoke without fear, without thinking. "She is not yours. You cannot have her!"

The fog around us growled.

The darkness intensified. Fear, cold and bitter and stark, sank through my skin and into my bones.

"No." I spoke again. My eyes were closed, and I envisioned Nina and me, sitting out back, the sun shining, the ocean a soft murmur in the background. There was no fog, no shadow, and no presence other than me, and Nina.

"You have no place here. You are not welcome."

The cold felt like knives piercing through my skin, down to my soul. Not just my bones, but seeking out my soul.

In my vision, a door appeared before me. Red and black and with anger seeping frcm it, it shuddered and creaked.

You can stay closed. You are not welcome here.

The door bowed out toward where we sat.

In the vision, next to me, Nina put her hand to her forehead. "It hurts," she whimpered.

This was my vision. My home, my turf.

Taking a deep breath as I stood, I threw out my arms, bringing in the sun and the sky and the energy of the sea. I felt Goldie on my arm, and somewhere behind me, I could feel Florry. It was as though the energy from the three of us combined to make something tall and strong and far more lasting than this ugly door that had shown up unannounced.

The words of the scrying hex fell from my mouth, each word a note, a slash against the hate behind that door. "In the name of the gods, my ancestors, and the creatures of the Earth, the keepers of all that lives below and sustains us above. Cleanse this child of Earth of all magicks that do not belong, of all evil intention of harm."

A sound like screaming wind battered the other side of the door.

"You do not belong!" I shouted, feeling my hair whip around my face.

The door wavered, the reds and black becoming opaque and for a moment, I saw what was behind the door.

Like a whirlpool, it was a gaping maw of darkness. It pulled everything nearby toward it, taking it in, taking, taking, taking without thought or concern for anything but the hunger and the anger and the need.

Then the door faded.

I should have been scared, looking into that darkness that I couldn't see through, but I wasn't. I moved in front of Nina.

"You do not belong."

The dark whirlpool shifted and struggled, trying to hold itself in place.

The force of the anger from the whirlpool hit me, battering at me, demanding my surrender.

"You do not belong." At this point, I didn't know if I was saying the words or thinking them.

Like the door, the whirlpool began to fade. A shrieking started from its center, getting louder as the whirlpool itself got lighter, less substantial.

I held my position even as I heard Nina moan behind me.

Lighter and lighter, the whirlpool moved faster, trying to pull energy to it as it had been, but it could not gather enough strength.

I saw all this, saw behind the shadow of the dark, whirling blackness—and then it was gone.

My back garden was quiet. The sun shone, and the only noise was from the distant crashing of the waves.

Behind me, Nina wept softly, and then—

I was holding Nina as she slumped forward, limp and unresponsive. "I'm going over," I said out loud to no one in particular.

"Wynter!" Shelly was behind me, her hands on my shoulders.

Nina was lifted off me as Shelly helped me up.

I blinked. "Holy crow."

Elizabeth appeared beside me. "I am fairly certain that whatever was in that dark smoke—"

"The fog."

She nodded. "The fog, yes. Whatever was there is gone."

"Is Nina all right?"

Caro had pulled Nina to her feet, and Elizabeth leaned forward to touch the younger woman's face, murmuring something I couldn't hear.

Elizabeth met Caro's eyes. "Let's get her to the couch."

Together, the two women took an arm, and brought Nina to the couch.

Nina's feet moved on their own, trying to walk— that was a good sign, right?

Goldie? Florry? You two with me? I felt you, when I was wherever I was with Nina, but you were far away.

I am here.

Thank goodness! I was worried.

You should be. That dark energy was very strong.

I know. It felt as though I'd been hit with a large vehicle.

"I'm here," Florry appeared in the kitchen.

She wasn't as solid looking as she normally was.

What happened? Alarm flared around me.

"Keep your panties on. Whatever it was tried to draw from me. Take from me, really. Like a purse snatcher. I held him—well, actually, you held it off." Despite her brave words, Florry looked tired.

I did?

"Yep. Goldie and I tossed our hats in the ring to support you, but you held him off. What did you do?"

"I don't know," I said out loud.

"Don't know what?" Shelly asked as she got me over to the couch across from where Nina was now stretched out.

"How I got rid of it. Held it off," I nodded at Florry.

"Whatever it was, it was very strong. How one person pulled that much magic, that much negative energy together—" Elizabeth shuddered. "He, and I'm assuming it was a he because you were focused on her ex-husband, is very strong."

"Is it gone? I don't feel it anymore." I looked around, as though the fog might come back.

Elizabeth shook her head. "I don't feel it, either. I think you've banished it."

A sense of relief moved through me, like water freed

from a dam. I let myself sink into the couch cushions, weariness dragging my eyes closed.

"Wynter, I'm going to let you rest, and we'll talk tomorrow. I think you're safe." Elizabeth's voice floated above me.

"Okay. I might sleep until then," I said, pushing the words out.

"Go ahead." Shelly was still close to me.

Caro said something, but I couldn't hear her. Or couldn't focus on her. I wasn't sure which. The darkness—the soothing darkness of sleep this time, not the sucking whirlpool of hate—surrounded me, and I gave myself over to it.

When I opened my eyes, the sky outside the sliding glass door was streaked with gold and pink. I stirred, needing to stretch but not wanting to move.

"Wynter, are you awake?" Shelly was standing over me, her face full of worry.

"I am. What day is it?"

"Still Monday. But Monday late afternoon."

"Nina?"

"Sleeping, just like you. How do you feel?"

Pushing myself into an upright position, I took stock. "Good," I said. "Tired."

Shelly let out a laugh. "Good, thank god! I've never

seen anything like it!" She sat down at the end of the couch near my feet, one hand running through her hair.

"What did you see?"

"When you caught Nina, kept her from falling?" Shelly looked at me. "Do you remember that?"

I nodded.

"The fog whirled around you, like a whirlpool—"

"That's exactly what it was," I said.

Now it was Shelly's turn to nod. "Yes. And it swirled up, toward the ceiling. I could see you, see both of you, inside of it, but it was hard because the fog seemed like it was trying to obscure you." She looked into the distance, out the back door. "It was pulling you from inside. Like, pulling your insides outside."

"That's what it felt like."

Now Shelly looked at me. "Wynter, it was horrible. I wanted to grab you, pull you back, but Witchy Poo—"

"Who?"

"Elizabeth bossy pants." Her lips twisted.

I smiled. "You mean, Elizabeth didn't listen to you. I wouldn't call her that to her face."

"No, she did *not* listen, not even a little. I did call her that to her face, while I was yelling at her, telling her that you were fading, we had to get you out. Elizabeth replied, but she was not yelling." Shelly rolled her eyes. "She said that you had to cast this out, and if we interfered, we'd break the power of your spell."

"I didn't know that was a thing," I said.

"Well, she was probably right but I didn't appreciate it at the time." Shelly huffed. "I don't know how long it went on. It felt like a long time, and like there was screaming, a high pitched, ear piercing scream in the background. Just as quickly as the fog showed up, it was gone, and you and Nina pitched over."

"Thanks for catching me."

Shelly smiled then, a real smile of relief and love. "I'll always be there to catch you."

"I know," I said, and I leaned forward to squeeze her hand. "You're the best, lady."

She sniffed, her eyes bright. "Don't you forget it, now that you're all big and badass with the magical woo woo." Her fingers waggled at me.

I laughed. I couldn't help it. "Has Nina woken up at all?"

Shelly shook her head. "No. But Elizabeth said to tell you that Nina slept freely, whatever that means."

"It means that the thing that was holding her is gone."

"God, I hope so. Otherwise that was a lot of scary ass drama for nothing."

"Are you okay?" It wasn't like her to be so rattled.

"I'm okay, or I will be. Wine may be needed before long. A lot of it. I just thought I was going to lose my bestie for a long second, and I have to tell you, I don't like it."

"That makes two of us. But I'm not going anywhere, even though there are probably other people who—"

My words were cut off as Nina sat up.

Her eyes wide, her head whipped around. Then she looked at me and screamed, "Kira!"

CHAPTER EIGHTEEN

I was off the couch before I even realized I was moving. "Nina! It's okay!" My hands went to her arms, steadying her.

Her eyes were still wide and wild, but as they met mine, and she stared a hole through me, I saw them calm.

"He's... he's gone?" Her voice was scratchy and soft, as though she'd been yelling.

"Yes. Whatever it was, however he had you, it's gone."

Nina's head dropped, her hands running down her front, along the tops of her legs.

I stepped back, letting her take stock.

Her hands went up to her face, through her hair, and then down her arms, coming to rest as her arms wrapped themselves around her, hugging her.

"He's gone." Still a whisper, there was a thread of

something more than had been there a few seconds prior.

"He's gone," I said again.

Nina's head lifted and she smiled at me. Her eyes shone with happiness and relief.

In looking at her, it was like there was a light within beaming out, a light I'd never noticed before.

"It's back!"

"What is?" I asked.

"My magic. I can feel it. It's like a... it's like a dam broke."

Odd, that she should have the same imagery in her mind I'd had before.

"I didn't even notice the way it felt, just that I couldn't augment. But now, I can feel what was missing, because it's back." Her smile widened, and her eyes glistened with tears. "You got rid of him. You got rid of him!" Her hands came out to grip mine, squeezing them so tightly I thought my fingers might break.

"Good."

She fell back, letting go of my hands. "But goddess, I'm so tired."

"Elizabeth said you both would probably want to sleep. Like, a lot." Shelly was looking between me and Nina. "You want something to eat or drink first?"

"Food sounds great," I said.

"Water, please," Nina said at the same time.

Shelly moved to the kitchen and brought us both back glasses of water.

As good as I felt, it was tiring to even lift the glass to my mouth.

Shelly came back again with a protein bar and a banana for each of us. "Witchy Poo said this would help, so I'm going with it."

"I don't know that I could eat much more," I said as I peeled the banana.

Nina didn't speak, but tore open the protein bar wrapper and ate.

Together, Nina and I ate in silence. Shelly was next me, her worry almost a fourth person in the room.

When Nina and I finished, Shelly gathered up the trash, and our glasses. "All right, let's get you two upstairs."

It was a tight squeeze, but the three of us walked up the stairs together. It must have been a sight, Shelly holding each of us, and Nina and I hanging onto both Shelly and the bannister of the stairway.

Shelly got Nina into the guest room where she'd been staying.

"I'll get myself..." I stopped, waving a hand.

"Wynter, hang on." Shelly sounded exasperated.

I moved toward the door to my room, and then staggered to the bed. I fell onto it gratefully.

A few seconds, or moments later, I wasn't sure— Shelly was there, taking my shoes off, and pulling back the blankets to tuck me in.

"Get some sleep. I'll see you later, Miss Magical Badass."

My eyes were closing before she was even out of the room.

The room was dark, except for the moon coming in from the window behind my bed.

"Goldie?"

I'm here. How are you?

Taking stock, I realized that I was okay. Tired, yes. Feeling like I could sleep more, yes. But okay. "I'm good. Florry?"

"I'm here. You did good, kiddo."

"For someone who feels like a large truck ran over me."

"Magic takes it out of you. Watching you makes me glad my gift ran in a different direction." Florry was floating near the bed, the moonlight making her look translucent in spots.

It was kind of weird.

"Thank you," I said.

"For what?"

"I felt both of you. After I grabbed Nina, and we went wherever it was we went. I felt you, felt your energy."

We are always here for you.

I shook my head. "This was different. I know you're always here. This felt like the three of us working as one."

That's what it's supposed to be.

"No, don't give me that," I sat up, pushing myself further upright against the headboard. "It's supposed to be? Why don't you tell me these things until after the fact?"

"It can't be forced." Florry was the one to answer. "We are a team. We do work together. But you have to bring us all there, Wynter."

"Oh, for Pete's sake. Is this one of those find your own path things?"

"Yes," Florry said.

Yes, Goldie echoed.

"This really sucks."

"Complaining isn't going to do anything for you. Just accept that your life going forward will be a lot of learning," Florry said.

"Great."

"Accepting it will make it sting less," Florry added.

"Okay, fine." I thought about it, thought about learning. "So you two are good with me working with the coven, then?"

"It's not the norm, but yes, I am."

Yes, Goldie said. *The sooner you can manage your own power, understand it and use it, the better you will be. I have nothing against learning, as long as those teaching are in the right place.*

Are the witches in the right place?

I like their leader, Elizabeth.

Yeah, because she sounds a lot like you.

She is a wise woman. If he could smile, Goldie would be smirking.

I was sure of it.

"Okay, then. The coven here is a good thing. We're a team. That means what? I can call on you when I need the extra support?"

"Yes," Florry said. "We bring our energy together with yours."

"Good to know. I need to get up, check on things."

Neither of my mentors said a thing to stop me, so I got up and got a shower. I wanted to wash off all that had happened earlier, and start fresh going forward. Had I not been so tired before, I would have showered before collapsing into bed, but at that point, I was lucky I'd even made it to the bed.

By the time I tiptoed down the stairs, because the house was quiet in that 'everyone is still sleeping' way, the dawn was breaking. I could see the sun starting to lighten the sky from the back door.

I made myself some tea and sat at the island.

Watching the sun rise on a new day.

While I drank my tea, I wondered where Caro was. I hadn't seen her since before I did the scrying with Nina.

Someone had cleaned up last night. I could see the kiddie pool out back, and the tub and the rest of my supplies were clean, dry, and sitting at the end of the island, waiting to go back upstairs to the Oracle office.

Shelly had left a note.

W-

I tidied up, made sure all you sleeping beauties were tucked in, and I'm going home to make H wait on me. Call me tomorrow.

S.

I smiled as I made myself some oatmeal, curling up on the couch with a blanket around my feet as the room brightened with the rising sun. My friends were amazing.

Oh, crap. I hadn't checked my phone last night. I opened up my messages, and there was one from the blank number.

> Tommyknocker.

Logan was still safe. Things were still going well. I'd been so busy, I hadn't even had time to miss him.

While I was glad to be busy, I'd really like some down time. I stared at the text for a while, wondering where he was, what he was doing. Then I closed out messages. I still had things to do.

Starting with the things on the coffee table that I'd been ignoring. Today was the day for notes, apparently. There was an envelope on the coffee table, my name in bold black writing across the front. A small brown paper bag, like the ones I used to make my kids' lunches in, sat next to it.

But I wasn't in a hurry this morning, and I took the

time to finish my oatmeal before opening the letter. Inside was a piece of card stock.

Wynter,

I leave you in the capable hands of your friends. You've done well today. I'm looking forward to working with you.

I've composed the spell that I believe will help your spirit communicate with another. It's not complex on its surface, but you must be completely focused. I've put together a bundle of herbs that will help—don't worry, we'll go over them. Burn them in your burner. Once the smoke rising from the burner is white, call the spirit to you, tell them to focus on the one they wish to communicate with, and speak the words through the smoke. Make notes of the outcome. See you for our lesson.

E.

Below her initial was a short spell.

With these words, I ask to speak.
I see you true. May you see the same.
Together, we find the words we seek.
To hear is given to the few.
With this I call your name.
Hear me now, as I vow
I will always hear you, too.

This was interesting. I carefully opened the brown paper bag. A plastic baggie full of herbs and other things was the only thing inside. I opened the baggie and inhaled.

It smelled of summer at the beach.

I loved the reminders I kept getting every time I did something that I lived on a rock in the middle of the ocean.

This seemed simple, but Elizabeth had said that I had to be focused and concentrate.

"Florry?" I looked around.

"I'm here." She was in the doorway to the front room.

"Are you ready?"

"Always. For what?"

I grinned. "To talk to someone other than me?"

Florry stared at me, and then zoomed closer. "Are you kidding? Witchy Poo came through?"

"Don't call her that. It's bad enough Shelly does. She's helping me, and you and I both know she doesn't have to."

"Wynter, are you kidding? This will raise the status of Elizabeth and her coven. To be the ones who work with the Oracle of Theama? Even if she keeps it sort of under wraps, her fellow covens will know. This is a big deal."

"Well, if it gives them a leg up, or whatever, good. I need help with my magic, and they're willing to help."

A thought hit. I hadn't used what Elizabeth had called my gathering magic. I liked that term. It was better than 'Send people to their death' magic, anyway.

"Hang on, Florry. I need to grab something." Feeling more energy than I had since doing the scrying, I ran lightly up the stairs and used my thumb to open the office door. I brought my Oracle journal, plus a blank notebook. I also brought down my smaller burner, the one I'd first bought to scry.

Back in the kitchen, I rummaged through my junk drawer to find the markers I wanted. The heavy black stapler I'd had for years was in the back, and I brought that out as well

On the new notebook, I wrote 'Spellwork'. It seemed a bit brash to be all out in the open, but I did it anyway. This way, I could make notes about what happened.

As I opened the Spellwork notebook, I ran my hand across the smooth page. Like my Oracle journal, it was a plain black and white composition notebook. I loved them. When the kids were in school, I bought the note-books for them and always included one for me. They were still my favorite notebook, and in my opinion, better than any journal.

I made a note of the date, and stapled the card from Elizabeth in. This way, I wouldn't forget anything, or copy it incorrectly.

"You know, I have things to do." Florry's impatience spilled out of her.

"No, you don't. Stop being so pushy." I poured the contents of the baggie into my burner, and lit the flame.

A pungent, clean smell rose from the burner. Kind

of like when you walked into a room that had just been cleaned. I liked it, but it was strong.

Then I waited for the smoke to turn white.

"How long is this going to take?"

"What are you, five? It's going to take as long as it does. How did you ever get anything done when you're so impatient?"

Florry shrugged. "I don't know. All I know is that I'm ready to move forward, all the time. Maybe I was like this before? I don't remember. It's hard," she floated upward as she thought. "I have all the time in the universe in front of me. I don't want to waste it."

"That makes no sense. With all the time you could ever want, why hurry?"

"I don't know. I just don't want to." She crossed her arms.

Since there was no further explanation forthcoming, I let it go. Together, we watched the smoke rise from the burner. It was thin and opaque at first, and then it got thicker, darker, more solid looking.

"I think that's white smoke."

"What next?" Florry moved closer, her body dissected by the coffee table.

Pulling the Spellwork notebook close, I read the spell to myself. I closed my eyes. *I want Florry to be able to talk to Caro. Let Caro and Florry have open lines of communication.*

When I opened my eyes, Florry was right in front of me, eyes on the burner.

I read the spell, picturing her and Caro laughing and chatting.

"With these words, I ask to speak.

I see you true. May you see the same.

Together, we find the words we seek.

To hear is given to the few.

With this I call your name.

Hear me now, as I vow

I will always hear you, too."

The house was quiet. The smoke rose up, getting more white. Florry's eyes were wide.

The electric zing I'd felt a couple of times over the last week moved through me, making me jump.

"What?" Florry peered at me.

"I think it's done."

"You don't know?"

"It's not like someone waves a wand and says, *Congratulations,*" I said. "Why don't you go up and see if Caro can hear you?"

Florry just stared, and then she smiled. "You'll know pretty quick if it doesn't."

"I have no doubt of that. You're not one to suffer in silence."

With a smile that could be described as sweet, Florry winked at me and then zoomed away.

I let the herbs keep burning, just in case I needed them.

My head fell back and I closed my eyes. Magic was tiring. I might need a nap before I went over to the apothecary. I was debating what to wear, and what I'd need to bring—the grimoire would stay here, I decided. After seeing Elizabeth's reaction to other coven journals, I didn't think she'd be offended. The grimoire was the Oracle journal, for the Oracles only.

That settled, I was thinking about leggings when a scream rang out, breaking the peaceful silence in the house.

CHAPTER NINETEEN

"What the hell?" I raced up the stairs.

Another cry, from Caro's room.

Oh, shit.

I knocked on the door, calling out, "Caro?" and then opened the door.

She was in bed, pinned against the wrought iron headboard, the blankets pulled up to her chin, her eyes wide.

"Caro?" I asked again. "What's wrong?"

"Why can I hear her?"

"Who?"

"Florry. I can hear her. What is this? A cruel joke?" Her eyes focused on me.

"Don't you want to talk to her?" I looked around, seeing Florry in the corner. Her face... it nearly made me cry. Her hand was over her mouth, and she looked horrified.

And hurt.

I'd done this. How was I supposed to fix this?

What was that saying? Be careful what you wish for?

I met Florry's eyes, and held up a hand.

"Is she here?" Caro asked.

"Yes."

Caro nodded, looking around.

"Do you want to be able to talk to her?" I asked again. I didn't know how I'd fix it, but I would.

"Not if I'm not supposed to. She's gone. She can speak to you. Not to me. Wynter, I think someone's trying to do something to me to get to you."

I eased myself into a sitting position at the end of the bed. "No, no one's trying to get to me. No one's using you. I did this."

"What?" She stared at me, uncomprehending.

"Do you want to talk to Florry?" Shit, shit, shit. She'd said she did, and I'd taken her at her word, and now she didn't. What do I do now? Florry would be crushed, if the way she looked now was any indication, and Caro... what would this do to Caro? Panic rose from my belly, making me feel sick and choked.

"So this isn't something bad?"

I shook my head. "No, not if you don't want it to be."

The silence stretched out, fast heading for unbearable.

"Florry? Are you really here?"

"Yes," Florry moved from the corner to float beside the bed, laser focused on her friend. "As long as you want me to be."

"I can't see you."

Florry looked to me. "Can she see me?"

"I don't know. I don't think so, if she can't now. The spell asked for communication."

"I don't need to see you," Caro said. The panic was fading from her voice.

She was also less stiff, her shoulders dropping down.

"You sure? I don't want you freaking out again." Florry sounded better. The hurt I'd seen on her face a moment before wasn't so striking and raw.

"It just surprised me. You could have had Wynter give me a warning."

"You didn't used to be so negative about surprises." Florry glared at her friend.

"Well, you weren't gone before." Caro snapped back, obviously unwilling to take any sort of guff from Florry.

I got up. "I think my part of this is done. Caro, I did a spell to allow Florry to talk to you. Are you good with that?"

"I am, although I might regret it in five minutes."

Florry laughed, and the rich sound filled the room. The tension I'd felt when I'd run in was gone.

Caro smiled at Florry, although she couldn't see her.

I left quietly. The next part was for them to sort out.

Back downstairs, the herbs had burned themselves to ash. I cleaned up the burner, made notes in the Spellwork journal, and then brought all my stuff back upstairs. I'd just finished in the Oracle office—I loved calling it that, for reasons I couldn't identify. I didn't want to identify them, either—when there was a soft knock at my door.

"Come in," I said.

Nina's head poked around the door. "Is everything okay? I thought I heard shouting, but I was so slow, and couldn't get up."

"Yes. Everything's fine. How are you feeling?"

"Better. I managed to drag my butt out of bed."

"There's all kinds of food in the fridge. Help yourself. I think our resident chef is going to be busy for a bit. I'll join you once I've showered."

"Right on. See you later." Her head disappeared.

I took the hottest shower known to man.

It felt amazing and wonderful and like I was coming out of a dark tunnel, out in to the light.

When I went downstairs, the sliding glass door was open, the screen door in its place. Nina was out back, sitting with her back to me on the small settee.

Caro was nowhere to be seen. I was right. We weren't going to see Caro for a while.

That was a good thing you did for Florry. Goldie sounded tired.

There was a lot of that going around.

At least now it was tired in a good way. Because I'd

been doing the things I needed to, and not only fighting off megalomaniacal jackasses. It wasn't just the ex of my current consultant. Every single consultant had brought someone into my life who was trying to harm me.

Jackasses.

Hey, where have you been? I focused on my armband.

Where I should be. At your back.

Noted. Anyway, you approve? Of me doing this for Florry?

I do. Had her friend not been here, I would have cautioned against this path. But Caro is here, and it's hard for Florry to see her friend without being able to talk to her.

You do have a heart.

I care for all the Oracles. You know that.

Yes, you do. He'd made it clear in the past that Florry tried his patience. However, I didn't bring that up.

Don't let her slack on her responsibilities. She's here for you. She might forget that in her desire to reconnect.

Point taken. I think that I can offer her some grace today, though. Wouldn't you agree?

One day wouldn't be horrible.

I have my lesson with the coven today, anyway. I wouldn't want her there for that. I don't want them to get comfortable with my spirit guide.

I agree with that, Goldie said.

Okay, let me get on with Nina.

I'm not stopping you. His words were huffy.

Oh, the drama.

"Feeling better?" I asked Nina.

She turned to glance at me over her shoulder. "I am. Better than I have since I got here."

I smiled. I'd done it. But... the small sense of awareness, the click that told me that I'd finished the task set by my consultant—it wasn't there.

Okay. That meant that she needed to be here still.

"Nina, you're feeling better is wonderful. But I think you need to be here a bit longer—"

"I need to go get Kira."

"I don't have a protection spell for you yet. I'm seeing the coven tonight, and we'll work on that. What I was going to say was you need to stay here so that we can make sure you are free of the hex, that you're not going to relapse. Or whatever you want to call it."

Nina turned in her seat. Her face was thoughtful. "You're probably right. I'm so impatient, I want to see her, but it wouldn't be a good idea until I'm sure I've gotten rid of Rock's magic."

I nodded. "I think that's good." I sat on the chair to the side of the settee.

Nina got up, walking into the grass in her bare feet.

I could see her toes curling into the grass.

She bent down and picked a dandelion that had the nerve to be growing in my yard.

There were a number of them, in fact. I hadn't been out here enough lately to keep track, but now that I'd seen them? They were something I needed to address before they took over the yard.

Nina continued, "These are Kira's favorite flowers." She blew out a breath, and the white, fluffy seeds on one side of the dandelion puffed out. "She loves to blow on them." She looked up at me. "She calls them fairy hair."

I laughed. "Fairy hair is a great way to describe it."

Nina blew the rest of the dandelion fluff. "It's actually called pappus, all these seeds. I tried to explain that to Kira, and she said, 'No, it's fairy hair'." She smiled. "So fairy hair it is."

I could feel her longing for her daughter. "You're going to see her soon."

"When I first came here, I wasn't sure. I kept hoping, but I wasn't sure. Now, I think you're right. I will be seeing her."

We smiled at one another.

And for the next hour, we just sat outside in the sun, with the fairy hair floating around us.

Caro came downstairs, her eyes a little pink, but they were bright, and she couldn't stop smiling.

"Hey," I said. "How goes it?"

She walked toward me, taking my hands in hers as she got close. "Wynter, I can't thank you enough. Being able to talk to Florry is something I didn't think I'd ever get to do again."

"Still in the honeymoon phase," I teased. "Once

she's always in your head, you may be less inclined to thank me."

"You know I'm right here," Florry said.

"I know you're here. Why do you think I'm being so honest?"

Caro and I both laughed.

Florry crossed her arms, but I could see that she was struggling not to laugh.

"You two are all good? And you're not so freaked out?"

"Not at all," Caro said. "I'm sorry for that, by the way."

"No worries," I patted her hand. "I'm glad to help you. It helps me, too. Trying to translate between the two of you was making me insane. It cuts down on the conversations I have to direct."

"Well, I'm so appreciative."

"So am I." Florry moved closer. "All kidding aside, thank you. And good job, kiddo. You did great."

"Thank you." I felt my cheeks warm at her praise. It felt good.

"All right, now that the appreciation society has done its thing, what's next?"

Nina came in at that point. "Wynter, I think I'm going to go back to the rental place. Is that all right, do you think?"

I nodded. "Would you be willing to stay on the island until the end of the weekend? So I can make sure it's all good with you? I don't want to send you off without double and triple checking."

"I think that's a good call, even though I'm dying to leave. But I can wait a few more days." She smiled, and I could see a sense of peace around her. Not fully—that probably wouldn't happen until she was reunited with Kira.

But it was a start.

"Okay. Listen, I have that thing this afternoon, and then family is descending tomorrow." My words were casual, as though the meeting with the coven wasn't a big deal.

"That's right. Your husband's other wife." Nina grinned to show me there was no malice in her words.

"Exactly. The second wife." I pointed at her. "It takes all kinds here. I would not force anyone to be part of that. That includes you, too," I said to Caro. "But you're both welcome."

"I think I'll skip it. I have enough of my own drama," Nina said.

"You need to check in with me, then. Three calls during the day, just to make sure you're all right."

"Yes, ma'am," Nina gave me a salute. Then she stepped closer and hugged me. "Thank you." She stepped back, but one hand stayed on my shoulder. "In the Fire Ceremony, it mentioned something about giving you an offering for your help. I didn't even think about it before now. What sort of offering?"

"Well, it could be whatever you wanted to offer." I still found this part of the Oracle gig uncomfortable.

"Let me augment something for you."

"Oooh, that's a good idea," Florry interjected.

I waved a hand at her. "Can I think about what I'd like to have you augment? I don't have to make a decision now, do I?" I had an idea, but it needed some work before I took it public.

"Let me know as soon as you know," Nina said. "I have to do a little prep work before I cast it."

"Got it," I said. I had an idea, but I wanted to run it by the coven first, since this involved their magic.

Nina hugged me again. "Let me get my things and I'll get out of your hair for a while."

"You're not in my hair, and you have to check in with me."

"I will, I promise."

Within twenty minutes, she'd grabbed her belongings from the room she'd been staying in, brought her linens downstairs and put them in the washer, hugged me and Caro, and was out the door.

"So you're done with helping Nina?" Caro asked.

"I don't know. Normally, when I've completed the task, I can tell. I haven't gotten that feeling. That's why I want her to stay. I'm waiting for my sign."

Caro nodded. "Florry always said that, too. That she could tell when her job was done. But the hex is gone?"

I grinned. "It's gone. You want to come for a walk with me? I'm dying to get out of the house."

"Sure. Then breakfast?"

"Yes."

Together, we walked toward the beach. While I was expectant, nothing happened.

Tethys didn't appear. Scott Trenton didn't appear. No magic occurred.

Nothing happened.

It was glorious.

After we ate, I spent the afternoon taking care of my mundane, non-Oracle chores. The laundry was getting completely out of hand. I did some housecleaning, and got the two extra rooms ready for Natalie, Nathan, and Sophie. I went over the menu with Caro, and I called Shelly.

"How are you feeling, badass?"

"Much, much better. You want to talk about something less exciting, like the other wife showing up tomorrow?"

"Yeah, sure, why not? I mean, it's getting boring around here."

We both laughed, and I shared my plans.

"I think that's sounds great, Wyn. I still say you're a better woman than me, and that's fine. I can live with that. You want me to come over, be your moral support tomorrow?"

"You know, I really wanted you here. But you're so obviously on my side." I tapped my chin with a finger. "Caro's going to be here, and I don't want Natalie to feel like I'm lining up my troops or anything."

"It's not a bad idea," Shelly retorted. "Lining up the troops, I mean."

"She's already on my home turf. Stop."

"Your call, lady. All right. I'm going to relax and do nothing today."

"Thanks for all your help. With the planning, with all my Oracle stuff, all of it."

"Anytime. You know that. Hubie's great, but he's not enough to be exciting all the time."

"Oh, baloney. Since I know you adore him."

"Hush. I like to keep him guessing."

"Stop playing hard to get."

Shelly laughed. "All men like a chase. Remember that."

"Whatever. Can we plan on dinner after the other family leaves? Text me first, and we'll figure it out. I'll make you something special for being so accommodating."

"You got it. Later, Badass."

"That's not my name," I said to the phone, since Shelly had already ended the call.

I folded the last of the laundry, and then packed up my bag. I brought both the Oracle and the Spellwork journals. Even as I stood in my office looking around, I didn't see anything—oh, crap. I picked up the books Callie had given me. I hadn't gotten as much reading done as I'd like, but I tossed them in the bag as well.

When I went back downstairs, Caro was in the front room, reading.

Florry was hovering near the bay window.

"I'm headed to the apothecary. I don't know when I'll be back."

"I think I'm going to go out for dinner, if you don't mind fending for yourself."

"Caro, I'm delighted that you've been cooking. If you don't want to cook, you don't have to do anything other than tell me you're out for the night."

"Okay, okay. Message received. I'll be out for the night."

"I'll be fine," I said. "There's plenty in the fridge. Florry, once she leaves, keep an eye out, okay?"

"Don't I always? I'm the alarm bat in the belfry."

I was about to translate to Caro when I remembered that Caro could hear her, too.

So I waved at both of them, and left.

It was still sunny and warm, and I rolled down the window singing along with the radio as I drove. I had no idea what to expect, but after the past week, I felt pretty sure that it would be okay.

Which was as far as I was willing to go around expectations.

When I pulled into the apothecary, there weren't a lot of cars. Once I got to the door, it was clear as to why. The 'Closed' sign was up, along with a handwritten sign about having inventory this evening.

I knocked anyway.

A woman I didn't know answered the door. "Wynter?" she asked, her face neutral.

I nodded.

"Come in, and be welcome." She locked the door behind me, and then moved around me to lead me further into the shop.

We went down the hallway behind the curtain I'd noticed before. In a room off to the left, there were six more women. Callie and Nayla, the two I'd met before, weren't part of this group. I wondered how big the coven was.

The room was lit by candles, and at the back of the room opposite the door, was an altar.

"Welcome, Wynter." Elizabeth spoke.

"Welcome, Wynter," the other women echoed.

"Come and join us as one of us," Elizabeth continued. "To my sisters, we welcome our sister in the craft. We are all parts of the cycle of the craft, and while everyone's journey is a path of individual steps, we all are striving for the same place. Balance, harmony, and peace."

"Balance, harmony, and peace." The words were calm, easy.

A feeling of... ease... for lack of a better word, swept over me. I'd been so nervous, worried that the women I hadn't met wouldn't be accepting. I'd only met Nayla, Callie and Elizabeth. While I'd had more of the coven in my home, there had been a deliberate omission of names.

In some of my reading, I'd learned the reasons behind that omission. Even now, there were prejudices around those who called themselves wiccans, or witches. So secrecy was maintained until the person chose to share.

"As we hold the confidence of our sisters, we hold yours as well, Wynter. I have shared, with your permission, the obligation that you have chosen."

"Thank you," I said. Not having to go through it again was a relief.

"And we welcome you, welcome the chance to work with you, to share and to collaborate. To that end, tell us how we can help you."

This wasn't quite what I expected. "I would really like to bolster the protection spell you used on my house. Specifically, I'd like to cast..." I searched for the words. "I'd like to know how it's done. I have someone who can augment the spell, so I need to know the spell itself. If that's allowed." I didn't want to step on toes, but this was kind of necessary.

Elizabeth came forward. "That's an excellent ask, Wynter. Since we agreed to cast the spell for you, we are willing to share. Mari, let's get out our workings for that, if you please?"

A woman with light blond hair, younger than me, moved toward a set of shelves to the right of the altar.

We spent the next two hours going through the spell. The women, most of whom still were not named, talked me through the pieces of it. They were patient, and kind.

Finally, Mari said, "I think you need to try and cast it. You can cast it over me, Wynter."

"Oh, good lord. Will I hurt you?"

She dimpled. "No. That's the point, right? To keep me from getting hurt?"

"Well, yes."

"You can do this. You have a lot of raw talent, there is something really big within you."

All the other women, Elizabeth included, stilled.

"What?" Mari looked around. "We've all talked about it. We all feel it. I'd call it wild magic, the magic that comes from nature."

Or the sea, Goldie whispered.

"You have it. A lot of it. I want to see you be able to manage it, to use it. For good only, of course." She shook a finger at me.

"That's actually part of my job description," I said.

"Liz told us," Mari replied. "Which is the only reason you're here, really. I mean, can you imagine if people knew about you? Or about us? You've already seen how they can turn, get ugly."

I nodded. I hadn't heard from Hubie, but my lawsuit was out there, public knowledge, even as I did my best to ignore it. And Hazel Babbington wasn't going away until she took her final journey.

"So let's practice this. While this is designed for your home, in a pinch, you could cast it around you. And don't worry." The dimple returned. "We're going to basically take you back to school. This is just the first bit."

With that, Mari taught me the words, and I spent the next hour casting it over her. The other members took turns trying to cast spells on Mari, trying to bypass my spell.

Initially, every other spell that was cast made it through.

Then it was every fourth or fifth spell. The women of this coven were fast, casting one after the other. I had to focus on keeping my spell up, keeping it strong.

After I'd made it through two rounds of all the other members trying to break through and failing, Elizabeth said, "Let's take a break."

Thank god.

"Wynter, you can release the spell now," Mari said. "Good job, by the way. You're doing well."

"This is hard work," I said. I could feel the sweat running down my back, now that I had a moment to think about something other than my spell.

"It always is. But the more you practice, the more you and your magic will become known and comfortable to one another." She walked over to the far corner, pulling out a couple of bottles of water and offering one to me.

"I like that. Be known and comfortable to one another."

"It's a good way to see it."

Another one of the women approached me. "I'm

Tabitha. It's nice to meet you, Wynter." She held out her hand.

I shook it, feeling a thread of electricity running through her. Or was I reacting to her? "Is that me?" I blurted out without thinking.

"What?" Tabitha cocked her head.

"When I took your hand, I felt a shock. Not a big one, but like when you touch a live outlet."

"I didn't feel anything." Tabitha shook her head.

"It's me, then."

"You may be reacting to Tabitha's magic. It's not painful, or hurting you, is it?" Mari peered at me.

"No, it's just... there."

"Magic is different for us all. If I had to guess, and this is only a guess and could be completely wrong, I'd say this is your wild magic at work. One way for magic to protect the user is to let them know when another magic user is close."

"Is that part of gathering magic?"

"No, why?"

"That's what I have, according to Elizabeth," I replied. "Gathering magic."

"That's a really strong magic," Tabitha said. "So cool, Wynter."

"It is, but it sometimes takes on a life of its own. That's one of the reasons I asked for help."

"Asking for help is a good sign. A wise witch knows when she can't do it alone."

"I think that we're at a good stopping place," Elizabeth came over. "Wynter, I have a list for you of what you should be focusing on the books Callie gave you." She handed over a piece of paper. "How did the spell I left for you work out?"

I laughed. "After the recipient of the desired communication stopped freaking out, it went great."

"You had no trouble with the spell work?"

I shook my head. "No, it was within my skill level."

Elizabeth nodded. "I thought it would be. You need to give yourself both credit and grace, Wynter. You have, as Mari said, a lot of raw talent. There is power within you, and that means that you will be capable of a lot, unless I'm completely off base."

"I don't think you are," Mari said.

While it was clear that Elizabeth was the leader, what was also clear was that she believed her coven members were equals. Not like the necromancers I'd met.

Who had all been men.

I stayed for another twenty minutes, chatting and talking.

One of the other women went around and blew out the candles. Just before the last large candle was doused, the lights went on, and another coven member opened the curtains on the window, allowing the late afternoon sun to shine in.

There were eight small tea light candles along a table near the door. Those weren't touched, even though all the rest had been snuffed.

"This was a good lesson. I would be up for every other Tuesday, if you are." Elizabeth said to me. "Provided you get through your reading."

"I swear, I'm trying to," I said. "This week has been pretty packed."

"Fair enough. But you need the knowledge base for us to continue."

"I promise, I'll do the reading."

"I can't ask for anything more. Ladies, if you will?" Elizabeth looked around the room.

One by one, the other coven members walked to the door. Dipping their fingers into a cup with water, they each put out one of the tea light candles until there were only two left.

"One's for you, Wynter. It closes out the circle of energy you've used in here, keeps it from leaving with you."

"This drains me somehow?" I pulled my hands close to me.

"No, no. It's not like that at all. It's just part of finishing your work. The energy you used here is kept within the confines of the work. Nothing's taken from you. Think of it as more of a way to make sure that no one outside of this room can use your energy. We've expended a lot. Another magical user might feel it, and come seeking it. With us dousing it before we leave, we keep other magical users from taking that which is ours."

"That kind of makes sense," I said, trying to wrap

my head around the idea. I dipped my fingers in the water and then put out a candle, feeling the hiss and sizzle as the flame was extinguished against my fingers.

Elizabeth followed suit, and we walked out of the room. She closed the door behind her. "So go home and relax. When you have the augment near, cast the spell. And make notes."

"I brought my notebook—"

"We'll go over that another time."

"Oh, okay." I felt kind of put off. Tonight, while great, hadn't gone as I thought it would. Although that was on me, right? It was my expectations that were off. Not that I wasn't getting something I needed. I needed to beef up my protection.

That's what we'd done.

I couldn't wait to get hold of Nina and have her augment it for me. This was the spell I'd been thinking about when she'd asked about payment. I couldn't shake the feeling that the demon who had tried to break through wasn't a fluke. Even with the coven warning the demon away, I didn't feel as though that was the end of the matter.

Another thought hit me. This spell would be something I could use for Nina. To keep Rock from bothering her again.

Bonus.

I'd been planning on asking the coven to craft a spell for me, but I realized, after all the practice and learning the details of the spell, that I could cast this for her, she might even be able to augment it, and it would protect her.

Maybe like a continual loop? I bet if I did some reading, I could make it happen. The thought made me smile.

I came out of my own head to see Elizabeth smiling back at me. "That's what I like to see after we're done working."

"I like learning and I really appreciate you're willing to work with me."

"I feel the same. I'll see you soon," Elizabeth walked me to the front door.

And like that, I was back in my car, turning the notifications for my phone back on.

Within seconds, the phone began to buzz and ping, letting me know that the world hadn't stopped while I was busy.

Three messages from the kids, confirming that they would be here tomorrow on the four o'clock ferry.

One from Natalie, confirming she would be on the ten a.m. ferry.

And one from Logan.

Tommyknocker. Call?

Yes

I texted back quickly.

My heart raced at the thought of Logan. He was still all right. He was safe. If he wanted to call, it must mean things were going well. I didn't know this based on anything we'd talked about, but rather knowing Logan himself. He wouldn't call me if things were at a bad stage.

I drove home with a smile on my face.

At the risk of jinxing myself, today had been a good day.

Once I parked in my driveway, and ran up the stairs of the porch, I could hear yelling from inside the house.

What the hell?

CHAPTER TWENTY

As I raced into the kitchen, Caro was standing near the table, her hands on her hips, her face red.

"What's wrong? Are you hurt?"

Her head whipped around. "No, I am fine." Her accent was more pronounced tonight. "I'm just in an argument with my stubborn, pig-headed friend."

"You've got a lot of nerve, calling me pig-headed!" Florry shouted back.

"Überspann den Bogen nicht!!" Caro shouted as she stomped away from the kitchen and out into the backyard.

"What the hell is going on?" I asked. "And what did Caro say?"

"She basically called me a jerk and told me I was pushing it with her."

"Do I want to know?"

"No," Florry snapped. "You don't." She floated away, then stopped. "Don't worry, Wynter. There are things Caro and I need to clean up. But it's not anything that will get in the way of our work, yours and mine."

"Well, okay," I said. I wasn't sure what else I could say. I mean, this wasn't my fight. And given how angry both Caro and Florry were, I wasn't about to get in the middle of it.

Florry zoomed away, her anger trailing after her like a bad smell. I shook my head and went upstairs. Lying down on my bed, I pulled out my phone and dialed the number of the burner phone that Logan was using.

He answered on the first ring.

"Hey, you," he said.

"Hey, yourself," I replied. "How are you?"

"I miss you." His voice dropped down, the low rumble sending shivers down my spine. "What's going on?"

"Oh, the usual. A lot. I swear, this is like the never ending week for me. I don't want to talk about me, though. Tell me what's going on with you." I smiled into the phone as though he could see me.

"It's going better than I thought. So far, I'm just dealing with the banks, and the lawyers, and getting Evander Thane back into the world of the living."

"It's all the prep work you did," I said. I knew he'd been working on this with Mark for a while.

"I hope it's enough."

"When will you be back?" I asked.

"Not soon enough for me," Logan said. "Could you come here?"

"What?" I hadn't been expecting that.

"Come see me. Stay with me."

"I can't until Friday," I said. "I have things to do until then."

"Then come Friday, as soon as you're done."

I thought about it. "All right," I said finally. "I have to ask, though. What happened to worrying about keeping me safe?"

He didn't hesitate in his response. "I can keep you safe. I talked with Mark, and we worked it out."

"You feel comfortable with this?" I did, but I wasn't the one I had to worry about. Logan was careful and deliberate. Any plan he made would be the same. I knew that. I needed to know that he knew that as well.

"I do. But I have one request."

"Which is?"

"Don't take the ferry. It leaves you too exposed. Fly over here, right into the city."

"I can do that. I'll have to check the flights," I began.

"No, I got it. I'll send you all the info. But you'll come?"

"Yes. I miss you, too."

"Don't plan on a lot of sightseeing."

I laughed, eagerly anticipating what I could plan on.

We chatted for a few more minutes, and then ended

the call. I went back down in search of Caro, hoping she'd had a chance to cool down.

She was still sitting in the dark in the backyard. "Sorry you had to see that," she said as I walked out the sliding glass door.

"I don't care. Sometimes you have to fight with your friends. I actually wanted to make sure you were all set with the plans we made for tomorrow. I figure they'll want lunch after I bring them back, and then I'll take them to the beach. You are welcome to join us at all of these."

"I'm good. The menu is set, and I have all that I need. I'll join you if I feel up to it." While pleasant, it was obvious that Caro was still upset.

"Well, okay. I'm going to grab a sandwich and head off to bed."

"All right." She didn't move.

When I opened the door to walk back inside, Caro spoke again.

"Thank you, Wynter."

"You're welcome." There were a number of things this could be in reference to. I decided I didn't need to know any of them. I made myself a sandwich, eating standing up.

Once I finished, I took my bag and the scrying supplies from earlier up with me, locking up my notebooks, and making sure that none of my Oracle stuff was lying about. I didn't want to answer questions about it.

I was also glad that Logan wasn't here. While I wasn't ashamed in any way, and Derek's behavior absolved me from prolonged mourning, I sure as hell wasn't going to entertain any questions from his other wife about the state of my love life now.

She'd had more insight into it than I liked already.

Eventually, I wanted to introduce Logan to everyone I knew, shout out our relationship from the rooftops.

But with Natalie Chastain?

I wanted to wait.

If I was honest, I knew part of it was insecurity. I didn't want her to get a crack at another one of my men. Even as I knew, logically, that Logan wouldn't be interested. He wasn't the same kind of man that Derek had been.

"You know, if you weren't dead, I'd beat you with a shoe," I said to wherever Derek's spirit might be. "I can't believe I have to deal with this shit because of you."

No one responded to me. Which was a good thing. I'd had enough of near heart attacks lately.

I shoved aside all these thoughts and got ready for bed. I needed to sleep, and no amount of worrying tonight would solve any of this for me.

The next morning found me at the ferry terminal ten minutes before it was scheduled to dock. Natalie had texted me before they left.

Caro was at home, making sure her planned lunch was ready.

I was standing here, fidgeting and waiting.

As I gazed around, a dark sedan pulled into the terminal. After a moment, two men got out.

Oh, great. My least two favorite people in the world. Andy Dentwhistle and Scott Trenton. Andy saw me first, and he came around the car to steer Scott in the opposite direction.

Scott's head whipped toward me. The anger and hate in him focused on me with the intensity of a laser beam.

I stared back, willing myself to look calm and unconcerned. Let him say one damn thing. It would just add to the lawsuit. Speaking of which… I took out my phone and still watching the detectives, dialed Hubie.

"Wynter," his voice was warm.

"How is the lawsuit going?" I asked.

"You sound a little snappy. What's up?"

"I'm down at the ferry and Scott Trenton's burning a hole through me."

"Is he close to you? Is he saying or doing anything? Are you recording?" Hubie whipped his professional self into place without breaking stride.

"No, no, and I'm ready to if need be."

Andy pushed at Scott, who finally turned away from me. They both went into the ferry's administrative offices.

"He shouldn't be within one hundred yards of you. I just got the ruling back this morning. I was going to come over if you had time."

"I have company coming that I'd rather not discuss this in front of, if you don't mind. Can you give me the high points right now?"

"Both detectives need to stay away from you. If there is a legal matter in which the police department has to speak with you, the chief, along with me, will question you. Your lawsuit has been accepted, and all parties are being served within the next forty-eight hours." He snickered. "I'd pay money to see that service."

"You mean you're not serving them yourself?"

"No, it's not really appropriate. I'd still pay money to see it. Which is why I have my server recording it."

"You really are a petty man."

"Indeed I am. I wallow in it at times, and I will not apologize. I also want to see if any of the parties involved says something they shouldn't."

"Pshaw, the law. Secondary to the enjoyment of watching the other side get served."

"This is what makes you such a good client," Hubie said, approval radiating from the phone. "Any of 'em come near you, turn on record, and tell them to leave you alone. Repeatedly."

"Aye, aye, Captain. Anything else?"

"Those are the high points. I should have a court date set by next week."

"All right. Keep me posted, and love to Shelly." Initially, I'd asked Shelly to be part of today, but she and I had decided that she would stay home, even though she was dying to see Natalie in the flesh. I didn't want Natalie feeling like she was facing not only me, but my army. That wasn't the impression I wanted to give.

"Now why would I be seeing her?" Hubie asked in pretend surprise. Then he laughed as we ended the call.

As the ferry pulled into the dock, I put the phone away, and waited. Talking with Hubie, knowing that I was in the right in the things I was doing in regard to my concerns with the law—it had calmed my nerves.

Although I wasn't sure that legal shenanigans were the answer long term, I'd take it right now.

People began pouring out of the ferry, and I shaded my eyes so I could see better. Eventually, I saw Natalie's tall dark head. She was holding Sophie's hand as Nathan danced in front of her.

I waved and Natalie steered the kids toward me.

"Hi!" I greeted Nathan first.

He threw his arms around my waist. "Hi, Wynter!"

"How was your trip?"

"The ferry was awesome!" Nathan grinned up at me.

"Hi," Sophie said, more reserved than her brother.

I bent down to put my arms around her shoulders, giving her the chance to pull away, but wanting to offer her the chance for a hug if she was interested.

After a moment, she gave me a hug. "What about you? Did you like it?"

"The ocean's really big," Sophie said.

"It is. That's one of the things I like about it. Now let me give your mom a hug." I stepped through the kids and opened my arms to Natalie.

"It's good to see you," she said into my ear.

"You, too," I said, and meant it. Even with all the things, I meant it. "Come on. I brought the car, so we don't have to walk all the way home. And my friend Caro has a really great lunch for us today, after you get settled."

"Are we going to the beach?" Nathan asked.

"We are," I said, as I navigated home, ignoring the detectives who had just walked back out to their car. "And that we can walk to."

"It smells different here," Sophie said.

"Because we're on an island, and the sea is all around us."

"It's kind of scary," she replied.

"Sophie," Natalie began.

I smiled at Natalie. "Sophie's right. The sea can be scary. Everyone that lives around it or on it learns that. Some of us learn the hard way, and some of us learn by watching others learn the hard way."

"Which way did you learn?" This from Sophie.

"Well, I made some mistakes when I used to sail as a kid, and that resulted in me capsizing, and breaking my boat from time to time. But mostly I watched other people, and read a lot."

"So both," Nathan chirped.

"Both," I agreed.

We pulled into the driveway.

"Your house looks like the witch's house from Hansel and Gretel," Nathan was out of his seatbelt and opening the door. "It's so cool!"

"Nathan!" Natalie's face pinked.

"It's fine. It's an elaborate house. He's right. It is a witch's house," I said, laughing inside at the truth of it. "And you guys get to come inside and see it."

Caro was in the kitchen when we all tumbled in. I introduced her to Natalie and the kids.

"Are you Wynter's grandma?" Sophie asked.

"No, although I could be," Caro said. "I'm just her friend."

"She's a good friend," I said. "Not just a friend."

Caro smiled at me. "Good friends. Absolutely."

"She's prettier than I thought she'd be," Florry's comment was low key.

I mean, for Florry it was low key. She didn't shout. She wasn't being snarky. It was almost thoughtful.

She is pretty. I told you. I've always seen why Derek loved her. Much as I never wanted to.

While you don't always need to be forgiving, I think it's a wise idea in this case, Goldie said.

I think so, I replied. *Better for me, absolutely. Florry, can you keep yourself scarce? I don't want to accidentally reply to you and scare the hell out of them.*

"Okay, but I'll be watching. And we will discuss this later. Good luck, kiddo." Florry winked, and then disappeared.

I'll do the same, Goldie said, and a moment later, it was as though a door closed between us.

Huh. I'd have to make him show me how to do that. That was handy.

I was pleased to see that Caro and Natalie got along, although Caro was holding back a bit. I didn't think Natalie noticed, because she didn't know Caro as well, and because Caro was subtle.

But I saw it.

It took about an hour to get the kids settled and to get lunch served. Caro made linguine and clams with a white sauce. It was delicious, and I couldn't help but eat more than I should. After everyone ate, Nathan yawned.

"Mom, I'm tired."

"Why don't you nap for an hour?" Natalie asked. "Why don't we all nap for an hour and then we can go to the beach. What do you think?"

"That works for me," I said. "Whatever you want to do."

"When are your kids getting here?" Sophie asked.

"They're going to be here for dinner. They're really excited to see you," I added.

That made Sophie smile.

"Did you enjoy Pop Pop and Nanny?" I asked, knowing they'd been at Derek's parents for a while.

The kids regaled me with stories, and it was my turn to smile. Natalie cleared away the plates, putting them in the sink and getting ready to wash up until Caro shooed her away.

"Caro, would you like to come to the beach with us?" I asked.

"No, I have some things I still need to do. This dinner is not going to cook itself."

"You're a good cook," Natalie said.

"Thank you, I enjoy it. The love of something helps."

Natalie took the kids upstairs.

When we heard the doors close, Caro turned to me. "She's nice."

"She is," I agreed.

"You're a saint," Caro continued.

"I don't know. I struggle. Derek doing what he did has created some insecurities inside me, pretty big ones, and it pisses me off, if I'm being honest. I want to strike out sometimes, when I think about it too much. Natalie would be an easy target, but Derek lied to her just like he did to me."

"I don't know if I could do it," Caro said.

"You never think you can do the hard things. When you see my kids with them tonight, you'll see why I do it. The kids, both sets, really like each other. I think they'll eventually grow to love one another. When

Natalie and I are long gone, these kids will have each other, and that's a good thing for them."

"A saint. Listen, I got this. You go and rest, and fluff your hair, powder your nose."

"I will, but I have a favor to ask."

"Yes?"

"Logan invited me to fly over to New York to see him. I'd be leaving on Friday after my doctor's appointment. Would you be willing to have Nina stay here? I want to make sure she's all right."

"Is there something worrying you?"

"Yes. No. I don't know. I just want to be sure. It doesn't feel like this is over."

Caro nodded.

It made me feel better.

After they napped, I took my guests down to the beach. It was like when my kids were young. I still had the chairs, and the beach bags, and even some of the toys. Even though we had a lot of stuff, it was practiced and done with ease. Thankfully, we didn't have far to go to get to the town beach.

Natalie and I talked about nothing in particular for an hour or so, watching the kids in the sand and along the water's edge.

"How are you doing with forgiveness?" Natalie asked suddenly.

"What do you mean?" I needed more information.

She sighed, heavily. "You've been great through all this. Introducing your kids to mine, making sure that my kids know their grandparents, and basically being a damn saint." She stopped. It was clear she didn't mean to say that.

"I'm sorry," she continued. "That was crappy of me. It's just that I am so angry at Derek. So mad he took from me, from us."

I held up a hand. "Stop right there. If Derek was alive, I'd pummel him to a pulp. I'm angry at him as well. I have to wonder why I wasn't enough, why my kids weren't enough."

Natalie nodded, tears welling in her eyes. She didn't speak, but took my hand.

"What I keep coming back to, logically, is that we didn't do anything wrong. I didn't, you didn't and our kids sure didn't. Derek wronged us all, and we're left to pick up the pieces."

She wiped at the tears that spilled down her face.

"I don't know how long I'm going to be mad at him. I'm pissed that his actions have made me feel insecure in way I haven't felt in years. Why do I get to deal with this when he's the one that behaved badly?" My voice rose, and I stopped, feeling tears in my eyes now.

Then I took Natalie's other hand. "It's not me. It's not you. It was him. And it's okay that we're mad, that we want to kill him at times. He was a selfish baby, grabbing at both of us rather than being honest and telling me he wanted a divorce. Rather than telling you when you met that he was married."

A sob burst from Natalie's throat.

"I'm not a saint. I'm mad about him most of the time, and because of that, because I don't want to give Derek Damn Chastain any more of my time, I don't think about him. It's not healthy, I know that. I'm probably going to have to go to therapy, which also infuriates me. I've been really busy, but I know it's coming."

"I'm in therapy. I alternate between yelling and crying."

I hugged her. "I have to believe it's going to get better. We're trying, we're not ignoring what's happened. But it's painful. Dealing with pain takes time, and baby steps at first. Sometimes in the middle, too."

Natalie sat back down and dried her eyes with the corner of a beach towel draped on the arm of her chair. "I didn't think this was going to be so damn hard."

"It's because he's gone. It's because he can't stand here, in front of us, and take the heat he deserves." An idea formed. "Hey, after dinner, after my kids leave, and yours are in bed, let's tell him what he needs to hear. And try to let some of the anger go."

"I'd like that," Natalie said.

We smiled, a new bridge tentatively built. I had a feeling this would be a series of new bridges, being built as necessary.

Baby steps.

The kids were worn out after a couple of hours, and we went back to the house so they could get cleaned up. I showered quickly, as I'd gotten a text from Rachel that they were on the way and had boarded the ferry while we were still at the beach.

All three kids were laughing as they got off the ferry. I hugged all of them, happy to have my kids around me, happy to have some normalcy.

"How's it going?" Theo asked.

"It's been a nice afternoon. They're getting cleaned up. The kids were at the beach all day, so they've got a little too much sun and a lot of energy still."

"Mom, you were supposed to wear them out," Rachel mock frowned at me.

"I did my best, but I couldn't send them to the salt mines." I made a face at her.

"Everything okay with Natalie?" Kris asked.

"Yes, believe it or not. No claws came out, and we actually talked very honestly."

"About what?" Rachel eyed me.

"About being the wives of one man."

"Did you tell her about Logan?"

"No, and you aren't going tell her either," I said, making it clear I would brook no discussion on this matter. "That's my business. But she and I have things to talk about, things that need to be said."

"La, la, la, la," Theo said, sticking his fingers in his ears. "I do not need to hear another thing." He glared at Rachel, who opened her mouth. "Neither do you, Rach."

Rachel closed her mouth, but she didn't look happy about it.

Kris laughed. "Oooh, this is gonna be a long ferry ride home, bro."

Theo shrugged. "Whatever. Not my fault Rachel can't handle someone else being right."

All of us, even Rachel, laughed. I drove them home, and from the moment they walked in the door, it was non-stop laughing, talking, talking faster, and noise.

I had my kids roll out the butcher paper on the long dining table.

"What's this for?" Sophie asked.

"We're having a lot of messy food, and this helps keep things clean," I explained. Caro and I served dinner, a traditional seafood boil with lobster, clams, shrimp, and corn. Caro had also made fluffy, buttery yeast rolls—not entirely traditional, but something she liked. We set out rolls of paper towels, demonstrated how to deal with all the seafood so that you could eat it, and dug in.

It was one of the best nights I'd had in a long time.

After dinner, we played Pictionary, a family favorite. Caro made Boston cream pie for dessert, and Natalie had to limit Nathan from taking a third piece.

Finally, my kids had to leave. The last ferry would be leaving in the next thirty minutes, and after a lot of hugging, I drove them back to the terminal.

"Mom, that was fun," Rachel said from the back seat.

"It was," I agreed.

"I think this will eventually be okay," Kris said. "It's always gonna be weird, but it will be okay."

Theo, riding shotgun, nodded.

It had been a fun night.

Nevertheless, all three of my wonderful, amazing kids hugged me extra hard before leaving.

"We want to meet Logan properly," Rachel said. "If you don't mind."

"Well, we're both busy, but I will see what I can do," I said. It was hard not to smile and dance and sing. One of the things that had been so tough for me was feeling on the outs with my kids. Rachel and I had patched things up—but until they all met Logan, until I knew that they were all right—things were still going to be weird.

This was another step in the process of acceptance that I had a life that had nothing to do with them, or their dad, and that I could move on as any other adult.

Which was huge.

The smile stayed on my face as I stood on the dock, watching the ferry disappear into the night. Then it stayed on my face as I hurried to my room, an idea from earlier fermenting in my brain. I stopped to talk to Caro for a moment, who was enjoying a cup of tea in front of the fireplace.

I went to the grimoire. Sitting on my bed, clearing my mind, which wasn't hard because there was so much goodness all around me, I asked, "How to cut ties and let go? How to welcome peace where there was chaos?"

I wanted to help Natalie, and I wanted to help me. We were struggling with the same thing. It was a testament to both of us that neither had snapped and gone crazy on the other.

Turning through the pages, I waited for something new to appear.

Nothing did.

So I went through the grimoire again.

Nothing.

"Really? I need help here."

But after a third time with no writing appearing that wasn't already visible I had to accept that the grimoire wasn't going to help. What had Florry called it? The book of smug mysteries. It was living up to its name right now.

"Okay, fine. I'll make my own spell."

I went into the Oracle office, and thumbed through one of the books I'd gotten from the coven. In the section on herbs, I found a recipe for a mixture that would help to allow peace to come in. And to let go of anger.

Perfect.

Digging into the herbs I'd gotten from Nathanial, I mixed them up, and put them in my larger burner. I took the burner downstairs with me, and covered it with one of my plastic food covers, I didn't want the herbs to blow away.

About ten minutes later, Natalie came downstairs.

"What a great day. The kids can't get settled."

"Do they get up at night?" I asked.

"I think they're down for the night," Natalie said. "Why?"

"Because you and I are going to go out to the beach for a little while."

"I can't leave the kids," Natalie said.

"You can. Caro's here, and she'll listen for them. Come on." I picked up my burner, and a large grill lighter.

"What are we doing?"

"You'll see."

CHAPTER TWENTY-ONE

Neither of us spoke as we walked back out to the beach. I'd brought my phone to use as a flashlight, but the moon was bright, lighting our way.

I walked almost down to the water, then dug a hole and put my burner in it. Uncovering it, I clicked my lighter and set the herbs aflame. I stared at them for a moment, enjoying the smell, the sound and smells of the sea, and being out in the moonlight.

I was more of a witch than I thought. Everything I'd read said that these things were inspiring to witches.

The Oracle could be a witch as well.

I got up and reached out my hands to Natalie.

She didn't take them. "What are we doing?"

"I've been cultivating my meditation skills."

She stared at me.

"You know, meditation. I sit and think in silence, sometimes not thinking at all. Thinking about the spiritual side, the part of us that identifies with nature. And this is one form of meditation. You burn herbs, chant a mantra, and allow yourself to find peace."

Natalie still didn't take my hands.

"Natalie, we both need peace. We're both struggling. This is just one way of helping us find it."

Slowly, her hands reached out for mine.

I smiled, and squeezed her hands. She held on tight.

"We need to let this go. Both of us carry anger at the hurt our loved one has given us. Both of us hurt for our children, even more innocent than we are. Help us to let this go." I closed my eyes, and breathed in the herbal mixture. Along with the night air, and the tang of seaweed—I was home.

"Help us to let this go," I repeated.

"Please," Natalie said.

Even with my eyes closed, I could hear the tears behind her words.

"Let the wrongs of Derek stay with him. They aren't ours. We let the anger go, and allow our hearts to be open and loving. What died with Derek stays with Derek."

"What... died with Derek... stays with Derek," Natalie whispered.

We stayed, hands clasped, letting go of so many hurts piece by piece, inch by inch, until the herbs had burned away.

"Derek, you were a jerk to hurt all these people. But

I'm not going to carry that nonsense for you anymore," I said.

"I won't carry it either. I deserve better. My children deserve better," Natalie added.

When I let go of the hands of Derek's other wife, I felt lighter. I hoped she did as well. I had no idea if the things I'd said or done were proper, but they felt right.

And that was all I could hope for.

When she and the kids left the next afternoon on the lunchtime ferry, we were both feeling better. I saw it in the clearing of Natalie's forehead, in the brightening of her eyes.

"When can we come see you again?" Sophie asked me. "This wasn't long enough."

Since she was the one who had been so hesitant yesterday, this felt like a major victory. "Whenever you want," I said, giving her a hug and kissing the top of her forehead.

I hugged Nathan, who gave me a sloppy kiss on the cheek.

Then I hugged Natalie. "Be well. Be good to yourself."

"Thank you. And thank you for the meditation," she said.

"It was my pleasure. It was for both of us. We deserve it," I said.

As the ferry pulled away, I felt a door close. A click, if you will. Whatever I'd needed to do to let Derek go, I'd done it.

With his other wife, no less.

Maybe that had been the message. I couldn't do it alone. I had to embrace reality, and include all the people who were part of that reality.

It was enough to make my head spin a little. But I set the Derek issues aside. They were the past. Something inside was telling me they were settled.

I had more pressing concerns.

The moment I got home, I gave Caro a hug. "Thank you for all that you did."

"Was it me, or did something in the air clear?"

"It did," I nodded. "You can come out now," I called out.

"Whew. I was beginning to feel like the unwanted bat in the belfry." Florry appeared close to the ceiling.

"You're just batty," Caro remarked with no rancor.

"Thanks, toots. You're all sweetness and light. Wynter, what's on the agenda now?"

"Well, I need to work on making the spell the witches used on my house work for Nina. It's all right," I held up a hand to forestall questions. "I have an idea. If I need help, I absolutely will ask for it. But let me try this."

Florry closed her mouth and nodded.

"Then I have the doctor's appointment tomorrow. Then I'm flying to New York to see Logan. Caro's going to keep an eye on Nina, have her stay here to make sure that she doesn't relapse."

"I think she's doing well," Caro said.

"I agree, but something is telling me to be sure."

"Listen to your gut," Florry said.

"That's what I'm doing." I rolled my eyes.

"Bring protection to New York."

"That's—hey, stop it. I know what I'm doing."

"I'm not going to be a granny," Florry said. "Neither is Caro. Outside of our job description."

"Noted," I said as Florry and Caro hooted with laughter. "It's not that funny."

"Yes, it is," Florry got out.

I left and went to clean up after my guests. Once the laundry was working, I got out my books and studied the best way to make this spell work in two different directions.

I'd been nose down in my books for who knew how long when my phone's notification went off, for both text and email.

I checked the messages first.

Tommyknocker. On sch.

My heart leapt into the heavens as the rest of my body focused on more earthly concerns.

I also checked my email. It was an itinerary. I'd fly out of the Vineyard before noon, and be met at Teterboro Airport in New Jersey. From there, a car would take me to a hotel I hadn't heard of. The room number was listed in the email.

Oh, my god. I needed to prep and pack.

Which meant I needed to finish my homework.

By the end of the night, I felt like I could not only cast the original spell to keep my house safe, but I had a good grasp on how to use it for Nina.

Before I left for the doctor, I talked with Caro, and went over what to watch for in terms of Nina. "If she starts to look drained again, call me immediately. It doesn't matter what time."

"On your love nest vacation?" One of Caro's eyebrows went up.

"Yes. My consultant comes first. That's how it has to go. You know that."

Caro sighed. "I know. I was just hoping you'd say something else."

"I wouldn't be me. I wouldn't be doing my job."

"It's okay to take a day off."

"I am," I said, smiling. "But if you need me, call me."

"Okay, but I'm going to do my best not to call you."

"Deal," I said. I gave her a hug, grabbed my overnight bag, and left.

On my way to see Dr. Amberson Friday morning, I called Nina.

"Hey, how are you?"

"You're still alive," Nina said. "You weren't arrested."

"Ha, ha. Of course I wasn't arrested. We had a lovely time."

"Uh, huh. What's up?"

"I'm going to be away for a couple of days, and—"

"Oh, really? Where are you going, Wynter?"

"To see Logan, nosy parker."

Nina laughed. "Good to see I haven't ruined your love life."

"Since Logan knows what I am, I can't see that it would ruin anything."

"Yeah, you say that now." Her words held quiet bitterness.

I wasn't touching that with a ten-foot pole. Not even a twenty-foot pole. "I want to ask if you will come and stay at my house. You can keep Caro company. I'll be back on Sunday, and we'll cast the protection spell."

"You got it?" Nina's voice rose in excited anticipation.

"I did," I said. "Will you do that? I don't want to leave Caro alone." And with Caro also keeping an eye on Nina, all my bases would be covered. All my people would have someone looking out for them.

I could go on a mini-break and not worry my face off.

"Yeah, I can do that. Let me pack up, and let Myrna," Nina named the woman renting her the place where she was staying, "know that I'm leaving."

"Okay. I'm leaving right after my appointment. So I'll see you Sunday night."

"Use a condom!" Nina laughed as she hung up.

Why was everyone so concerned about using condoms? I mean, I absolutely planned to. But I couldn't get pregnant. I didn't think that Logan was seeing other women. Why would people assume I *wouldn't* use a condom?

Even in my most spontaneous tossing-off-my-clothes moments, I always thought about protection.

Because you had to.

Well, I did now, anyway.

Back to the matter at hand. I needed to see my doctor and figure out why I was losing my hair.

An hour later, I knew why.

Menopause. What else? I thought Goldie had said I'd come into my power when my hair went white. I'd have to have hair for it to turn white.

But according to my doctor, there was hope. After taking more of my blood than I thought was necessary, she informed me this was one more lovely piece of menopause, but that there was help to be found. Not a magic pill, unfortunately. But some kind of hope.

I left Dr. Amberson's office with a variety of what felt like very unsatisfying ways to help hair loss, to keep more of my hair.

Vitamins.

More vitamins.

Water.

Better sleep.

"Not helping!" I shouted out my window as I drove to the small airport in West Tisbury. We had enough people who took private planes that it was busy all year round.

I was the only one on the small plane.

"Mr. Thane welcomes you, Ms. Chastain," the steward helped me to my seat. "Can I get you something to drink? Mr. Thane also asked me to inquire as to whether the tommyknockers were awake?" He delivered the line without his facial expression changing.

"A mimosa? That sounds wonderful. And the tommyknockers are fine." I loved that Logan was adding our word, letting me know this plane, these people—they were safe.

He nodded and disappeared.

Within moments, we were in the air, and I had a delicious mimosa in hand.

"I could get used to this," I said quietly as I watched the Vineyard get smaller.

The flight was a little over an hour. I managed to fall asleep, but it felt like I'd only just closed my eyes before the steward was waking me up.

"Ms. Chastain?" A man in a dark suit and cap waited at the bottom of the stairs.

"That's me."

"Mr. Thane sent me to pick you up. He said to tell you the tommyknockers are quiet."

I smiled. More reassurance.

The ride from Teterboro to Manhattan was smooth, without too much traffic. The car pulled to a stop in front of a small hotel with no name. I only knew it was a hotel because a doorman leapt to open the car door while another took my bag from the trunk.

I bypassed a discreet check-in desk as the doorman

led me to a small elevator off to the side of the larger ones in the middle of the lobby.

"Just tap the key on the pad," he said, demonstrating, "And the elevator will take you up."

He handed me the key, which I took, slightly dazed.

"What floor am I going to?" I asked.

"There's only one floor, ma'am." He smiled, touched his cap. The doors slid closed.

I was alone.

When the elevator door opened, I held my breath.

As it opened fully, I saw that Logan stood in the doorway, wearing dark pants, sharply creased. He had on a button down shirt, bright white, also crisp. His hair was neatly tamed.

We stood, just staring at one another.

Logan's hunger was evident.

Mine roared into life.

I was in his arms, my bag skittering across the tile floor.

He picked me up, his mouth on mine, demanding, hungry, blind to everything else.

We were moving, but I couldn't pay attention.

Then Logan set me down, and I realized he'd brought us to his bedroom.

I pulled my shirt off over my head, then wriggled out of my pants. I was unfastening my bra when I saw that Logan hadn't moved.

"Is everything okay?" My hand stilled on the back of my bra.

"I just forgot." His voice was hoarse.

"Forgot what?"

"How truly beautiful you are. That you want to be with me." He blinked.

"Says the most beautiful man I've ever seen."

"Me? With all my scars and—"

I put my hand up to his mouth. "Yes. The most beautiful man I've ever seen."

"You deserve nothing less."

"I have everything I want." I reached for him.

That moment, where I reached for him, and he took me in close to him, that was in slow motion. I saw every detail. The expression on his face. The tender way he brushed my hair behind my ear. The way my body thrilled at the touch of his thumb on my lips.

And then it was a blur.

Sometime in the night, we ate. I didn't remember much because we were feeding one another, and then we were back in bed, immersed in one another's bodies, saying so much with our hands, our lips, our tongues.

All without a word.

Later, as the dark surrounded us, I whispered, "I have so much to tell you."

"There's much to say between us," Logan whispered back, sounding a lot more formal than I would have thought possible at this moment. "We have time tomorrow." He kissed me then.

We could talk tomorrow.

The last thing I remembered was curling into him, feeling safe and warm and happy and satiated.

The shrilling of...something filtered through my head.

"What?" I muttered, rubbing my eyes.

The shrilling sound continued.

Once I got my eyes open, I saw my phone. That was the noise, the screen bright in the early light of dawn.

I scooted over, working around Logan's arm draped over me.

It was Caro.

"Hey," I said, trying to clear the frogs from my throat. "Caro, what's up?"

Her sobbing drowned out whatever she was trying to say.

CHAPTER TWENTY-TWO

The flight back to the Vineyard was quiet. Logan sat next to me, his arm around me. I kept crying, unable to believe what Caro told me on the phone, in-between her sobbing. How was it possible?

We landed, and I had no more answers than I did when we'd left, grabbing clothes and my bag and racing for the airport.

Logan was speaking into his phone the entire time, only putting it away after the plane took off.

I was so glad he was with me, but in the end, it didn't fully help. It couldn't fix what I had done.

What I had ruined.

The lives I'd lost.

Because she was lost.

Kira was lost.

All because I'd failed.

Failed.

Logan tried to take the keys from me after we landed on the island's airport, but I clutched them to me without speaking. He got into the car, and held my hand as I drove home, trying not to speed. The last thing I needed was a ticket.

Besides, if I sped up, the wheels would just repeat the message even faster.

You failed.

You failed.

You failed.

You failed.

You failed.

Your fault.

You lost her.

You did this.

You.

You.

You.

The worst Oracle ever.

Everyone fails, Wynter. Goldie's voice broke into the repetitive thoughts.

Not now, Goldie.

You need to hear this. Everyone fails. All the Oracles have failed. All of them.

Please, just stop. Please.

He didn't reply.

After what felt like hours, I turned onto my street, and whipped the car into the driveway, flinging open the car door and running toward the porch.

I had to see it for myself. To see my failure.

I could see the outline of the gargoyle. Racing up the path and up the stairs, I skidded to a halt next to the gargoyle, my hand on its hunched back.

"Nina," I whispered.

Logan had gotten out of the car when I did, but he wasn't up here. He was still down by the car. Why wasn't he here, with me? I couldn't focus on him right now, though.

All I could see was the gargoyle who had once been Nina. I set my hand on the hunched back of the stone creature, unable to process my thoughts.

I had to try. I had to try and fix this.

Caro had said that Nina went gray, like she did before, when the hex on her was draining the life from her. But unlike before, she was having trouble moving, getting slower and slower. That she'd made her way out to the porch, and when Caro went out, Nina's cup of tea had been knocked over, along with the chair she'd been sitting in.

All that was left was the gargoyle, clinging to the porch, clawed hands gripping the railing. As Nina must have when she realized what was happening.

I started to cry.

This was why I hadn't been able to feel the click of finishing a quest. Because the hex wasn't broken. I hadn't broken a thing. What had I done? What hadn't I done? I'd failed her. I'd failed Nina in every way.

And what about her daughter?

My hand tightened on the gargoyle, even as I had a hard time seeing because the tears poured out of me like a faucet at full blast. My poor Nina. We thought we were on the right path.

All along, it was a trick. "You bastard," I breathed. "You utter bastard." As I looked around, I saw a man out of the corner of my eye.

Without him saying a word, without being told, I knew this was Rockledge Davenport. He stood on my walkway, hands in his pockets. He looked like the man I'd seen briefly in my scrying.

And he had the nerve to turn up here.

I glanced to either side, wanting to make sure no one else was about and that's when I saw Logan. He was frozen next to my car. His eyes had gone golden, and his face was stern and chiseled. His arm reached out, stuck in the moment where he'd been stopped in time.

This was all Rockledge.

"You did this," I said, and I was startled to hear the growl in my voice.

This man, who was a rotten, horrible, nasty little turnip of a man, sneered at me. Within the sneer was gloating triumph as he looked at the gargoyle and then back to me.

Watching him, my anger rose.

Perhaps feeling my anger, the turnip known as Rockledge smiled. It was gross and creepy. If you saw it on the street, you'd cross to the other side. How could he look so normal when he was such.. such a creep?

"I always told her, you will never win. I always win. Always." Rockledge shook his head. "Nina wouldn't listen. I hope you do, because otherwise, you see your future," Rockledge said. He was silent for a moment. "At least, I hope you see your future. Because unless you do as I ask, you'll face a similar fate. You can't win. You thought you *were* winning, didn't you? You thought you released her?" He shook his head, making a tsk-ing noise.

"What do you want?" My teeth were clenched as I spoke. "You just cursed with silence the only person who might be able to tell you where Kira is. Maybe you're not as smart as you think. You're never going to find Kira now."

Rockledge laughed. "I don't think so. I think that Nina had a contingency plan. That's her style. I haven't found it yet, but I know how she operates."

I shook my head. "No. No one but Nina knows how to get to Kira. You utter fool."

He stared hard at me. "I hope you're wrong. I want my daughter back. Through you, I shall have her back. Until I do, this decoration can remind you of your failure and what you have done. How no one wins against me." He turned to walk down the path that led to my house, then stopped.

Slowly, he turned back to face me. "If you take too long, Nina will not be the only one decorating your porch. How about three of your children? The man here," his hand waved dismissively at Logan, still frozen. "Who is so determined to protect you. He could also pay the price for your delay. The old woman who lives here? Yes," he smiled nastily at me. "I know who surrounds you, who is important to you." He looked away, up at the sky.

"What's also important is that you know what it means to lose. That you understand what you will lose. And you will know these things intimately, if you ignore my demands." He completely ignored the part where I'd told him I didn't know where Kira was.

What an asshole.

My mouth fell open, in anger, in rage, and, I hated to admit, a dash of fear. The fear was sharp and hot and cut through me to my heart.

"I see that you understand. Tick tock, little Oracle. You have less time than you think." He turned away once more, walking down the path and onto the sidewalk.

How did he know I was the Oracle?

I looked at the gargoyle. It was weeping, the sadness pouring from the stone. When I looked back to glare at Rockledge Jerkface Davenport, he was gone. It wasn't that he'd turned left or right and walked quickly.

It was as if he'd never even been there at all.

My street was quiet and still.

The fluffy white tufts of a dandelion, pappus, Nina

had called them, with her daughter Kira calling them fairy hair, drifted by on a burst of wind. They swirled up, and then over across the face of the gargoyle, and were gone before I could blink back the tears that obstructed my vision.

"I'm sorry," I whispered.

A crash and a muffled exclamation told me that Logan was no longer frozen.

I had no idea what to do next.

And I couldn't stop the sinking feeling in my stomach.

The End

Thank you for reading the latest installment with Wynter! But there's more to come, in book five, Incantations & Insomnia. Read on!

Available in the Amazon store!

Two weeks ago, I logged my first failure as an Oracle. Two days ago, I learned that magic is a fickle thing. Two hours ago, I unleashed a posse of the undead.

Chapter One

Four Days.

It had been four entire days.

Four days since Nina was turned into a gargoyle, and I had done nothing to rescue her. It wasn't for a lack of trying on my part.

I'd been through the grimoire multiple times. I'd called the local coven and asked for ideas. I talked Logan's ear off. At least until he had to leave.

And Goldie's.

And Florry's.

I'd cried to Caro and Shelly.

Even with all that, I'd still failed.

And now, four days after the biggest failure of my life—I was in bed. The blankets were up around my nose, and my eyes were closed.

I couldn't face the day.

Not another day where Nina sat on my porch, silent in the condemnation that I could not escape, not that I wanted to. I'd earned all condemnation.

I found that after thinking of nothing but helping Nina, freeing her, I couldn't face another day where the dandelion fairy hair flew around in the gentle wind that came from the sea. Or another day where a little girl went without her mother, in danger from her father.

Not another day where this was all my fault.

I pulled the blankets up over my eyes and tried to shut out the morning sun.

I just couldn't face it. Or anyone. Or anything.

Click here to get the next book,
INCANTATIONS & INSOMNIA!

Whew! That was a ride, wasn't it? I'll be honest, that wasn't where I planned for things to go, but sometimes,

I am not the one in charge. Keep reading to see if and when this resolves.

AND - at this point, there are ten books in this series. I planned for six, initially. But remember right above when I said I wasn't always in charge? This series has been one of those times. Wynter keeps talking to me, telling me her story. I'll keep sharing as long as she does.

Xoxo,

Lisa

About the Author

Lisa Manifold is a USA Today Bestselling Author of fantasy, paranormal, and romance stories. She moved to Colorado as an adult and has no plans of living anywhere else.

Lisa writes the things she does because she really, really wants to live in a world where these kinds of stories happen. This could explain her room of costumes, addiction to fan conventions, and her hope to meet the Goblin King (if he takes her away right now, she's staying).

She lives in the mountains of Colorado with her children, two amazing dogs, even as one has no respect for personal space, and one murderball cat. She camps as much as she can.

Sign up for her Newsletter to keep up with the latest releases!

You can also follow her on her website:

www.lisamanifold.com

Also by Lisa Manifold

The Oracle of Wynter

Hexes & Hot Flashes

Magic & Menopause

Necromancy & Night Sweats

Hoodoo & Hair Loss

Incantations & Insomnia

Witchery & Weight Gain

Charms & Chin Hairs

Grimoire & Gum Disease

Familiars & Fine Lines

Mystics & Migraines

Occult & Osteoporosis

Conjuring & Crying Spells

Tarot & Toe Tingles

An Otherworldly Midlife Medium

Hocus Pocus & Headaches

Batwings & Bloating

Tales of a Midlife Mortician

Cursed by the Corpse

Bewitched by the Bones

Dirge for the Departed

Abra on the Cadaver

Gods of Thunder MC

(A Shared World)

You Can't Fight Lightning

The Ouroboros Society

(A Shared World)

Shift in the Blood

Vampire Mates

(with The Midnight Coven)

Immortal Darkness

The Mostly Open Paranormal

Investigative Agency

Dark Pact

Dark Night

Dark Fates

Vampire Brides

(with The Midnight Coven)

Forever Blood

Deadwood Sisters

Hellborn: The Unlucky Book 1

Hellfire: The Unlucky Book 2

Hellfury: The Unlucky Book 3

Dragon Thief

Dragon Lost

Dragon Found

The Realm Series

Heart of the Goblin King

To Wed the Goblin King

Realms of the Goblin King

Rise of the Dragon King

The Companion Tales, Volume I

The Companion Tales, Volume II

The Aumahnee Prophecy

with Corinne O'Flynn

Eamonn's Tale

Marigold's Tale

Watchers of the Veil

Defenders of the Realm

Tales From The Veil

with Corinne O'Flynn

The Portal Keepers

The Gimcrackers

Djinn Everlasting

Three Wishes

Forgotten Wishes

Hidden Wishes

Sisters of the Curse

Thea's Tale

One Night at the Ball

Casimir's Journey